I0544798

pSycho theRApy

ALAn SpenceR

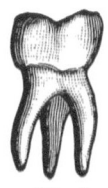

Bizarro Pulp Press
an imprint of JournalStone Publishing

Bizarro Pulp Press books may be ordered through booksellers or by contacting:

Bizarro Pulp Press, a JournalStone imprint
    www.BizarroPulpPress.com

    ISBN: 978-1-947654-10-5

Printed in the United States of America
JournalStone rev. date: July 26, 2017

    Cover Art: Justin Coons

    Interior Formatting: Lori Michelle
        www.theauthorsalley.com

Advance pRAISe foR pSycho theRApy

"*Psycho Therapy* is a fright-filled rocket ship that will blast you into a new world of terror."
—Shattered Ravings

the wAITIng Room

CRAIg hoRSy touched the wet bandage taped to his forehead when he woke from a deep sleep. The tip of his finger was stained red. He was confused by the mysterious wound.

How did it get there?

Who did it to him?

He didn't remember coming here. He was slumped upright on a brown leather couch draped in a layer of thick plastic. Confused by the situation, he attempted to stand up and walk. His cranium was jolted by a shock of pain that delivered him right back down onto the couch.

He gathered up enough saliva in his mouth to speak. "Is anybody out there?"

Slowly, he inched up to a standing position. The dim light above him gave the room the dank yellow color of a chicken incubator. The room failed to jog a memory of how he came to be here until he noticed the red plastic hazard box for dirty needles propped on the wall. Today was his court-appointed visit with the psychiatrist named Dr. Richard Herbert. Now he regretted waking up. There was no way to prepare himself for the session of psychobabble and forced self-reflection, especially in his banged-up condition.

Craig winced at the blinding-white headache flaring up behind his eyes. He was in the right place to cure the pain, he thought. Dr. Herbert could write a script, and off to the drugstore he'd go.

He braced his throat to speak again when a young face peered into the room. Her lipstick was a shade too pink, costing her a decade of her youth, even though she couldn't be a day over thirty. The woman's cheeks were sucked in, as was her midsection. Her auburn hair was styled in a bun, and her black skirt and blue button-up top were freshly ironed, creating a secretarial look, even though she was wearing black running shoes.

"Mr. Horsy," she said in a sultry voice, "how do you feel?"

He clutched his head in demonstration. "My head's killing me. Can you tell me what happened? I can't remember anything before I woke up here."

Without saying a word, she guided him out of the small room and into a carpeted hallway. Each door was closed, but the waiting room flagged his attention. It was a square with eight oak chairs and a coffee table. The front reception desk was a hole in the wall with a frosted glass window. An aquarium to the right displayed cichlids against a background of a fake deep sea. The blue-black fish swam among the remains of a submarine. There were no other patients waiting.

"Take a seat, Mr. Horsy, and I'll explain everything momentarily."

He smiled at the kind woman. "Call me Craig."

She had a soothing, reassuring voice.

"I'm Dr. Krone's assistant, Rachael. It's nice to meet you."

6

"Dr. Krone? I thought I was seeing Dr. Herbert. Am I at the right place?" He laughed. "Did I get the wrong information in the mail?"

"It happens." Her eyes fell on his bandage. "But I have your appointment in the books. They gave you the wrong doctor's name, but, thankfully, the right address."

She touched his shoulder, and when she bent down, he couldn't help but enjoy the cleavage she presented. "About your head, you took a mean spill outside. Dr. Krone saw it happen from his office window. You were walking up the steps, and you simply slipped on the ice. He said you landed hard. You smacked your head on the guard rail." She turned her head down to him in sympathy. "Poor thing, you look so confused. Can I offer you a drink? How about a soda?"

"I'd love one." He perked up. "And thanks for being so nice to me."

"That's how we do things around here." She walked into the back of the office, turning her hips in a practiced strut.

She must really enjoy getting sodas for people.

He looked over the table at the magazines, each of them up-to-date: *Time*, *People*, *Cosmopolitan*, *The New Yorker*, *Highlights*, *National Geographic*, *The Reader's Digest*, and *Mad* magazine.

"What, me worry?" he laughed under his breath, but then paid the price. He clamped his teeth, cursing and squeezing his eyes shut. A yellow flash of razor wire exploded in his cortex.

"Christ, I might need X-rays. That was brutal."

He rubbed his head as a cheap remedy. *Maybe if you were being careful walking up the steps, you wouldn't have fallen on your head.*

3

Last night, three feet of snow had fallen, and it wasn't melting, it being ten degrees outside. Winter in Franklin, Indiana, was bitter.

Rachael returned with a soda. "Dr. Krone's ready to see you. You can drink it while you're talking to him. This is a consultation. The first round is kept simple, so don't be nervous."

She pointed at his bandage. "You've had a bad morning. This will be easy. Afterwards, we'll send you down the street to St. Anthony's to double-check you haven't suffered any serious damage."

She then kindly ushered him down the hall to meet Dr. Krone.

dR. dAnieL kRone

RachAel opened the last door on the left, and Craig entered of his own accord. The door closed behind him shortly after he crossed the threshold. The room was a study. Bookshelves were lined with encyclopedias, each volume of the DSM— a book of diagnosed mental disorders, he recalled from *Gray's Anatomy*—and a wide variety of psychologist's aids. One caught his attention: *Psychology and the Criminal Mind*.

An acorn-brown leather chair was positioned in the center of everything, and across from that, another of the exact chair. No couch, Craig was happy to note.

A calm, professional voice beckoned him, with what he imagined to be the tone of a seasoned Harvard professor. "Please sit down, Mr. Horsy."

The doctor rose up from behind his desk to shake his hand. "Stubby" was a good start to describe the doctor's appearance. He was over three hundred pounds and five feet tall. His double chin was a marshmallow tire around his neck. His head was small, his chest was bigger, his belly wider, and his pelvis was the largest tier, and then his legs thinned out. A shock of gray hair topped his head, though it was thinning, leaving parts of his scalp visible. His upbeat voice didn't match his hard countenance. The man was in his late sixties, Craig guessed. The oddest feature of the package—he wore running shoes.

"I'm Daniel Krone," he introduced himself, shaking Craig's hand vigorously and not letting go until he was well into the next statement. "I'm glad you're here. I'm sorry you took such a mean spill outside. I looked you over. It's not bad. It's merely a scrape that won't require stitches, but I'll send you home with bandages and antibacterial ointment. I'll also point you to that clinic down the street, just to be certain, and I'll foot the bill. I want my clients to be A-okay."

And not sue the pants off you, right?

The doctor pointed to one of the leather chairs. "Now have a seat. Enjoy your cola. Let's talk."

Craig dreaded the coming moments. The visit itself was an admission he'd done something criminal. And he had. This was better than jail time, as Judge Ingram mentioned three weeks ago in court. "Yeah, let's talk. I have things to," his fingers made quotes in the air, "*hash out.*"

The doctor gathered a thick manila folder and plopped down across from him with a twin pop of the knees. "I don't let my patients sit on a couch facing the other direction. I want to see their faces. There's nothing to be afraid of, Mr. Horsy, and there's nothing to hide from me. I'm a professional. Everything shared between us is confidential."

"I understand."

The doctor removed his glasses and rubbed at his eyes. "Listen, I know you don't want to be here. Some judge sentenced you to chat with me for," he peered at his sheet, "six months. Let's make the best of this. You might even get prescription drugs out of it." He gave Craig a smirk. "Would you like that?"

He laughed awkwardly, caught off guard by the strange offer. "Well, now you're talking. I like the way you think, Doc."

The doctor shuffled through the paperwork and located what he was seeking. "I'm going to read off your past criminal record. This is to get us on the same page as to what we need to discuss in our sessions. You admit what you've done, and we can continue on with the truth. This means I can better help you. The truth is key, Mr. Horsy. Without it, I'm not only out of a job, but the point of me being here is wasted." He dabbed a crawling bead of sweat from his forehead with the back of his hand. "I must have the truth from you, if nothing else."

Craig mentally turned over the deeds of his past. "I only have one offense besides traffic tickets. This'll be a short conversation."

"Maybe not. I have access to detailed files, Mr. Horsy." He turned over many pages before stopping to read one. "I'll start with your childhood."

"My childhood?"

What he heard had him reeling.

"In the first grade, you punched Tim Morgan in the stomach during lunch. He knocked over your lunch tray, and you slugged him. Tim was a bit of a bully, I understand."

Craig threw his head back in one long, nervous guffaw. "That was a long time ago, Doc. I mean, *wow*. Tim and I made up afterwards. I couldn't play at recess for two weeks, and I had to write him a letter of apology. I was really hungry, man. He knocked over my food on pizza day. *Pizza day*. And it wasn't the first time he'd done it to me on the good food days."

Dr. Crone moved on, satisfied by Craig's reaction. "Third grade, you placed a whoopee cushion on Mrs. Steinman's chair."

"And she said 'Whoopee!' She was asking for it. So book me, Dr. Krone. I can't believe they documented this. Now I'm really interested. What else you got?"

The doctor rattled the list off like a preacher at the pulpit. "You pulled the fire alarm three times at Parker Elementary. You lit a cherry bomb in the bathroom while you were being watched by a babysitter. Fifth grade, you removed a fire extinguisher from the wall and doused three girls as they were walking out of the bathroom. And then—"

Craig cut him off, overwhelmed by how funny his record was. "I didn't understand why the girls always wanted to go to the bathroom together. They mentioned makeup, so I decided to apply my own kind of makeup on them. Makes sense for a fifth grader to do. So I did it. I know, I know, I'm a jerk. But I was a kid. It's not like I seriously harmed anybody. And I didn't do it again."

The doctor became stern. "Seventh grade, you broke Drew Massey's nose."

"Drew Massey, yeah, I remember that jerk. Middle school sucks, man. You understand. Kids make new friends. Old friends break apart. People form their own cliques. I won't make excuses. Drew was pushing a kid in the locker room with a developmental disability. He punched the kid in the gut when he couldn't work his combination lock open. Drew denied it. But I protected Jake the whole year. Drew backed off after I elbowed him in the nose during a flag football game in gym class. The bully deserved it. Kids can be cruel. I was crueler."

"But you're an adult now. You can't win fights by starting them."

"What kind of philosophical talk is that? I was a prankster. I played jokes when I was little. I've gotten into fights. Who hasn't?"

"Tell me about Willis Young."

Willis Young was his best friend, and maybe still was, but he wasn't sure.

"I met Willis at Indiana University. I dropped out during the second semester. You know how it goes. You don't know what degree you're after, so you take your general education courses. The problem with me, I lost interest. Willis got his business degree and opened his bar called Half-Time. It's a sports bar. I visited the place all the time.

"I lost my job working for the city. I picked up garbage. I came in late too many times, and off with my head, right? So Willis offers me a job, and I really need the money. What happened, Willis's brother also wanted a job. He gave it to Joey without telling me. I depended on that paycheck, and man, the tips would've been awesome. Willis offered me free drinks the night he told me about not getting the job, so I was drunk. I lost control, and, um," he loosened his collar, "I threw a barstool at him. I broke his collarbone and nose."

Craig jumped to defend himself. "Hey, it's nothing I'm proud of. I felt horrible afterwards. I had no right to do that. I lost control. I'd been drinking too much. I was lucky my sentence was just time served, and of course, these counseling visits."

The doctor scribbled notes actively. "So what are you doing for work now?"

"Unemployed." He wasn't proud of it. Thirty-two years old, and no job, the next step in his life was undetermined, and a midlife crisis loomed on the horizon. "It sucks."

Dr. Krone finally made eye contact. "I'd worry about getting your house in order before pursuing a job. Unemployment can foot the bill in the meantime. We need you clear of mind. I wish the government would truly focus on the people who need time. They should give you a few months to recuperate from your ordeal. Visit me daily, for one. It'll take more than a few visits to cure you—anybody, Mr. Horsy. Nobody wants to spend the time anymore to be well. That's American society. Instant gratification, throw some pills at me, maybe shock therapy, and boom, you're good again."

He wasn't sure what the soapbox spiel was about. A mantra of the field, he supposed. He'd already touched upon a lot of old memories and fresh wounds in a matter of fifteen minutes. Dr. Krone wasn't doing a bad job so far, he admitted.

He'd shortly change his mind.

"Let's go back to your prior record."

"Prior record? What other minor offenses have been recorded in the history of Craig Horsy?"

The doctor simply stated the name, "Alice Denny."

The name ripped the smile from his face. How did he know about her? There was no official police report involving her. What happened between them was private.

The response shot out of him as a threat. "I don't want to talk about her."

The doctor weighed his reaction with calibrated eyes. "I can see your blood pressure rising. You're a new shade of red. I've hit an important topic, haven't I?"

"Watch it. I don't want to talk about her. Your receptionist promised this would be easy today. What's my favorite pig-out food, what's my favorite color, that kind of bullshit. How would you know about what happened between Alice and me? Nobody does."

Cherry bombs and fire-extinguisher stories didn't sound so ridiculous now, he thought.

Dr. Krone removed a handkerchief from his pocket and waved it like a flag. "Surrender. I'm trying to flush out what brings out your anger. Be honest with me. I've done my research on you, Mr. Horsy, to assure positive results. I know who your friends and family are. So I've taken the liberty of doing some preliminary interviews. I'm hard at work for you. My patient's success is top priority. You do have an anger problem. That's why Willis was sent to the emergency room. I am correct, yes?"

"Yes," Craig admitted. "I'm quick to anger. Isn't it obvious? I'm a hothead. Impulsive. I overreact, yes. You're right."

"Then let's hash out the issues, like you said. It can only help. Do it for Willis."

What's with this guy, Craig thought. The doctor forewent the niceties and lunged straight for the throat. Craig couldn't leave the session. This was court-ordered. Mandatory.

The doctor licked the tip of his Bic pen. "You have a lot of reasons to be angry, Craig. The issue is you need to learn how to manage yourself. If you can harm your best friend, what will you do to a stranger—or, perish the thought, me?"

"I wouldn't harm you. Are you rattling the cage and seeing what you can shake up?" Craig popped his knuckles unconsciously. "Rachael said this wouldn't be so intense."

"You're a special case."

"And what the hell does that mean?"

"You require immediate assistance. Everybody in your shoes does. You may not show the symptoms, but early prevention is the best thing to avoid the sickness."

In that moment, he wanted to beat that self-satisfied smile from the doctor's face. *No. That'd validate my requiring immediate assistance. Maybe I am out of control. Maybe I do require 'immediate assistance.'*

"I don't want to talk about Alice, not yet. Maybe some other time when I know you better, okay?" He checked his watch. The digital face had cracked and turned black. "Is this session over yet?"

"No." The doctor slapped the file onto the ground, and one side of his face sneered hard. "None of this Q&A matters now." He bent in closer, leveling with Craig. "My treatment is revolutionary. I won't sling drugs at you or talk your head off. This is a mere preliminary to what we're about to accomplish. You won't have an anger problem when I'm through with you." He rubbed the small patch of saliva from the corner of his mouth. "Do you have regrets, Mr. Horsy?"

"Who doesn't?"

"Do you wish you could've done things differently? We make a lot of choices in our lives. I'm sure you'd like to relive some of those choices and change things—even if it's just in your mind. And let me say, I've done it before."

"Done what before?"

"Never mind." The doctor placed his fingertips together. "What I've begun to say, we'll address later. I think I'll head straight into my next step of treatment." He raised his head to meet Craig's eyes. "It's the most effective."

"Why not jump right into it if it's the most effective?"

"My line of questioning serves to open up that brain of yours. It stirs memories to the surface. Good ones. The ones I can use."

"What the hell are you talking about?" He didn't expect the visit to be so out of the ordinary. He'd been on the verge of tears thinking about Alice, and now he was genuinely concerned as to the effectiveness of Dr. Krone's program. "Use my memories for what? Can you give me a little bit of information here? Layman's terms."

Dr. Krone's eyes went small, and then they went soft again. "First, would you talk a little about your wife's death?"

He was unable to curb his outburst. "I'm done! And fuck you! I want to see Dr. Herbert. You're a crackpot. I'm here for twenty minutes, and you're already asking me about Katie. Aren't you supposed to build up to that? Yes, you are. This is ninth-inning shit, not first pitch."

The doctor was pleased, speaking above a whisper. "This is how you're supposed to react."

"Oh, here's more psychobabble talk. Do you have a self-help book for me to buy? Will it explain to me how to fuck my own brain? And let me guess, you'd like to watch?"

The doctor clapped his hands together once. "Oh, this is splendid."

"I won't go to jail." Craig bolted from his chair and hovered at the door. "I'll tell them about you. I'll visit Dr. Herbert. According to my documents, I'm supposed to see him anyway. I'm sure it'll hold up in court."

"Absolutely, but you won't be leaving to do those things anytime soon."

"And why the hell not?"

"Go ahead and leave. I'm done with twenty questions. Do as you wish. I've got you worked up. You're ready for the machine."

Craig refused to play into the doctor's game. He prayed every psychiatrist wasn't this unprofessional, or else he was prison bound.

He stormed out the door and slammed it closed, hearing from the other side a set of plaques collapse from the wall.

There goes Dr. Krone's well-established career all over the floor.

He rushed to what he guessed was the exit, taking wide, fast steps, the escape being fifteen paces north of him. Rachael wasn't in sight, though he didn't bother to glance at the main desk to say goodbye.

Then a cold drop startled him. It stained his eyebrow. Blood. Touching it, he found the bandage was sodden through. Why hadn't Dr. Krone said anything? Was it bloody during the interview?

This is one of those places that will inevitably be closed down. I'll hear about it on one of those investigative news programs.

He decided he could better inspect the bandage in his car. Closing in on the exit, he reached out for the doorknob.

The knob was the only part of the door that was real.

Staggering back a step, he muttered, "You're kidding me."

He jangled the doorknob, and it ripped from the wall, plaster pieces crumbling to his feet. It'd been glued in place. The door frame was painted brown. A faded purple drape shielded a fake glass pane. How had he not noticed it before? Obvious was too light of a word.

And then something sharp nipped him in the back. "*Ahhh!*"

Rachel's soft smiling face turned maniacal. She wheezed from a cracked-open mouth.

She was laughing, enjoying his shock as he faltered to the floor. "This'll be a simple visit. *A summer's breeze, Mr. Horsy!*"

She shoved him down the rest of the way to the ground with a kick to the back of his knees. He landed face-first against the carpeted floor. She straddled his back, and another cold prick to the neck later, he plunged under those ripples of water into unconsciousness.

Dr. Krone stepped into the waiting room and looked down at Craig's body. "Another patient for the machine, and this one shows serious promise."

Rachael knelt down and stroked Craig's hair, stretching out the individual curls and letting them bounce back into their natural position.

Then she smiled up at the doctor. "He does show promise."

the mAchIne

An **Ammonia tablet** was broken under Craig's nose, rudely waking him. The room buzzed with rusted gears grinding against each other, dueling against the chug of a roaring diesel motor. A blank screen on the wall directly in front of him glowed bright with artificial white light. He imagined the gates of heaven opening, it was so blinding. The remainder of the room was cast in pitch-darkness.

Ca-clink. It sounded like metal catching metal.

He attempted to speak, but his lips were numb. Craig couldn't shift his tongue. Trying harder to feel his body, he vaguely sensed his arms pressed against two wooden panels. Leather restraints strapped his extremities firmly into place. He couldn't move at all.

A metal object touched down around the circumference of his head. It felt like a crown. The metal was ice cold against his skin. The ticking of the machine increased, and something swung down fast in front of his face. His skull was pricked by dozens of needles. He stiffened involuntarily. He twitched. His arms began to spasm. His back tightened, vertebra by vertebra. His head radiated warmth. His ears buzzed with mechanical locusts. A copper tang filled his mouth. His eyes leaked hot tears. He'd describe the overall feeling as being plugged in and hooked up to electricity.

The machine grinded faster, humming, churning, clanking, and working. A startle escaped his throat after a pair of red binoculars was lowered in front of his eyes.

Wuuuuuuuuuum.

The machine revved itself.

The binoculars exuded golden light. Pain flooded into his eyes. The gates of heaven were opening once again.

A voice echoed in the room, emanating from the walls, rising up from the floor, and reverberating inside of him. "It's going to get uncomfortable, Mr. Horsy."

You're too late if you were trying to warn me, you bastard.

"Calling me a bastard won't solve anything," Dr. Krone laughed. "I can hear your thoughts. They come out of that speaker in the corner. I'm hooked up into your mind."

Jesus Christ. He really is.

"Yes, Jesus would be impressed. Now calm down. I need you to relax."

The doctor peered into the magnifying lenses over his face and twiddled a circular knob. The change lowered the brightness of the light, but only by a slight degree. Everything was bathed in electric white, the concentration of dozens of computer screens. The headache worsened by the second. His brain was heating up.

"I should let you know that when you signed the court order, you consented to this treatment. It's a brand new therapy. I'll have you a changed man in less than four hours, I promise you."

I didn't consent to torture. This is illegal. I'll sue. I'll burn this fucking place to the ground!

He stopped thinking. Each word sounded harmonized.

Dr. Krone guffawed. "You're hearing yourself think out loud, you fool. Do you really plan on burning my practice to the ground? You'll be thanking me by the end of the day. You'll shake my hand, or maybe you'll buy me a beer. I love any ale on tap."

I'm not buying you shit.

"You should read the fine print. This is for your own good. You'll see."

What about the fake door? Why is this place set up like a trap? Did I really take a fall outside and hit my head?

The doctor stood behind him, punching what sounded to be computer keys. "This is an overwhelming procedure, but it's also overwhelmingly effective. There are no fake doors on my premises. The door swings both ways, like anybody else's. You're talking nonsense, Mr. Horsy. Let's reel you back into reality. Do you remember breaking that stool over your friend's body?"

Before Craig could protest, the screen ahead of him lit up with an image. It glowed around the edges with purple flashes of light. The screen crackled with sharp static, but then shortly after the crackling, a scene played out—

Half-Time pub's television screens displayed the Giants versus the Patriots football game. The scene was what a pair of eyes would see—Craig's eyes. Next, the bar's varnished oak counter snuck into the picture. Hank slid a frosty mug of Pale Moon Ale at him. Hank had that special talent of delivering beer five stools down without disturbing the froth or spilling it.

This is a memory of mine. You can't be doing this. It's impossible!

"Keep watching." The doctor put his hands on Craig's shoulders. "You'll see."

The memory skipped a scene. It showed Willis pleading with him, cowering backwards from him in fear. "I'm so sorry. I know you're mad, but Joey is family—you're family too. My best friend. I'll tell you when something else opens up. I'm sorry I can't give you a job. I'll give you a hundred bucks, and you don't have to pay me back. Have another beer. Please, you can't understand how disappointed I am that I can't help you."

"The hell with you!"

"Craig, you're drunk. Take a deep breath. Hear what I'm saying. Go to the unemployment office. Use me as a reference. If you have to crash at my place, then fine. It might even be fun, huh?"

"I don't need a place to stay," Craig's voice erupted, "*I need a fucking job!*"

The room tilted, mimicking his drunken experience.

The image jumped time again.

Shouts and screams clashed with the bar's banter. Willis cried out, tears welling in his eyes. Genuine fear turned Willis into an unfamiliar person. He wasn't real. He was a caricature of himself. The seat of the barstool slammed into his nose. The metal leg connected to his collarbone with an aluminum rattle.

Skipping ahead again. Willis was sprawled out on

the floor and unconscious. His nose gushed red. Then Craig was tackled from behind by a bar patron and driven onto his stomach. Someone asked someone else to call the cops.

The typing of computer keys came from behind him, and the image became a blank screen.

Craig was stunned.

"Imagine how many of these horrible memories you have stored in that cerebral cortex of your mind, Mr. Horsy. I'm not suggesting you take them out. I want you to confront them. I can put you in that moment again, physically. You can change the way you reacted."

But I still hurt Willis. What will reliving it prove?

"It's a way of forgiving yourself."

A female voice nearby added, "It's like changing your past. Why not act out what we meant to do and not what we actually did?"

Dr. Krone snipped, "*Quiet.* He'll learn what we're doing in due time. I'm the one in charge, not you. Keep your mouth shut and watch."

Is Rachael watching? What does she know about this? She hasn't been hooked up to this torture device.

Rachel tried to correct him. "In fact, I—"

The doctor angrily cut her off. "That's not your concern, Mr. Horsy. You're the patient. You're the one with the ailment. You're the one with the court order. I'm in charge."

I want off this fucking machine.

The doctor stepped in front of the screen. That self-satisfied smile dominated his face. The doctor was slick with sweat, his face shining like melting wax. The entire room was stifling hot. The machine exuded warmth like a space heater from hell. The doctor was enjoying the beauty of his creation, as if experiencing an intellectual orgasm.

Craig feared what Dr. Krone could produce on the screen next. *Is this your treatment? Showing me images on a screen?*

The doctor's face clenched. "This is a preliminary. My procedure is meant to drum up old memories. It's to percolate memories and events from your personal history."

The doctor stalked back to the machine, shortly after punching another series of computer keys. The screen flickered and then stayed bright, the golden rays piercing into Craig's eyes and lighting up his skull.

Turn it off, my God, just turn it off!

"Hold on and watch, Mr. Horsy."

Rachael added, "This is going to be better than your last memory."

"This'll take a minute." Then the frantic typing of computer keys. "I'll tell you something while we're waiting. Haven't you ever thought how cool it would be to see and hear what somebody else is thinking? Nobody can truly explain in words what's transpiring in their heads. And human beings have a tendency to lie or stretch the truth. Nobody's accurate in real life. This machine is one hundred percent accurate. I can analyze what's injected the anger into your life, and I will coax it from your system."

But you said this therapy wasn't just putting images on a screen.

"I did. And I wasn't lying. You'll see. That's the next step of the process. Soon, you'll be living the process."

Craig was helpless to watch the memory unfold—

"It hurts, Craig—I'm bleeding! Why did we turn on this damn highway? Why did we take your piece-of-shit car? I don't want to die. Not like this."

He watched his hand clutch his wife's. Both of his hands were slathered in blood. He was positioned on his knees outside the Toyota Camry to catch the baby. Various shades of crimson soaked the car seat. Katie's thighs were sodden in brown-red birth fluids. She clutched the back of the driver's side to abate the pain, but her shouting and yelling didn't stop.

"You can't push so hard," Craig pleaded. "Remember Lamaze class? Breathe in and out and push, but not so forcefully."

"Fuck Lamaze, and fuck you, Craig!"

"Stay calm, Katie, I love you. We'll get through this."

"You're not the one pregnant. And why did you take the highway?"

"It was only lightly snowing when we started driving. I couldn't know the storm would get worse . . ."

"You should've checked the weather. This car has about had it. We should've taken a cab! What the hell is wrong with you?"

"None of this is happening as we planned."

"Oh, no shit!"

Snow pelted his head. Sheets of white whipped across the highway and blinded the horizon. The below-zero winds pierced him unmercifully. Gusts of air were so fierce, they rocked the car and the shocks squealed.

The engine had quit. It was Saturday at three in the morning. He called a tow truck and an ambulance, but the weather was so bad, they were taking forever to arrive. Sirens wailed in the distance. No other cars had passed them the entire time they were stranded beside the concrete median.

"You waited too long to call for help," Katie accused him. Softer now, demurring into a dying voice, she said, "*It's too late.*"

So much blood had been lost, it dripped from the edge of the seat and spattered the road and colored the snow. The red soaked into his clothes, his skin, and somehow flicked onto his lips.

He did his best to keep her conscious. "Hey, stay with me."

She passed out.

He shook her body. "Katie, *stay with me!*"

Sirens blared from nearby.

Help had arrived.

You sick son of a bitch!

That was the last he'd seen Katie alive, with blood staining both her cheeks in handprint shapes from when he touched her. She died three hours later at the hospital from an internal hemorrhage. Jenny was miscarried.

Dr. Krone and Rachael clapped in unison.

What the fuck are you so happy about? You enjoy watching my wife suffer?

"This is progress," the doctor rejoiced. "Please understand. Your mind is accepting the machine's impulses. This means my treatment can be effective. Not everybody's mind allows my machine to enter their memories."

Take me off of this machine right now!

The doctor moved into Craig's line of vision again, Rachael standing beside him. They were side by side, the woman hugging the doctor with one arm. They were delighted.

Dr. Krone said, "Do yourself a favor and calm down. Like what you said to Katie, correct?"

Fuck you. You have no right to talk about Katie. You don't know her. You don't know me.

The doctor's eyes lit up. "But I will know both of you very well in time."

The doctor removed the binoculars from Craig's face. The screen went blank. The golden rays vanished. Purple and white blotches corrupted his vision. He couldn't see anything for five minutes.

Doctor and assistant were busy at work. The time to chat had concluded. The mechanical whir of a metal fan matched the grinding of gears. The device was warming up again. Burning hot now, Craig's skin absorbed the heat, and he couldn't do anything to abate the rising agony. Computer keys were tapped at ninety words per minute. What Dr. Krone was instructing the machine must have been intricate, as intricate as navigating the depths of his mind.

Rachael pushed a syringe into the back of Craig's neck where his spine and brain stem connected. She was lost in her work.

"What's wrong with you people?"

He could talk again.

Dr. Krone sighed. "Inject him with a numbing agent. We can't have him yammering while we work."

"Stop this right now." He couldn't move his limbs. The fresh injection served to further numb his processes. "I'll call the police. You can't silence me. People will miss me. They know I've gone to Dr. Richard Herbert."

And that was the problem.

"This isn't a real clinic. I'm not where I'm supposed to be."

"It sure is a clinic," the doctor said. "You're required by law to stay. You signed the court document. It's the best decision you've made in your lifetime. I'm saving you and the public any future harm. Now, let us get to work. Give my treatment a chance. You'll enjoy it, Craig, I promise."

"I didn't want this. *Stop what you're doing to me!*"

Rachael seized his jaw. A needle pierced his lips, clacked against his jawbone, and he was instantly anesthetized.

He yipped in his throat when she unbuckled his khakis pants. She dragged them down to his knees. The room was colder now. He shivered, holding his breath without realizing it.

"He's very serious about helping you." Rachael removed his underwear and installed a catheter. "You don't have to be scared. This will be a therapeutic experience. You'll thank us later."

Dr. Krone inserted an IV needle into each arm. One was a morphine drip, the other a feeding tube.

Rachel stared at him apologetically. "This looks intimidating. This is the hardest part of the process. Please, try your best to relax. We'll be done shortly. I know you're scared. But don't be."

A blanket was draped over his legs.

Ca-clink. The machine was charging up once again. It was like eleven furnaces kicking on to fight the dead cold of winter.

The metal gears churned faster. *Crrrrrrrrink.*

The seizure was one swift motion. Two steel prongs swung down, connected to robotic arms. The plastic at the ends of the arms were fingers that pried open his eyelids.

25

"This is the hardest step," Dr. Krone warned. "Brace yourself."

The machine worked at deafening levels.

The doctor had to raise his voice to be heard. "Stay strong, Mr. Horsy!"

The spinning motor's hum now sounded like a dentist's drill held up to a microphone. Two new robotic arms were poised before his eyes. At the end of each arm was a metal circle. Thin needles lined the circumference of each circle.

Oh God!

The needles pierced the wet tissue around his eyeballs and dug two inches deep. They touched specific parts of his brain. New nerves were activated, while other functions were terminated. Electric impulses seized him, circulating into his bloodstream, his nervous system, every vital process hooked up to a power source. His skull crackled and his hair popped with static electricity. Drool spooled from his lips. Tears trailed down his cheeks.

Dr. Krone stepped into his line of vision, beholding Craig, before he flipped on the final switch.

"*Now* the therapy begins, Mr. Horsy!"

LAke jAcomo

RAIg cLutched the rope in both hands. It was soaking wet and slippery. He was standing on one of the shagbark hickory tree's thickest branches that extended over the surface of Lake Jacomo. The scent of dead fish was kicked up in the breeze, and he took it in willingly, that dose of nostalgia he so much enjoyed. The lake extended for half a mile in each direction, the surface muddy brown. The water would be the source of numerous ear infections in Craig's future.

J.J. Kidd, one of his best elementary school friends, hollered at him from below. "Hurry up, Craig. I'm swinging next!"

Neil Jablanski was already scaling the tree, ready for his turn after Craig's. And there was Alice Denny, who wore her one-piece bathing suit decorated with watermelons. She sat on a boulder far enough from the boys to be ignored. She'd have nothing to do with the high dives, but she liked to watch them.

Craig stood on the branch like a king of the mountain. If his parents knew about this, they'd cut the rope down. His father, Brandon, had scolded him previously, *"You remember Junior Conners? He broke his leg falling from that branch. I don't want*

27

to pay expensive medical bills because of your stupidity."

His father's warnings vanished. Lake Jacomo begged to be jumped into. He had to muster a cool dive first, but before Craig could decide, it was too late. Neil grabbed the limb by both his hands and shook it, ruining Craig's footing.

"You're going down!" Neil cheered. "You know the rules. You take too long, you go *down!*"

Craig teetered, then, losing his balance, he crashed on his side into the lake.

"Yeah, fall!" J.J. cheered, clapping his hands. "Did you see that, Neil? You're awesome. Knocked him on his ass. He went *down!*"

"I said I was next," Neil bragged. "I warned him he'd go down."

The slap of landing awkwardly against the water had him near tears, but Craig couldn't lose it, not in front of his friends. When he touched down, his feet graced the mud at the bottom. He imagined a creature grabbing his ankle and forcing him down. The mud monster. The images of the mud monster impelled him to the surface so fast he almost lost his blue swim trunks. He lifted them back up fully to his waist, and once he stepped onto shore, he waited for another chance to perform a cool dive from the tree.

Standing there, Alice eyed him shyly. The boys were ten years old, and she was eight. She tagged along with them. It was an unspoken neighborhood kid understanding that she could hang out with them as long as she didn't interfere.

"Good landing," she mumbled, her best attempt at making conversation. "You okay?"

"No thanks to Neil." He balled up his fists. "Jerk."

Neil launched down from the tree limb in a ball. The cannonball landing shot water onto land, pelting Craig and Alice.

J.J. was already halfway up the trunk, ready to follow up with a better midair trick. Craig waited for his turn again, thinking that these summer days were the best of his life. He didn't really know how much he enjoyed himself back then until he relived it with the benefit of adult hindsight . . .

Lake Jacomo's fetid waft of dead fish was refreshing compared to the brazen winter cold in Franklin, Indiana. Winter offered no natural smells. Everything was buried under ice and rendered characterless by the cold. This was the perfect escape from the city. The warmth of summer, the thriving of life, it was so easy to absorb and experience a reinvigoration.

This is what Dr. Daniel Krone enjoyed as he canoed the lake and watched the children play.

bRAndon hoRSy

CRAIg wAS cRouched beneath the basement stairs inside the crawlspace, clueless as to how he arrived in the dark place. He spent his time observing the scene rather than trying to pick at the mystery of how he showed up here. The plastic Christmas tree, the Halloween decorations crammed into one bulging box, the second-hand clothes, and old records were all stored in the claustrophobic corner. Dusty sheets draped the items.

He once discovered birthday presents in here, including a Huffy ten-speed bicycle. Craig learned later that his dad, Brandon, had worked overtime to afford it. The man worked for the city repairing potholes and broken water pipes, and performed basic street maintenance. Brandon wore a neon green vest and thick brown overalls to work. He'd stamp out his black leather boots on the porch after work and dirt clots would be strewn about the steps. He was a hulking man, and Craig feared his father's temper. He hid here when his parents argued, and that's what he was doing right now in the crawlspace.

The basement was his father's getaway. It was off-limits and mysterious to a nine-year-old. The bench press, the rack of free weights, and the treadmill manned one corner. Posters of bikini-clad women and other lesser-clad women highlighted the walls. The refrigerator in the corner was a giant-sized Budweiser can, which stood adjacent to the pool table and dart board. Brandon's friends often joked and lounged down here. The place exuded a mystery that compelled Craig to search it when he was home alone.

Overhearing his parents argue in that special room, he peeked out of the crawlspace in the desperate hope his mother didn't get harmed by the giant who was now shouting at her, both of them in the grips of a heated fight. Brandon towered over Craig's mother. Broad shoulders, thick chest, a modest pot belly, he was two hundred and thirty pounds. Tina, Craig's mother, had the opposite figure. She was only one hundred pounds, and closer to five feet tall. Craig was nine at this moment in his life, and he was already more than half his mother's weight, and almost as tall. Her dark auburn hair was cropped at her shoulders.

Today was a Friday, he recalled. What his mother called "Clean House" day. She overhauled every room in the house, including Brandon's bachelor pad— that's what Craig referred to it as after his parents divorced when he was twenty-two.

His father shouted, the source of their argument coming to light. "Where the fuck is my Cindy Crawford poster? She doesn't even show her tits in that one. What's the big deal?"

"It leaked downstairs," Tina said, defending her choice to throw away the poster. "They were damaged. They would've mildewed."

"You mean the ceiling leaked? I know it rained,

but the rain doesn't sneak in through the ceiling. Are you dumb?"

She was caught in a lie. "I-I just don't want so many nudie posters up, okay? Craig wanders down here. He sees them."

"And so what? It'll grow some hair on the boy's chest. He doesn't know what these mean. Big deal."

"But he'll see women as objects."

"So you're saying I see women as objects?"

She hid her face in her hands then dared to look at him again. "It's not healthy for him to look at them. Kids learn about sex too young. He'll knock up some girl, and who'll take care of the kid? *Me*."

"I'm a good father." He swigged the remainder of his Budweiser can then placed it on the edge of the pool table. "I'm a man. I'm an adult man, Tina. I don't tell you what you can or cannot do. I enjoy myself. I don't cheat on you."

It slipped out of her, "You did once."

"Ah, fuck this!" He swatted the can off the pool table. It slammed into the wall, froth shooting up like spit and striking them both. He grabbed her by both shoulders and shook her hard once. Craig winced, praying she wouldn't be hit.

"That was two years ago. I said I was sorry. Forgive me or leave me, but don't hold it over my head. It was a mistake. God, you piss me off so much sometimes when you bring that shit up."

Craig once overheard Tina talking to their neighbor in the backyard about how to protect themselves. She too had a husband who lost his temper and the control of his fists. "Clutch your head," Jill had advised Tina. "Don't let him bruise your face. Hank hasn't hit me after our counseling sessions, but I know what to do if he ever hits me again. And don't get me wrong, I'd leave his ass. I have a suitcase packed in case he ever does and enough money to last me three month's rent in some crackerjack apartment. You should have a plan too, Tina."

They formed an abused wives club, didn't they, Craig thought.

Hey, wait—!

Craig stared at his hands. They were so small. His palm was patched with a Snoopy Band-Aid. He'd cut it on the lava rocks in his front yard. He got tackled in a frenzied game of tag and landed on them. He was dressed in Nike shorts and a green T-shirt with the *Slice* beverage logo across the chest. He was an adult in a child's body.

Tina wept and wrapped her arms around Brandon. "I'm sorry. I'm sorry I brought it up."

He patted her hair and released a great breath of air. "It's a stupid poster."

She gave up the fight. "It's fine."

Craig sensed her disappointment. She'd conceded to her husband once again. "I shouldn't have taken it down." She softened her words. "I'm prettier than them, aren't I?"

He stroked her hair. "Yes, you are. They're stupid posters. It's a man thing. It's nothing."

You're a goddamn liar. You like the posters better than my mom. All you care about is sex.

Craig locked his fists, channeling rage into them. "I'll fucking show him." The words were strange—morbid—escaping from a child's throat.

He launched out of the crawlspace, throwing open the door so hard it snapped the top hinge. Stomping toward his parents, he questioned what damage he could do to his old man. He located the rack of pool cues. He cradled one like a baseball bat and charged toward his dad with fury escaping his throat. "*No-mooooooore!*"

Brandon was shocked, his eyes bulging as he took in his oncoming son. He finally let go of Tina and tried to intercept his child, but Craig was too fast. He slammed the cue over his back three times, his dad shrieking in pain, the stick snapping after the last thwack.

Brandon was on his knees and clutching at his back. His face twisted up at him, his buzzed head glistening with new sweat. "Boy, what the hell is wrong with you?"

"You cheated on Mom!" Craig shouted, cracking his throat to unleash his contempt. The child's body couldn't translate the adult emotions. "You fucked those ugly hookers at the strip club. What's her name, you told me once after you divorced Mom—as if I'm supposed to be proud of you! Temptress, yeah, that's it. And you've slept with Paula again since your first affair. You can't keep your mind off snatch. And that's what you called it, you called it 'snatch.' You don't deserve Mom." He turned to his mother. "Don't put up with his shit on my account. Don't stay in this marriage for me, not for this asshole."

He was unleashing his father's future secrets, but at this point, they had yet to happen.

Collecting his lung capacity, Brandon growled, "You brat, you're making shit up. I haven't cheated on your mom—not what you're saying."

The giant rose up and twisted Craig's arm around his back and shoved him against the wall. "Now why are you saying those things about me? I taught you common sense and respect. You don't disrespect your elders, and you sure as shit don't disrespect me."

"Because everything I'm saying is true." Craig's lips were wedged against the wall. He was inches from a poster with bare breasts—the breasts were all he could see, shiny, and glossy, and flat. "You told me about it all when you two finally divorced. You tried to treat our talks as a confessional. You tried to keep your boy from hating you for the rest of your life. You're a scumbag, and you know it."

Tina was puzzled, but somehow, she was able to speak, though meekly. "We're not divorced, kiddo. Your dad hasn't done any of those things. Craig, what's gotten into you? You've never behaved this way. And those words, who taught you to talk like that?"

She stole Craig from Brandon, wrenching him from the man's hold, and hugged him close. She was trembling. A deep-down part of her knew what he was saying was true, but this was the earliest stages of her doubt, and she couldn't act on her instincts yet.

"You shouldn't pamper him. Answer your mother. Who taught you to talk to your father like that? Speak up."

"You did, Dad."

The man landed the back of his hand across his face. It hurt as much as it did in the past. The mean tingles. The blood beneath the skin spread the pain. The emotional overcame the physical, and he stared at his dad with venom seething in his eyes.

"You hit me like you hit Mom. And you like it, don't you? Once a deadbeat, always a deadbeat. Hit me so you can shut me up. Hit Mom so you can shut her up. You can go to hell, you *bastard!*"

Tina charged up the stairs, wailing. Craig's protector had fled the scene. It wasn't long before he was wrestled to the floor by the shoulder and neck and flung down hard. He landed stomach first, every ounce of fight dashed to nothing in two seconds. Brandon shoved his knee into his back to anchor his son in place.

"You're not going unpunished for this." The man was beside himself, confused and fighting the guilt of harming his child. "Boy's making up shit about me. It's not true . . . not true at all. What would possess you to say those things?"

He unloosed his belt, and Craig imagined what his father was thinking—*How do I punish this kid enough to silence him in the future?*

But Dad doesn't know he'll cheat on Mom in the future. Why the hell is he so worked up? How does he know what I'm saying is true? It should be nonsense to him.

Brandon was wrapping the leather of his belt around his fist, the stretch audible. "This is unacceptable. Children live in their parents' shadow, boy, not the other way around."

The belt was raised, prepared to deliver an expedient punishment. Brandon's face was locked in an absent expression. He was moments from landing the animal skin across Craig's back when the words came as a deadly warning, "You leave my son the hell alone."

They both turned to Tina.

She cradled a .28 Brown Eagle pistol.

Brandon lowered the belt and stood in awe at the wife who finally stood up to her husband.

Dr. Krone furiously jotted notes onto his steno pad. He hid behind the crawlspace door, listening in. He completed his notations. What else would pop out of Craig's mind, he wondered, knowing the machine would soon answer him. Enough had been accomplished in this moment that he decided it was time to move on to the next memory . . .

LAke jAcomo

The **Snow wAS** falling in thick downy flakes. Lake Jacomo was frozen over and thick enough to ice skate on, though it was absent of people. Standing there on the lake, Craig was dressed in the same thing he wore at Dr. Krone's office—a dress-up shirt, khaki pants, and black leather Hanover shoes. The bitter winds were howling, but he didn't feel any of it. Shrugging the odd sensation of being numb to the elements, he scanned the area once again and caught the man standing behind the wooden bench two feet from the frozen shore.

Dr. Krone.

Craig bounded forward for the opportunity to beat him down, but he slipped. He teetered forward, landing on his hands and scraping his palms on the ice. A hand reached out to help him up.

"You're upset," Dr. Krone said matter-of-factly. He'd somehow cleared the distance between them in seconds to give him a hand. "The treatment is intense. But you're over the difficult part. I even placed you in one of your favorite places to talk to you. You enjoy Lake Jacomo during the winter, right? It's calming. Serene."

He refused the man's hand and worked back to his

feet by himself. He was enraged, but questions replaced the urge to strike the doctor. "How did you know that?"

"I'm a professional." The doctor removed a pack of cigarettes from his pocket. They were 80's Milds. "And these are your favorite cigarettes. Even though you detest your father, he smoked these. You stole a few from his stash in his toolbox every now and again. You wanted to emulate him. I guess that's the best quality he had to emulate. It's so sad."

The air was sucked out from his lungs. "My God, you know everything about me. It's like you're—"

"—In your mind?" He handed Craig a cigarette. He put it in his mouth, and the doctor lit it with a match, guarding the flame with his hand. "I'm traveling these memories with you. The machine simply displays your catalogue of experiences. My job is to determine the most productive route to take for your treatment, and I stand back and observe."

"So you're really in there? In my head, I mean."

"Plugged in, is all."

The cigarette seemed real, and it was all he could trust at the moment. "I'd call this situation, what, a mind fuck?"

"That's a bit harsh."

"I haven't forgotten about the fake door in your office. This is still against my will. I can't trust you. You trapped me. You built a psychological prison around me, or something."

"No, it's not like that at all. And this fake door you keep mentioning, it doesn't exist. I gave you your treatment. I did drug you to get you strapped into the machine. It was to calm you down so you didn't hurt yourself. Maybe you're imagining these other things.

The drugs can make you do that. It's that scary, my treatment, I admit it, because it's intense. You were terrified even while drugged up, so imagine your experience without sedatives. I was doing you a favor. Your reaction isn't uncommon. Past patients say exactly what you're saying. They have delusions before the treatment—like your said 'fake door.' But this is very real. The drugs are vital in other ways too. The early testing of the machine, patients had seizures, heart attacks, and panic attacks. You're lucky you came along after the machine was perfected."

"I can only imagine what other snafus occurred before I came along." Craig refused to take his eyes off the doctor. "Did patients lose their eyes, or maybe their brains bled to death? So right now, as we speak, there's needles in my eyes and needles in my skull, and I'm sitting in that dreadful room hooked up to a piss bag."

"Your physical body is, but right now, you transcend the hemispheres and lobes of your mind. It's an endless labyrinth. The machine keeps you where you want to be. I'll level with you, Mr. Horsy. You're a pent-up man on the verge of criminal violence. You already harmed your best friend. You remember poor Willis, don't you?"

"You saw it happen ringside. You don't have to remind me."

"I'm here to break you of becoming a violent individual. I'm what's going to keep you out of prison. You'll come out of this feeling renewed. The burden on your shoulders will be gone. I've arranged for you to meet with your mother after my treatment. It's too bad your father died in that traffic pileup a year ago."

"A real shame," Craig sighed, the sentiment real,

though there was a piece missing to his grief he failed to understand. "But I hadn't seen him in forever before he died. I might as well not have had a father. That sounds awful, saying that."

"It's too bad you feel that way. But you have a mother, and she needs you. You'll rekindle old feelings—good feelings—about your family once we're finished here."

A problem struck Craig. How was the doctor here talking to him? Craig reached out to touch the man. He was physical. Solid.

It tickled the doctor. "You're looking at me like I'm an alien being. How am I in your head with you, is that what you're thinking? It's a fair question." He stepped closer, and Craig could smell the cigarette on his breath. "I, too, am hooked up to a machine. Does that put you at ease? I went through the same process as you did. I do every time I receive a new patient."

"So who strapped you in?"

"Rachael, of course."

"Oh." He paused, reconsidering his approach to the man and his machine. "How come this treatment is so secret?"

"It's a privacy issue. And it's a controversial method. It's safe, but hardly mainstream. This one can be tough to endorse too. It's not as pretty as taking a pill."

Craig wandered out to the ice. His steps were slower. The ice was slick and covered in white powdery snow. The sky was a dark slate gray. This was the true dead of winter.

He retraced what happened with his parents earlier. He had lashed out at Brandon as a child. Then

Tina pulled a gun on him. Both those things didn't happen in real life.

"How is the machine determining all of this?" He sucked in several breaths, challenging the winter's cold that wouldn't settle into his skin. "My memories have been changed. New things are happening that didn't before. It's . . . altered."

He lowered his defenses, though he still didn't trust the doctor.

Dr. Krone stepped out onto the ice with him. "Your mind sets up a scene for you to react to in a specific manner. The memory can change. Your father didn't strike you with a belt. Tina never pulled a gun on your father. But in your deepest id, you wanted these things to occur. You wanted to smash a pool cue over his back and shout at him that he was a terrible husband and a terrible father. Your parents won't understand what you're saying in every situation, but they will react to it with the best of their ability. It all depends on what your mind can produce."

He rubbed at his eyes. "This is so confusing."

"It tends to be. The reason I put those images on a screen previously was to see if using the machine would be productive." He came closer. "Your mind is *very* productive. So productive, I want to reward you. Consider it a break from your therapy."

"Wait, how long have I been in treatment?"

He had no concept of time. He had no job to answer to or wife or girlfriend who'd check up on him. Most of his friends inhabited Half-Time bar, though he was temporarily banned from the establishment because of what he did to Willis.

Dr. Krone caught him at a crossroads in his life. This was supposed to be a stepping stone to a normal life.

His temper shut him out of a lot of opportunities. He was skeptical of the doctor, but also dependent. If this was the cure he needed, he would leave the practice a better man. And if this quack was bullshitting him and keeping him here against his will . . .

He'd have to find out the truth and soon.

"I'm not a bad guy," Craig said. "Sure, I seriously harmed Willis, but I mean well otherwise. I'm a pretty solitary guy these days. I don't have a lot of friends."

"But that's the thing. You're a social butterfly—at least in the past you were. You've been altered because of your temper. You seclude yourself to subdue your beast. This temper is something you learned. It's time we unlearn your temper so you can truly be yourself again."

"Then I'm open to what you've got in store for me next. I have no choice, so I might as well give it a shot. I can't fight you."

Dr. Krone *tsk-tsk*ed. "I wouldn't put it like that."

"It is what it is. So I guess we should continue on."

Dr. Krone's eyes lit up. "Wonderful. Here goes." He smiled. "But first, I give you my reward, to show you my good faith."

the SIngLeS cLub

he SIngLeS cLub met every Friday night. It was a night that created the sense of a relationship, or the dating experience without actually dating. The group frequented Quivers, a hip dance club, and tonight was '80s night. Blue, yellow, and red squares painted each wall in wild rotations, the disco ball refracting silver light in overlapping dimensions. The dance floor was jam-packed with partiers as *Duran Duran* blasted the song "Girls on Film."

Craig had sweated on the dance floor for long enough, and now he retreated to the bar for liquid refreshment. A whiskey and soda.

"You're a camel when it comes to drinking," Susan, his friend and fellow club member, chided him from a nearby table. She raised her voice to match the music level. "Sit down. Let's hang. How the hell have you been?"

The singles meeting played out differently tonight. Their four other friends couldn't make it this time. Later, Craig learned Susan arranged for their absences. The others really went to see a movie. *The Terminator*, if he recalled correctly. Susan wasn't the kind of girl he wanted a relationship with. She was

44

more of a friend, but with new hindsight as an older Craig Horsy, he had a completely different take on the situation.

Susan was gorgeous. Her blonde hair was silky smooth in the club's lights, the locks flowing down to her shoulders in golden waves. She wore a silver sequined dress that bragged generously of her borderline D-cup cleavage. She had a sleek body shape at one hundred and twenty pounds. Susan wasn't thin to the point one questioned her diet, and he liked that. There was plenty to grab from her hind quarters too, and he especially liked that.

She said, "I'm not drunk yet, but I'm working on it. The night's young."

The waiter brought her another round. A sea breeze. "Here you go, ma'am."

Taking it to her lips, she asked, "Who ordered this for me?"

Craig raised his hand, being the guilty party. "I saw you before I hit the bar and ordered it. I owe you a drink, right? If you weren't here, I would've shown up alone. How embarrassing, huh? The singles club would've been, well, one single guy."

She clasped his hand. Looking at her, her eyes shined more than they would normally, as if on the verge of happy tears. She glowed. Susan was perked about something, and with that valuable insight from the past, he understood she had a crush on him. He was an idiot not to realize it at the time. He was twenty-eight in this memory. Three years after he lost Katie and his unborn child. Relationships were still tricky. Time had failed to heal his wounds.

Or you were simply a chicken shit. You have a right to enjoy your life. Why didn't you see her for

45

who she was instead of letting your goddamn emotional baggage get in the way?

Kevin and Brice, the two other men in the singles group, grilled him the following day because he'd turned Susan down for a nightcap. "You were cold to her." "Are you that stupid? She's head over heels for you, man." "She practically wants to be your wife." "You could've turned her down easier, or given her an honest chance first." "Susan's such a nice woman. And she's been married before. She's in the same boat as you." "She's a corporate secretary for a law firm, and you're a garbage man. And she doesn't care. She's not fickle like those other bitches out there." "You're an asshole, Craig. Why don't you forget our meetings? This is a support group, or did you forget?"

Susan reached out and touched his cheek with three fingers. "You're blushing."

"But it's so dark, how can you tell?"

Every ounce of her was trying to hold back her true feelings for him. She couldn't stop smiling at him. Her eyes were so soft, it was endearing.

She plucked the cherry from her drink and rolled it up and down in her mouth. She tied the stem, then she stuck out her tongue and showed him her hard work.

You were such an idiot. She's screaming for you to throw her a hint.

He never said this to Susan the first time this happened. "Of all the women I know, Susan, I'd want to get to know you better."

Rod Stewart's song played, *If you want my body, and you think I'm sexy . . .*

He'd read her correctly. Susan's face lit up at his words.

What he really said that night was, "*I don't like it when women hit on a man without knowing if he has feelings for her first. It's a sign of being kind of a slut.*"

That was it. He was embarrassed by his behavior. It was the fear of commitment talking. Susan shut down after that. It was too late to fix the damage. Susan later dated Kevin in the group. They married a year later. He wasn't invited to the ceremony; Brice told him after the fact, and by then, the singles club had officially disbanded.

Susan slugged the sea breeze down, giving him a pair of lustful eyes. "I've got better booze at my apartment. How about a nightcap?"

Thank you, Dr. Krone. I owe you one.

Maybe you're not so bad.

Maybe.

"Yeah," he agreed, standing up and taking her by the arm. "I'd like that very much."

The ride home was fast. She lived six blocks from Quivers. They were making out in the hallway of her apartment building, her legs wrapped around his hips as he carried her to her room. "I don't care if the neighbors wake up," she whispered in his ear. She was giggly, and he was pressing all the right buttons, caressing her shoulder blades and cupping her ass and kissing between her neck and ears when he could, though doing all of this carefully so as not to drop her.

Arriving at her door, he placed her back onto her feet so she could unlock her apartment, and shortly after, they spilled inside, practically racing for the bedroom.

"This way." Susan threw the door closed and stepped out of her sequined outfit. She was draped in shadow, the curves along the small of her back and the top of her buttocks visible, taut and muscular hard lines and soft flesh. A monarch butterfly tattoo had been inked on her right shoulder blade. Her car seats were draped in monarch butterfly covers. She often wore butterfly necklaces and earrings too.

Following after her, he observed her bedroom, the bed itself surrounded with a silk net like some kind of French sex palace.

God, why did I turn down Susan? I'm such an idiot. I even liked her. I liked her a lot.

"I can't believe this is happening." She sauntered back to him with a strut, her arms outstretched to snatch him back into her grip. "I didn't think you shared the same feelings."

"I should've owned up to them." He hugged her close. Really embraced her. He whispered, smelling the sweetness of her hair and the wanton saltiness to her flesh, "It really means a lot to me somebody like you could take an interest in me. It's very flattering. I'm lucky."

"No, I'm lucky." Susan kissed his lips tenderly. She started to cry because he was crying. They wiped off each other's tears. "You don't have to be afraid of relationships anymore. I know you are. I was too."

He pressed his face against hers. "It's hard to move on. Damn hard."

"I know what happened to you." She stroked his hair, curl by curl. "And you heard about Mark."

Mark was shot down during a gas station robbery. He was paying for his gas and a robbery got out of hand, and a random bullet came his way, ending his life.

But that was the end of talking.

Susan unbuckled his belt, and Craig slid down his boxer briefs. He was painfully hard, each throb an indication he hadn't been laid in a long time. They grinded against each other and built up the sexual tension. She kept whispering for him not to penetrate, urging him to tease her. Her mouth roamed his neck, ears, and up and down his chest. Every girl had her special moves, but he had moves of his own. Craig cupped one side of her buttock. He reached his finger between her legs, checking. She was already wet, and he massaged her, spreading that wetness.

Overtaken with the heat of passion, they fell backwards onto the bed. He was already inside her. She cooed upon the first thrust, reaching out her arms and grasping the iron headboard, her muscles taut and stretched to their maximum. He kissed her breasts, biting at the budding nipples, and he might've bit too hard, he thought, when she yipped, "Oh, Craig!"

"Oh, I'm sorry."

She pushed his head back down to her chest. "No, it feels *fucking* good."

He rocked gently inside her, careful not to test his endurance. She was tighter than Katie. He was ashamed to form that distinction, but it happened unconsciously. Her kisses tasted different too. The flavor of her skin was saltier. He could smell her pussy, and it aroused him. Susan reached around and played with his balls, tickling them, carefully raking her nails down the circumference.

He was surprised by how much she liked to play with him. "You like to touch them, huh? Most girls find them unattractive."

"They bring you satisfaction," she purred, bearing

a hint of what else she wanted to do to "satisfy" him. "I hear touching them during sex increases the potency of your orgasm."

Susan wrapped her legs around his back, reclaiming her prey. "Now fuck me."

So a few thrusts later, he was on the verge of finishing, and he had to take it slow. "It's hard to hold back," he grunted, knowing she'd notice his hesitation.

They slowed down, relishing the moment, grinding at a slow rate. She eyed him with zeal as she lay flat against the bed and began touching herself. She kept her orgasm in the running, and she talked about her body. "I don't get the big orgasm. I get little ones. It's like a small step up a long climb. Each step brings me closer to the top. It's all good, don't worry, Craig."

"Then good, because I think I'm ready to pump you hard again . . . *maybe*."

He cradled Susan. She was asleep. She was at peace, her face tranquil, and maybe dreaming. He played his fingers through the strands of her hair, enjoying her. She shifted, moaning softly, and drifted back to rest. "This is what could've been, huh?"

Susan didn't wake.

Craig looked about the room. There were acrylic paintings of monarch butterflies and one of those 3-D optical illusion pictures. *Ah, let me guess, it's of a butterfly*.

He could never see those things. He couldn't cross his eyes hard enough.

The vanity mirror was sixty percent covered in 3x5 pictures. Friends, her two sisters, and the singles club mostly. Her closet door was open, showing the dresses, work clothes, and an ironing board folded up inside. It was strange how realistic all this was, making it easy to forget none of this had actually happened. Dr. Krone's machine was ingenious. Whatever allowed this to exist, it was amazing. He felt alive. Relieved too. Deep down, he regretted the way he had treated Susan.

The idea of what could've been was bittersweet.

He relaxed in bed, letting the scene play out as it was going to play out, and he closed his eyes to sleep.

If he made a sound, Craig would hear him, so Dr. Krone kept his movements to a minimum. The treatment was coming along nicely. The patient was accepting his medicine, so to speak. He stood in the hallway by the door outside the bedroom. He'd tucked his pad of paper in his back pocket a long time ago. It was useless now. His clinical observations ended when the sex began.

He liked to watch.

Those moments were his favorite.

Almost his favorite.

Katie

CRAIG OPENED HIS EYES. He wasn't at Susan's apartment anymore. He was in another room altogether. A gray coverlet was wrapped around him, keeping him warm. How he got here, he wasn't sure. It just happened. He closed his eyes for a moment, and here he was. But he wasn't about to deny the privilege of what was provided. It was wonderful to be with Susan, and now, he was with his wife. The actuality of it was overwhelming.

Katie was on her side of the bed, and he was spooning her. He smelled her dark brown hair, what was a mix of day-old hair and the remains of her pomegranate lavender shampoo. They were pressed up against each other, naked.

They'd just made love. He was having a lot of sex; too bad he didn't enter the scene sooner to fully experience it. She was exhausted from working another evening shift at Bryer's Pharmacy as a pharmacy tech, but as Katie put it that night, and other nights like this, "I'm too wired to sleep, let's have sex. That always puts me to sleep." It was a compliment despite the way it sounded.

He was spent, the post-sex moment at a

comedown. Craig battled to stay calm. He wanted to break down and cry and tell her he loved her and everything else a person said when a person they loved died.

What she said removed him from the reverie. "How was Susan?"

There was no accusation in her voice.

"Excuse me?"

"You just had sex with her, so was it good?"

Confused by the question, he couldn't do anything but tell the truth. "Yes, but how did you know?"

"Let's not talk about that—talk about Susan. Was it hot? Did she give it to you good?"

"Wait, whoa, how do you know about Susan?"

Katie stared at him, waiting for the answer to her question first.

"Yes, she was good. I-I enjoyed it. But I love you. You know that, right?"

She waved him to be quiet. "I know that, honey. I want you to be happy and horny." She giggled. "It's fine. I'm sure you'd want the same for me."

He was stunned. "Did you see us or something? How do you know about what happened?"

Katie brushed off the question. What she said next he recognized from a previous conversation. "Do you ever think about other women during sex?" She always asked introspective questions, like little post-coital quizzes. But now Katie wasn't speaking of Susan anymore, and according to Katie, she now didn't have any knowledge of her. He had difficulty grasping on to the moment, but he tried to anyway. Every moment with Katie was precious.

She gave her opinion about her own question. "I think about other men. There, I said it."

He scoffed, thrown off by the admission. "Yeah, like who? Fabio?"

"Fabio's gross," she gagged, sticking her finger in her mouth. "He's not real. He's too primped and manicured. I like real men. Paul Reiser."

"Paul Reiser? Who's that?"

"You know the show *Mad About You*? He's Helen Hunt's husband on the show. Curly black hair, smartass charm, he's cute."

"Wow, Paul Reiser. You think about *him*."

"Come on, you think about other women. It's okay. I'm not mad."

"I'm not *Mad About You*."

"Oh, shut up." She nudged him with her elbow. "You're just going to make fun of me."

"Well, yeah," Craig teased. "I'm no Paul Reiser."

"You're better than him. Would you stop bringing him up?"

He wrapped his hand around her belly. She was twenty weeks along in the pregnancy. He enjoyed touching her belly. It was an extension of her, something extraordinary, something he created. He leaned down and kissed her stomach above the navel.

"You're kissing our baby."

"I know."

Katie petted his head. "You're just a big softie."

He kissed behind her ear. "You tamed the beast."

"You got into so much trouble as a kid. What made you that way?"

He shrank back to his side of the bed. "I never figured that out."

"Maybe you should."

"Psychiatrists are full of shit."

A muffled laugh resounded from the left wall. Craig asked her, "Hey, did you hear that?"

She wrapped herself up tighter in the blankets. "No. I think you're ready for bed, though. You've got work in the morning. Sometimes sex makes you forget that."

She rolled over in bed and fell asleep. He tried to wake her, but he couldn't rouse her, no matter how hard he nudged her or said her name.

"Come on, honey. I want to talk longer. I haven't seen you in years. You're not alive anymore so wake up, Katie. *Katie!*"

She was still and at peace. Like she was dead again.

She's not waking up.

This is Dr. Krone's fault.

Craig bolted up from bed. He rushed into the hallway to pursue the location of the muffled laugh. The laugh had to be the doctor's. He ignored it earlier simply to be with Katie that much longer.

I still don't trust him.

"I know you're out there, Doctor. Why don't you face me?"

He burst through the hall and into the kitchen. The screen door to the backyard clapped shut. "Oh, I've got you this time, you fat fucker!"

Craig ejected himself into the twenty-degree cold, and he shivered against it, the effect a burning slap to the face. He stomped through three-feet-high snow and spotted him. The doctor stood beside a shed, caught.

"You were watching me. You pervert!"

Dr. Krone stepped into the porch light. He was stone-faced. "But you knew I was watching. It's my job."

"You were watching me with Susan." He leapt at the doctor and landed a wild punch to his nose. "You pervert!"

Dr. Krone spilled onto the ground with a crunch of snow. Blood bubbled from his nose. He snorted it out and chortled, smiling wide, his lips colored in red. "You can't hurt me. This isn't my mind. It's yours."

"But you're bleeding."

"It's everything you want to see. I'm not in pain. But you can feel pain. You can feel everything because we're in your brain. This is very real for you." The man's eyes went small. "Be careful what you do here."

"Is that a threat?"

The doctor raised his hands up in surrender. He dug into his pocket for his kerchief and dabbed the blood from his face. "We're getting on the wrong foot again. Susan was supposed to be enjoyable to you. It's a regret in your life, and you fulfilled that regret. You can check it off your list."

Craig was flabbergasted, just like he'd felt during their consultation. "This is too weird. Whatever you're doing, I'm not so sure it's working. I want to be with Katie again."

It wasn't fair. She was alive one moment, the next, asleep. "Please wake her. I-I can't make her wake up. You can. I know you can wake her up for me."

Dr. Krone trudged through the snow and patted his back. "You have a lot of things to work out with Katie. I don't think that memory was the correct one to put you in. That's why I ended it. I know it's a cold thing to do. You're a very courageous man. You've been through a lot, Craig. There are a lot of things that happened you didn't really ingest. No sane, red-blooded person could. Now you have the chance to ingest them with wisdom, and with my help."

"I just want Katie back," he pouted. "Forget my childhood. My parents can go to hell. Give me Katie."

"I can't," the doctor sighed. "It's not helping your treatment. There are other moments you need to explore first. Then I'll reward you again. It's for the best, I promise."

He seized him by the collar and shook him, the doctor's blood flecking onto Craig's shirt. He was losing himself to his trademark temper. "Look, you asshole, Katie's all I want! You've taken her away from me again. How many times am I going to lose her? How many times?"

The doctor pried Craig's hands from his collar and clasped them in his, squeezing them hard and sternly reminding him, "Remember why you're here to begin with. You haven't done physical harm to that many people, Mr. Horsy. But you will. You're on the course to serious violence. I'm going to stop you. It'll take time, but I'll remove the urge and replace it with a sense of calm."

He wiped at his eyes, but the cold had frozen his tears. "You're doing a shitty job of calming me down."

"I tried to give you another peaceful moment with your wife. I'm sorry it didn't last long enough for you. It wasn't productive for your treatment."

"Don't talk about my wife anymore." He pounded his fists against the shed and kicked the snow in a wild demonstration. "*I don't know what's real anymore!*"

He wanted to pummel the doctor into the ground. Really hurt him. The man was manipulative, and most of all, in charge of him. The bastard was in his mind.

He missed Katie already. Years he'd been without her. He'd been alone since then, except for Willis and his buddies at Half-Time and the singles club before it disbanded. Drinking buddies weren't true friends, he reminded himself. But Willis was a real friend.

"There's something not right about the way you're going about this." Craig rubbed his neck and tried to relax. "It's intrusive. I don't like you watching, especially when I'm having sex."

"I understand." Dr. Krone lowered his head. "But you have to understand, it's my job. Try and shut me out. I'm a professional. It's for your own good." He redirected the conversation. "I see you're eager to get back to business. Let's get serious again. This process doesn't go without its emotional challenges. Tell me, Mr. Horsy, how did you meet Katie?"

Craig stared into the yard next door, the Montaveys' yard. The above-ground pool was covered with a tarp. The dog house was piled in snow. The scene was so real, he kept thinking.

He replied to the question without animosity, "Why don't you put me in the memory, and you can see how we met."

Dr. Krone understood his patient's abrasiveness. "Then let's get on with the treatment, but it's my way, Craig. You'll learn to understand it's the only way we do things here."

the bLue RIde

CRAIg'S fAtheR CALLed the city bus "the blue ride." Brandon only used it when his '81 Ford Cruiser broke down, and this time, it was because the alternator was shot. The family only owned one car in order to save on auto insurance and gasoline. The supermarket and post office was within two blocks of their house, and Tina liked to walk for those trips—except during the winter, but she did so anyway. Craig was disappointed this was where Dr. Krone had placed him next.

This wasn't how he met Katie.

He was eleven years old in this memory, he remembered, shifting his backpack strap so it was secure between his shoulder blades. During most of their normal car rides, his father was quiet. He sipped his coffee and played the rock station, the eighties hair metal his favorite—*Def Leopard* in particular. But today, the journey was on "the blue ride."

Craig looked up at his dad and knew the man was hatching a plan, and it had nothing to do with taking his son to school.

The bus was jam-packed at this hour. The air was stale. Somebody wasn't wearing deodorant. Somebody had farted. Despite the distractions, Craig waited for the moment to happen, what had happened all those years ago. He wanted to warn his father, to tell him not to say anything to anybody, but he couldn't. The childhood fear of the man prevented him from acting out before it was too late.

He wouldn't interfere with Brandon's extra-curricular activities.

He followed his father's gaze, and there she was, walking up beside him, then staying inches from him. She was much too close to be a casual patron. She wore a leopard-skin coat, knock-off quality, black high heels, and a gray sheath dress underneath the coat. She was in her mid-thirties. She had applied spider-black eyeliner and her eye shadow was a shade of green. The woman clutched the bar overhead, working even closer to him. When the bus stopped, she over-exaggerated the impact and brushed up against his father.

"Oh, sorry," she apologized, holding his arm briefly. "I didn't mean to bump into you."

Brandon ogled at her cleavage. The man was suddenly knocked from his morning routine. The man liked to flirt. He was a true cheater, and it couldn't be any more obvious to Craig, especially now.

You really fucked over Mom.

"Oh, I'm sorry."

"Damn bus drivers," he joked. He held her arm gingerly. "I guess I can't let you go. The driver might take another sharp turn, and down you'll go."

Craig predicted it. Brandon peeked at her cleavage yet again. Her breasts were small. He supposed the chest wasn't the most important feature to his father. The plumbing was number one.

She licked her dark brown lips. The shade was

between cinnamon and dark spice. Craig knew the distinctions because his mother sold Avon products for a brief spell. She tested the application process on Alice Denny, his next-door neighbor and friend. *"Doesn't she look pretty?"* Tina would ask him during dinner sometimes. *"She looks very nice, Craig, yeah? You should ask her out. Oh, it'd be so cute. Dad could drive you guys to the movies."* He talked a lot to Alice now that J.J. had moved to Cincinnati and Neil had made new friends.

Craig found himself distracted, so he focused on the woman on the bus again. She was sleazy. A child's eye refused those details in the past, but now Craig could see her for who she really was. She practically had her hands reaching into her purse for a condom to flash at his father.

"What's your stop?" She forced a lisp. It was intended to be sexy. "I'm off work today. I haven't eaten breakfast. I know a place. It's the next stop."

She pulled the cable above them, and the light dinged overhead. The bus soon pulled over and stopped. The location was between a long strip mall and a Denny's.

"Missing summer school won't be such a bad thing, huh, pal?" Brandon relayed the fact without expecting a response from his son. "Let's call today a wash. And don't tell Mom. I'll buy you that Atari game you wanted. We'll have fun later together, okay? Promise."

He turned to the woman without waiting for his son to respond. "What's your name?"

"You can give me a name." She batted her eyes seductively. "Pretend I'm somebody. Whoever. It's funner that way."

"I'll call you Tina."

Craig's grip tightened on the pole. Butterflies gnawed at his stomach lining when he was ten, but now, he was fuming.

They walked out of the bus, Craig following behind them. Brandon would've forgotten him otherwise. He tagged along with the two, battling to decide what course of action to take, if any.

Brandon said, "I'll call in sick to work, and I'll buy you some breakfast."

He thought his father was talking to him, but he was engaging "Tina." Once his father completed the call to work, the woman sauntered to the back alley of the strip mall. "Forget breakfast." She beckoned him with her pointer finger. "Come here."

Brandon stalked after her, playing into her game. "You stay here, Craig. Don't move. Don't follow me. I'll be back soon. I promise. Just stay here."

He watched the philanderer at work. Craig walked to the mouth of the alley beside the closed-down bookstore and the hind end of Denny's. Laughter echoed to him, a woman's giggling. It made his stomach turn. This was the same man who'd make love to his mother and claim her as his wife.

Get a divorce, you dickhead, if you want other women so bad.

Craig hid behind a Dumpster. He dug his nails into the brick wall to abate his anger. The woman had somehow removed her panties and twirled them on her finger. "What are you going to do with me now?"

Brandon reached to caress her when a man in a white undershirt and faded black jeans leapt from behind the other end of the alley, armed with a Louisville Slugger. A superman tattoo was inked on his left shoulder. The man was nearly a foot shorter than his father, but he was burly and wore the face of lunatic. "Throw me your wallet and put away your hard-on. This is my woman, so back the fuck off!"

His father's fantasy abruptly crash-landed. Brandon cowardly tossed the man his wallet.

You deserve this.

For some reason, Craig couldn't stand by like he did back then no matter how much of an asshole his father was. The incoming scene that would occur was brutal and unnecessary. He remembered the scene from his childhood with alarming clarity.

He thought he could move, but Craig stayed hidden. The robber pounded the bat into Brandon's rib cage. His father grunted and faltered to the ground, moaning, the worst look on his face playing out in dramatic fashion like a person drowning and helpless to reach air.

"I think I want more than your wallet. You're a bit too grabby with my lady."

"Fuck him up," the woman shouted. Her eyes were ignited by the prospect of violence shed in her honor. She hovered around Brandon waiting for the action to play out. "Beat his skull in. He was lookin' at me funny. He was going to rape me. Behind a Denny's, Rob, is that what I deserve?"

"Were you going to do something with my lady?" He aimed the baseball bat at Brandon's crotch. "You're not even that good looking, but my woman can pick 'em. The dumb men with small dicks and big wallets."

"No!" Brandon held up his hand in surrender. "I meant no harm. Take my wallet. She talked to me first. She flirted, man—honest. I meant no harm."

The incident had ended with Brandon suffering three broken ribs and a concussion. He was bleeding from the head afterwards. He hid his face in shame from Craig who came to his aid when the two strangers finally fled the scene. Brandon even made Craig lie about it to the cops and his mother. "*I took you to Denny's for breakfast, and I was robbed. That's how I got hurt. Simple as that, and that's all you say, Craig.*"

Rethinking the situation and its outcome, he wouldn't allow the scene to escalate this time. Something was triggered in him, and he refused to remain on standby as his father got pummeled. He searched the alley for a weapon. The best he produced was a chunk of the curb the size of a baseball. He aimed for the assailant's head. One throw was all it took, Craig suddenly able to pitch the piece with perfect control—for a moment, he wondered if Dr. Krone had anything to do with the newfound ability—and it struck the assailant's skull with a sick crunch.

"*Agggghhh!*" The man spun backwards, bleeding from a gash in his head the shape of an upside down triangle. He dropped the bat with a hollow ringing sound. Brandon picked it up, and charging at him, he slammed it onto the man's back repeatedly. "Throw my wallet onto the pavement. And give me yours while you're at it." He raised the bat to the woman, pointing it at her face. "You keep your pussy to yourself. You keep acting like that, someone's going to slit your throat one of these days, and your man won't be able to do a damn thing to stop it."

He glanced at Craig as relief washed over his features. "That's my boy! You should pitch for the

Yankees. Holy shit, you were dead on. Dead. Fucking. On."

The robber tossed his wallet at Brandon's feet, fearing another blow. Half his face was red with trailing lines of blood. "*Please, don't hurt me . . .* "

His father recovered the wallet, but after bending down, he clutched his ribs. "That's going to leave a bruise. I should shove this up your ass."

The woman bit at her nails, pacing the same four steps, left to right. She noticed Craig and snarled. She mouthed something Craig couldn't understand, even this time.

The second wallet was offered up, the woman digging it begrudgingly out of her purse and throwing it underhanded in their direction.

"Now get out of here before I really fuck you up." Brandon enjoyed his victory. *Testosterone*, Craig thought, *is working its magic*. "This bat looks too new. I want to break it in some more. What do you think, son? Knock her head around a bit, and it'll be ready for nine innings, huh?" He swung it twice in the air at head-level and shouted his final warning, "Now get out of here before I really do hurt you!"

The two fled the scene, the woman helping the man to his feet. His father called Craig over, then lowered to his knees and hugged him close. Brandon kissed his forehead, and that was the first time that'd happened without Tina instructing him to do so. His face beamed with pride. "That's my boy. You saved my skin. You're a hell of a shot, kid. Anytime you want to play catch in the backyard, you got it."

You're lying, but I'll accept the compliment.

"We're skipping school today. We can't eat at Denny's. We have to book it out of here, so how about

Homer's Donuts? I'll take you to the mall afterwards. We'll pump quarters into those arcade games all day." He counted the money in the robber's wallet. "Yes we will."

Here came the equivalent to a court's swearing in, the man saying, "Promise you won't tell Mom about this. She wouldn't understand. This is between us."

His father placed his hand on Craig's head. "I love you. I don't say that enough. Now how about breakfast? All the donuts you can eat."

Craig nodded, a childlike giddiness overwhelming him. "Yeah, let's do that."

This was a better ending than Craig crying on the street until somebody finally called the police and Brandon was rushed to the hospital for head trauma.

***

Rob cradled his forehead. The blood wouldn't stop issuing from the gash. It stained his shirt and hands, both dripping with red. Misty kept him on his feet, though she struggled not to tip over due to his weight leaning against her.

She was crying, hysterical, shaking, and speaking so fast. "He got your wallet. He got my wallet. You're bleeding. It's all over you. That fucking kid. He did this. We can't let them get away with this. But look at you. Oh God, Rob, look at you! They got our money. That goddamn brat fucked everything up."

"We'll find them," Rob encouraged her, closing his eyes because he was so dizzy. He thought he was about to puke or pass out. "First, get me home. I need a drink. I need to lie down. I'm woozy."

"It's barely nine in the morning. You shouldn't be drinking."

"To swallow some pain killers, you stupid bitch."

They were at the end of the alley where it fed into the street. Their Chevy truck was parked nearby for the quick getaway.

Then a random voice called out to them. "*I suggest you wait on that drink.*"

"Who said that?" Rob was forced out of his daze. He feared it was the police. "I didn't hurt anybody. I'm the victim. The guy who did this, he's with a boy. Maybe ten years old. The dude assaulted me."

A man in a white lab coat was leaning against the wall. He was a portly man. The double chin was prominent, like a glazed fleshy tire. He sweated in the morning sun. It dripped down his face. He was waxen in the yellow glare, melting in the heat. The man smiled at them with recognition. Delight played upon his face.

Rob called out to the stranger, "What are you smiling at, asshole? You know me?"

"You don't know me." He started toward them, marching slowly. "And you don't need to."

Misty called out to him, praying she could reason with the man or coax him to help her boyfriend. "Are you a doctor? Would you help him? I can't stop the bleeding."

"I won't be able to assist you," he replied coolly, but then his face became the color of a blocked artery, and he shrieked, "*because I want to continue the bleeding!*"

Misty screamed. The stranger raced toward them, advancing quickly for an overweight man. He extended his fingers to Rob's throat, and the force was so unreal, Misty thought she'd seen it happen the wrong way, her mind registering the events through a grief-stricken mind. But she blinked, shook her head, cried, cursed, turned away, stared harder, concentrated with every ounce of her being and the outcome didn't change. The man's fingers had punctured through Rob's neck up to the knuckle with quadruple pops of her boyfriend's trachea. The connection sounded like a corer being driven through an apple.

Rob's eyes threatened to spill out of the sockets, they were so wide, stretched to shed maximum terror. He gargled, choking on fingers and blood. "*Grah-gaaaaack!*"

Removing his fingers, the doctor slapped a wad of tissue onto the pavement.

Rob faltered to his knees, aspirating on blood. It spurted in gobs out the concave holes in his neck. His larynx gushed in the blaring sunlight.

She fell to her knees beside him, erupting in panic. "Rob!"

The stranger wiped the red off onto his lab coat. "It's going to be a scorcher today. Perhaps I can ask you to step inside that building behind you to cool down."

""W-what are you saying?"

The lascivious smile was like a slithering worm. "We'll need to stay cool for what I'm about to do to you."

blessed

he didn't have a chance to enjoy an afternoon of arcade games or the breakfast of donuts because Craig was displaced yet again. He didn't realize the transition until the change was completed. It was instantaneous.

This time, he was sitting on a chair in his childhood bedroom. Moments after he arrived, he closed his eyes without willing it. He sensed others in the room. Hands were rubbed together. A throat was cleared. A nervous tension floated about the room.

A man's voice spoke, "Are you ready, Tina?"

His mother replied, though she was nervous. "Yes, I'm ready."

It was Parker Stevens's voice asking the question. He was the pastor at Neiman Heights Non-Denominational Church. He was also their next-door neighbor.

He was eight years old at this time. He was also scared. His mother tore him from playing outside just moments ago. It was two thirty, he remembered, and the time was very important. Brandon would be home from work soon. Craig later learned today was the only day Parker could perform Craig's indoctrination into the church. Today, he was being blessed. And if

Brandon learned of this blessing, he'd punch a wall—and later punch Tina and possibly Parker.

His father was a devout believer in nothing. Craig asked him when he was older if he was an atheist. Brandon's response was, "That'd mean I believe in some organized belief, and I don't. Only thing I believe in is a dick in a pussy."

The sense of haste was evident. Parker had skipped reading the scriptures he'd planned to recite. Parker touched both hands to Craig's head. They were wet with holy water. "Lord, I invite Craig Horsy into our congregation. He is a young boy with potential to do good in the community and in his life. Guide him with your Holy Spirit and allow him to overcome sin in its many forms. Love him with your grace, support him with your infinite knowledge. Do you accept Christ into your life, Craig?"

He hadn't been aware the question was addressed to him. The adult in the child's body waited. He'd forgotten how he'd reacted to the private blessing back then.

Parker repeated, "Do you accept Christ into your life?"

Tina whispered, "Say yes."

"Yes," he said, too loud.

Parker wasn't pleased. "Come to Christ willingly . . . come to him."

The front door opened. Brandon was home. Tina gasped, startled and ready to panic.

"He's already home. Damn it."

Parker turned up the heat and shifted into prayer overdrive. "God, guide this creation into your arms. He's been blocked by a man worthy of your love and divinity. He has lost his way, but do not give up on this man. Watch over the Horsy family in the future and pray they can one day embrace your Holy Spirit together."

Dad's not going to embrace any Holy Spirit.

He snickered on accident.

Tina elbowed him. "Craig, stop it."

Parker continued unaffected by his outburst or Brandon moving about downstairs. "Come to Christ willingly, Craig, come to him."

Sssssssst.

Brandon had opened a can of Lark's beer. He concluded the day of patching pot holes and cutting up the roads with a cement saw with liquid refreshment. Again, Craig had to stifle a laugh.

"Let me talk to him," Parker urged her. He failed to end the prayer without the habitual "Amen." Did that mean the blessing wasn't sealed, that the stamp wasn't placed on the envelope and wouldn't ship to God, he wondered. "He's a sensible man."

"No," Tina whispered insistently. "He won't understand. He is *not* a sensible man. You can't leave through the front door. I'm sorry. He'll hurt you. Do it for me, okay? He'll take it out on me and maybe Craig."

Craig kept his eyes closed. The worried feeling increased. It was an unwanted force field of heat surrounding his skin. Tina was truly frightened. She feared Brandon and his repercussions, and with good reason.

"Okay," Parker digressed. "I'll go down the balcony. I can crawl like the best of them."

"This is so embarrassing. You've been so nice to me. I'll have to make it up to you. Let me make it up to you."

He heard the rub of cloth. The two had hugged. "God bless you, Tina. Stay vigilant in your journey to find God."

"I promise I will."

The window was cracked open. Craig finally opened his eyes to catch the man in street clothes crawl out the window and onto the balcony and jump down into the backyard.

Tina looked at him, frazzled around the eyes. "I'm trying, Craig, I really am."

"Trying to do what," he asked in his kid's voice. He stated the same question back then.

"I'm trying to raise you right." She looked downstairs with disgust. "I wish I could do something to convince your dad to go to church." She muttered, "I can't go on like this."

Craig agreed. He wanted to offer words of encouragement, but he was distracted by the blemish on her face. Her cherry blush lipstick was smeared.

Come to Christ willingly, huh?

Before he could comment on the observation, the scene cut to another part of his life.

hAppy hALLoween

CRAIg heAved the last two eggs in the carton at Mrs. Neilson's front door. They cracked and then exploded, spilling thick yellow yolk down the wood. His high school keyboarding instructor failed him last semester, and this was his revenge. The old bag had it coming, he thought, with devilish delight.

Alice Denny handed him another egg, saving it for him special. "I kept this one back for you. Make it count. Imagine the hag's face when you throw it this time. Really make her pay."

"Oh, I will. The bitch is getting it real good."

He aimed the egg at one of the draped windows. Craig hoped it was her bedroom window. Maybe she'd think the spirit of Thomas Hayden would be knocking and wanting to come in and pay her a visit. Thomas Hayden was a local serial killer from twenty years ago. He hung his victims from their ceiling fans and dismembered their extremities. After they were only a torso, he'd turn on the fan and the limbless corpse would spin around and splatter blood about the room. Thomas also left the eyes alone, believing they harbored the soul. If he kept the souls intact, it wasn't true murder, Hayden reasoned, though it didn't prevent the state from administering the death penalty on him.

"Happy Halloween, bitch!" Craig launched the egg, the object smashing against the window. "I hope that keyboard keeps you warm at night. You can stick that mouse up your butt too!"

He was minutes into the next memory, and he finally acknowledged the change. Craig was no longer in his upstairs bedroom. Parker Stevens and Tina were long gone. But this was a better memory already. It was Halloween night, and he didn't wish to end the current festivities.

They fled down the street, escaping the scene of the crime. They didn't wear costumes, but instead, all black. They were ninjas of the night. Lit jack-o'-lanterns bobbed on both sides of his peripheral from front porches. The demon eyes watched as if cheering them on: "Make mischief!" "Raise hell!" "Entertain us!" "Satan approves!"

Craig and Alice completed a block of sprinting and then stopped. Together, they hunkered behind a mulberry bush, checking if the coast was clear. Mrs. Neilson opened the front door, her expression furrowed as if she'd been disturbed from a session of late-night reading or from working on one of her famous hard puzzles. The prudish woman stepped onto the broken eggs in her slippers, cursing, "Aw shit!"

She clutched a broom in both hands, raising it in the air. "*Damn kids.*" Watching both ends of the street, she gave up the witch hunt. "Forget it. I'll clean this mess up in the morning."

Mrs. Neilson slammed the door, choosing to turn in rather than scour the neighborhood for the culprits.

"Dumb bitch," Craig laughed so hard his throat ached. "It's all worth it. That's the last time she'll mess with me."

Alice chimed in, "I wish I had a teacher I detested with such a passion."

He was in the ninth grade, Alice in the eighth. They planned tonight's festivities for months. They were too old to trick or trick, but not too old to trick, as Alice had stated on many occasions. She had bloomed this year. Breasts arrived in a generous package. They were as big as a twenty-year-old's. But Craig was best friends with her. The breasts were something only his eyes enjoyed. The great part about having a girl best friend, he believed, was how she shared all the girl secrets. She told him about her first period: "It sucks because you have to buy all these feminine products. I'm already tired of it, and I won't be done until menopause. My mom gave me the longest spiel about periods. 'Always carry a tampon in your purse everywhere you go.' 'Menstrual cramps are different for everybody.' My cramps are like somebody shoving a hand up my cooch and trying to rip out my stomach."

Knocked from thought, a darting pirate paused at the house two ahead of them. Craig vaguely recognized the person because of the costume. It was Dennis Brockman. He was the equivalent of a class clown from hell. Laugh at his lame jokes or else become barraged with mean pranks.

"What the hell is he doing?" Alice studied the yard, opening her mouth and stifling it with her hand. "Don't tell me he's doing what I'm thinking?"

Dennis bent down as if taking a seat on a pair of concrete steps. It was an extended walkway, so he wasn't right up against the porch but instead closer to the street. He hiked down his pants.

Alice pressed her hands to her face. "He's pooping in a jack-o'-lantern."

Craig reiterated, "Dennis is pooping in a jack-o'-lantern."

Dennis caught them watching. He cackled, throwing his head back. After he lifted up his baggy pants, he ran toward them, proud of his excursion. "Man, I have to rush home. I need some toilet paper ASAP. A group of us are pooping in as many jack-o'-lanterns as possible. This is cool, right? It was my idea. I'm putting a patent on it."

"Oh, I believe you," Craig joked. "Now go wipe your ass."

He saluted them both. "Happy Halloween, boils and ghouls!"

They walked by the defiled jack-o'-lantern, both of them pinching their noses. Alice turned to him. "It's strange that we've been next-door neighbors since kindergarten, and we've barely started talking until two years ago."

"You didn't talk much when you were a kid," Craig defended himself. "You hung out with Neil and J.J. and you watched us do stuff."

"Life's easier that way. You can't mess up." She thought about Neil. "And since when did Neil become such an asshole? He won't talk to us anymore. Mr. Popular."

"It's just you and me," Alice reiterated. "It's too bad J.J. moved to Tennessee to live with his uncle."

Alice mulled over something as if concerned, and Craig pressed her to speak, "You're thinking about something? Are you thinking about lighting something on fire? Forking a yard?"

"My parents are out of town, you want to get drunk?"

Now I get it. This is why I'm living this memory. Another life-changing decision. I get it, Dr. Krone. Real smart. Regrets are a bitch. I'm not sure where this is necessarily going, though.

That night, Craig feared his father would notice his absence and punish him accordingly. Alice read into his hesitation. "You're afraid your dad will smell booze on your breath? Hey, we're next-door neighbors. Check in, and sneak out your window. I'll unlock the back door. They won't notice. They'll be asleep by now." She widened her eyes, emulating a ghoul. "The night is ours."

She was correct by mentioning his parents. Brandon often stayed up late on Saturday nights, but after midnight, he was passed out. He normally watched late-night Cinemax while Tina was asleep on the couch.

"They'll probably both be asleep." Alice was building him up to drink with her. "I have something I want to tell you too." Her eyes widened like a witch before her cauldron. "I want to make a pact."

"What? Like with one of those Ouija boards?"

"Something like that." Her lips twitched. She bit them to subdue a grin. "Just do it. I'll wait for you. It'll be worth it, I promise."

They walked the rest of the way home. He checked his watch, and it read three in the morning. Arriving in his yard, and Alice going to her house, they split up. Walking to his house, Craig peered into the front bay window. Brandon was unconscious in front of the television, sprawled against a stack of pillows. He caught two bare-chested women necking in a hot tub on the television screen. Craig stifled a laugh, and then noticed Tina was on the couch asleep as well, her head resting in Brandon's lap. The two had a party of their own. A bottle of vodka, a carton of orange juice, and two cans of pineapple juice were strewn on the coffee table.

"Now it's my turn to party."

Noting the scene was clear, he skipped to Alice's house next door. What did she want from him that night, he had always wondered even into his adult years. Now, he was going to find out the truth.

He was starting to enjoy his treatment. How many more mysteries would be unraveled by the end of this session?

Walking into her backyard, standing outside in front of the sliding glass door, Alice stood on the opposite side. She pressed her face against the window, and using her open mouth as a suction, she turned her mouth into a huge gaping maw. The expression always made Craig belly laugh.

She pushed open the sliding glass door after enjoying Craig's amusement long enough. "Let's get fucked up."

He air-toasted, tipping his head back, then bellowed in an accent like Bela Lugosi's, "Happy Halloween, my darling, can you tell me where the open bar is?"

Inside the house, the kitchen was decorated with black and orange balloons taped to every surface. A plastic tarantula and a black cat poster were on display, a background of cheesy Halloween fun. The sound of screaming echoed from the other room, and

Craig followed the alarming noise. A guy in his late teens was watching *The Exorcist* on television, sitting on a recliner with red glazed eyes. Craig heard a demented demon growl, "Your mother sucks cock in hell!" and he lost it to a fit of uncontrollable laughter.

He composed himself, and then asked, "Did I miss the part where she masturbates with a crucifix?"

The guy watching the TV was unaffected by Craig's question. He enjoyed another toke from his joint, and then he raised it to Craig. "Here y' go."

Alice nudged him. "Don't be a chicken shit. It's Halloween. It's a toke, it's not like he's asking you to smoke his pole."

He accepted the offer despite himself, despite knowing his father would smell it on him from a mile away and beat him to an inch of his life. But now he didn't care about his father's wrath. He sampled the joint. Waiting for a big change, he didn't feel anything different. No hallucinations or munchies. What he really wanted was a shot of booze from the table behind the stranger. Five kinds of off-brand whiskey stared him down. The amber-brown fluids refracted the television's light, begging him to take a nip. Craig had sampled many bourbons and whiskeys from his father's collection in the past and accumulated an appreciation for hard liquor. He learned if he sipped a little from each bottle, his father wouldn't notice his dwindling reserves.

After finishing another round of smoking the jay, Alice introduced the guy watching the movie. "This is Jake. He's my cousin. He lives out of town, but he stopped by to say hello. He visited his girlfriend, but they broke up tonight."

Jake enjoyed another toke, his eyes refusing to

leave the screen. "Ah, whatever, she wouldn't put out anyway. After a month of dating, what's the point if they don't put out?"

She motioned for him to leave the room, and Craig swiped the bottle of Brown Barrel Whiskey.

He aimed to get drunk. It was happy Halloween time. And he was ready for the secret he never learned from his past. She had something to tell him, and he was ready to hear it.

They walked upstairs to the kitchen. Alice wore a concerned expression on the way. Her eyes were glazed, and she hadn't smoked that much weed. Was she going to cry? His concerns were proven wrong when she removed a four-inch kitchen knife from the kitchen drawer.

"Take a drink," she insisted, running her finger down the dull side of the blade. "And I'll have one too."

Craig threw back a swig, scrutinizing the blade. "What's wrong? You look really upset. And, um, what's with the knife?"

She smirked, though she only briefly wore the expression. She drank with purpose, swallowing it like water. "You mentioned Neil. It got me thinking, what's it going to be like when we graduate high school? Will we move on and not see each other anymore? If so, I think that's bullshit."

He was honest—and this was the adult talking, "People get jobs and married, and it's hard to stay in touch. We'd have to be next-door neighbors for the rest of our lives. How about that? That'd be fun. You could borrow my scotch, and I could borrow your whiskey."

"Yeah." Her eyes spaced out on the knife. "So let's make it official. Really seal the deal."

She slit the underside of her forearm, inches from her wrist, and it cut deep enough to bleed a good deal. She extended the knife to him, the tip red with her blood. "Now you do the same." She wrinkled her nose, experiencing the first inklings of pain. "We'll make a blood pact not to lose touch when we graduate."

He eyed the knife pensively. *This is what she wanted. After all this time wondering what she was going to do that night. You idiot. You thought she wanted to ask you out on a date or something. She really wanted to make a stupid pact.*

He slammed another mouthful of whiskey, preparing to watch skin part via a sharp edge. He seized the handle, placed the tip of the blade on his forearm, and guided it, parting enough flesh that blood seeped free.

Seeing blood, she offered her arm to him. "Rub your blood against mine. Doesn't it make sense to form a blood pact on Halloween?"

They grinded arms and the blood mixed together, the connection warm, metallic, and binding.

He offered another thought on the future, "Even if we don't live in the same area, there's always the phone or a weekend getaway trip. It'd be nice to escape the wife and kids—whoever they may be."

"I'm not having any fucking kids." She took her arm back, smeared with two types of blood. "They can suck somebody else's tits for milk."

"Right on."

They toasted to the anti-child cause, enjoying a nip straight from the bottle. Afterwards, they washed off their arms and bandaged the cuts. Craig asked, "Where did you learn to come up with a blood pact?"

"The Boy Scouts used to do it for tribal stuff before AIDS and hepatitis became such a serious concern."

They overhead the screams from the basement, and Alice suggested, "Let's get high and finish watching *The Exorcist*."

Before he could answer her, she hurried to the other room, and Craig followed after her, enticed by the prospect of watching Linda Blair levitate.

Dr. Krone poured himself a screwdriver because the Horsy residence had the ingredients right there on the coffee table. He looked down at Tina and Brandon fast asleep, then he peered at the television screen. A man was smearing whipped cream and pouring chocolate sauce on a naked woman in a chef's hat. They were romping in the kitchen of a greasy spoon. He turned down at Brandon and asked him, "Porn is ageless, isn't it?"

He parted Tina's hair, his hip popping to bend down to her level. The doctor caressed her hair with a feather's touch. He didn't want to wake her. He focused on her and the bruises on her arm from where Brandon had grabbed her the other day during an argument.

He whispered to her, leaning in so Brandon couldn't hear him, "*I know about the things you always wanted to do to your husband*."

MASON OWENS WOODS

CRAIG CHECKED HIS ARM. There was no healing mark, or wound, or scar. The drunken sensation vanished. The stench of weed was missing too. He watched Linda Blair on the screen one moment, and the next, he was riding his Huffy bicycle down the bike path in Mason Owens Woods. The overhead Shagbark, hickory, and oak tree limbs draped him in shade. He caught a white-tailed deer shoot through a pair of trees. He kept pedaling. His destination was Lake Jacomo. He wanted to swim, even if it was alone. Neil and J.J. were at Boy Scout camp, and he was alone right now for the summer.

His mother thought he was riding in the neighborhood, but he changed course without telling her. Three blocks of the same street was repetitive, but this bike course was much more adventurous.

I'm not sure what memory this is. I can't remember.

He looked around, sensing a person was following him. Craig slammed the brakes and listened. The ruffle of leaves and the soft breeze circled him, and he trained his ears harder, trying to hear his stalker's mistake. Perhaps the follower would step on a twig or crunch over a patch of leaves. After a time, he gave up and continued to ride his bike. But there it was again. The roll of his tires against the path, it was matched by another set of tires.

He hit the brakes again and turned around sharply. "*Is anybody there?*"

Craig was scared. Tina advised him not to venture out too far from the house. There were strangers out there, she warned, and he was not to talk to them.

What if a stranger really was following him?

He pedaled in retreat, not knowing how to escape. Craig looped back the way he'd come. The matching roll of tires didn't change.

He peddled faster.

Craig shouted, his voice cracking, "*Leave me alone!*"

Then his bike chain snapped. He tipped over and slammed onto his side.

With the rush of pain arriving, now he remembered this memory.

"*Ahhhhh!*"

He cried so loud it hurt his own eardrums. Craig bounced three times onto the bike path. He turned his ankle and slammed his knee into the pavement. A large gash bled from his knee. He couldn't move his right leg. The ankle was broken. The agony was threefold in a child's body. He wept, unable to move, his back flat against the pavement, saying, "*Help me, help me, help me, help me, help me!*"

The mysterious stalker didn't show up to nab him. The wind brushed on the gash, and it burned in increasing conflagrations. "*It hurts,*" he complained to nobody. "*Ouch, it hurts, it hurts.*"

And then there she was, standing above him—Alice Denny. The woman had regressed from

84

blooming post-puberty woman to an eight-year-old. Her hair was fashioned in two ponytails, fastened by lady bug hair clips. She wore purple sweatpants and a purple top. Alice was the one following him on bicycle. Ironically, the bicycle was purple too and had a banana seat. Pink streamers shot out the handlebars, wildly whipping in the wind.

She was shocked, viewing the blood. It stole what bravery it required to confront him. She stood still as a statue. The only things moving were her widening eyes and jaw that steadily dropped. Finally, she managed a question. "A-are you okay?"

He stifled his initial response to cry some more. She wanted to help—to be his friend. He sensed now that he was thinking through an adult mind. "I'll go tell somebody," she relayed, speeding off for help. "Hold on, Craig!"

Before anything else happened, he was now sitting in his backyard. How he got there, it was blink-instant and without explanation. He rested on the patio furniture in his backyard with his bad ankle propped on a plastic bucket, his foot wrapped in a splint. He was bored and punished to house arrest. It was two days after the bike accident. Alice eyed him through the notches of the wooden fence. Craig noticed her but didn't say anything. That's when she started randomly throwing things into the yard—a beach ball, baseball, aluminum bat, football, and then a yo-yo.

"What are you doing?" he asked, looking over the array of toys. "Hey, come over here."

He was desperate for company and was delighted when she raced around the other side of the fence and opened the gate. She was eager to play. She too was experiencing a droll summer.

Craig smiled at her, and this was the adult in him. "I'm bored."

He knew those two words would send her into game mode. Alice picked up the aluminum bat and politely handed it to him. "You swing, I'll pitch the ball. You don't even have to get up out of your chair." She raised her voice to a shrill, putting her entire body into the statement. "Knock it out of the park!"

This was the beginning of their friendship. Craig loved this moment. But he never thanked her for saving him in the woods.

And now was his chance.

Dr. Krone walked the bike path in Mason Owens Woods in a calm swagger. Again, he couldn't get enough of the summer air. The present winter was miserable in Indiana. Bitter cold. It was hard to wake up from bed, it being so frigid. He wanted to stay under the toasty blankets and sleep the winter away until spring. Summer and spring were perfect, he kept telling himself. But fall was the best season, especially with the rain. It wasn't anything an umbrella couldn't fix. It brought people closer together, the rain.

But the mind is the greatest escape, he thought.

He sighed, enjoying the wistful moment by keeping his easy pace down the path. "I'm very comfortable in here, Mr. Horsy. I think I'll stay for a while."

Nobody utilized the bike path. He willed them to go away. He could do that.

He could do a lot of things in Craig's mind.

Dr. Krone completed his trek. Stopping, he bent down onto his haunches. "Ah," he announced jubilantly, "fresh air!"

He dipped his two fingers in Craig's spilt blood from his bike crash and tasted it.

tRApped

"**Stay the heLL In theRe!**"

"You're drunk again."

The throaty roar replied, "*Woman*, you're controlling me. Why don't you go out more? You can fuck around with Betsy. Go shopping with her, whatever it is you women do without your husbands around. You're always home, and I'm tired of it. A man needs time to himself, but that's something you don't understand. Stay in there. Don't say anything either. Shut your mouth. I don't want to hear a word."

Tina was startled by the *fu-whump* of the mattress being wedged against the bathroom door. She tried to open the door, but she second guessed herself. Craig observed purple-black bruises on her arms. She slid down the door and closed her eyes, her breath expelled in weak gasps as if afraid to breathe at all. "*I'm safe here*," she whispered under her breath, "*he's outside . . . he's outside.*"

Craig hid under the large wicker laundry basket during the ordeal. It tipped over when he fidgeted, his legs tingling, losing circulation. She was startled, but then relieved. She drew him close, pressing his head up against her chest, her arms bringing him in smothering tight. Her trembles abated the longer she

87

cradled him. She smelled of body odor. He also recognized another smell, categorized from an adult olfactory index. Sex. Her undershirt clung tight to her. She had no bra underneath. The top button of her blue jeans was undone.

"He's drunk is all," she murmured trancelike. Her lips were so close to his ear every word was clear, though she didn't mean for him to hear. "He gets horny. And then he gets angry. He's dropped from the greatest feeling after we're done, and then he's brought back to reality. It makes sense. He doesn't mean to hurt me. He doesn't mean to . . . "

He listened with anguish, cringing on the inside. Dr. Krone was a genius to drum up this memory. This is what gnawed at him on a subconscious level. How many scenes like this were saved up and shoved into his psyche and stewing about his brain? He was bound to burst at some point in time, and Willis, his best friend, had been the victim.

An overwhelming sense of appreciation washed over him for this gift bestowed on him. It was as magnificent as it was unbelievable. This treatment would be effective. He'd come out of it a changed man, even a bettered man. The first thing he'd do after his treatment had concluded was to visit Willis and hug him. He would apologize and mean it.

Tina kept chattering, inducing her own form of therapy. "He's wonderful when he's sober. If he could stop drinking. He's not happy with his job. That'd make anybody moody. As long as he doesn't hurt Craig. No, I wouldn't stand for it. He needs time alone. I have lots of time alone. Every time he's at work, I'm alone. I could start a new job, if he would let me. No. Forget it. He won't listen to me. He wants to be the sole breadwinner."

Craig had listened to the words without comprehending them as a child. He was maybe eight or nine then. Old enough to start absorbing their marital mess, but not decoding it.

He was about to speak up and boost her confidence when she added, "He can do whatever he wants. I can forgive him because I have secrets too."

pReAcheR StevenS

RAIg SCRAmbLed to stay in the moment, but it wasn't possible, because the change was as inevitable as it was jarringly fast. He was disappointed the change happened when it did. Tina was about to reveal something, and here he was in his backyard, away from the important facts. Now, the sun was hot against his back. Alice wasn't in the backyard. He was alone. He kicked at the grass and clods of dirt shot up.

"Damn it, what was she going to say? Dr. Krone, you asshole, why did you pull me out of there when you did?"

The doctor was watching him from somewhere nearby. Perhaps on a computer monitor, because the man said he was hooked up to the machine. And how did the device pick out the memories? Did he have a mental locker of juicy history, a membrane in his cerebellum that contained this psychosomatic bullshit? Psychobabble talk was one thing, but to actually rip open the mind and relive these moments was an attack on his personal history.

Craig was disoriented, and the backyard spun around him, the sky tilting and the sun blinding and golden white. He landed on all fours and wretched at the assault. He was around thirteen or fourteen, he guessed, as he clutched his aching head, sucked in a round of breaths, and stood up again. He wiped the side of his mouth dry. The nauseous sensation stayed in the pit of his throat, and it would make its home there for a time.

A stifled laugh breeched the silence, rousing his attention. He peeked through the wooden slats of the fence at his next-door neighbor's yard. It was Parker Stevens's house. But what was Tina doing there? They were both exiting the sliding door together. Tina's face was flushed pink, and her smile, her face was conquered with the glowing sentiment of joy. It was a womanly thing he recognized with Katie as the after-sex glow.

This is getting interesting.

Parker was dressed down in black basketball shorts and a Celtics shirt. He dyed his gray hair brown. Tina wore a black tube top and cut-off whitewashed jeans. They hugged each other and punctuated it with a friendly kiss. The fence border was up on Parker's property, and Craig supposed they were comfortable with the backyard display of affection.

The gate to their property opened. Craig ran back to the swing set and acted like he was minding his own business. Tina waved the man into the yard after spotting Craig. She whispered something in his ear, and there he came, edging toward him to have a talk.

I remember this. But now it makes sense.

Parker relaxed on the swing beside him. "Hey, kiddo. What're you up to this summer?"

"Nothing."

He smirked, thinking a second on what to say

next. "All the kids say that. You're doing something. You're swinging." He snapped his fingers. "You're having a swinging summer."

Good one.

The joke was lame even as a kid. He couldn't think of what to say in reply. It was the on-the-spot feeling he couldn't shake.

"You ever think about going to church?"

Craig had a good response, and this was his original statement. "My dad doesn't believe in it."

He placed his hand on Craig's shoulder. "But do you?"

That's a heavy question for a kid. Tell me your religious faith, kiddo, and while you're at it, how do you feel about the Middle East and yoga?

"I like to see friends there," he said, shrugging his shoulders. The adult in him added, "That's about it, really."

Parker moved on. This was a test, and he became more intrusive. The point of the entire conversation was about to happen. "So how are things, Craig? Are you happy? Anything you're concerned about? You know you can tell me anything."

He did say this back then, and he said it again now, "My dad yells at Mom a lot. He gets mad easily."

"Do you love your father?"

"Yeah. He's my dad."

Parker understood, looking at him from the corner of his eye and then training his focus on the house. He caught Tina standing in the window. Parker admired her. She gave them a quick smile and went about what she was doing in the house.

He initiated conversation again. "Do you love your mom?"

"Yes, I love my mom."

"She's good to you. And she's a wonderful lady. Your dad's a lucky, lucky man. The good Lord will see to it she gets what's due to her."

After a stretch of awkward silence, he asked another question. "Is there anything at all you want to talk about?" He crossed his heart. "I swear it's between you and me."

And the good Lord, and my mom . . .

He stayed silent, and Preacher Stevens prompted him, "You wish the best for your mom, right?"

He shook his head, baffled. "What do you mean?"

Parker realized he'd asked too deep of a question for a kid. "You know your mother loves you no matter what."

He was frozen, confused, and couldn't say anything. Ten seconds later, Parker gave up the battle, but adult Craig refused to let him off the hook. "You said I could ask you anything. We're friends, right?"

He perked up. "That's right, pal."

Craig rolled his eyes, though Parker didn't see it.

The question slipped out of him. "Are you fucking my mom?"

"The mouth on that brat! With a father like that, no wonder he's talking to a priest with such language." Parker muttered this on the way to his kitchen in a frenzy. The taste of Tina was on his lips—her saliva, her skin, and the potent flavor of her sex. "I guess it doesn't matter. Woman's stuck in a dead-end abusive marriage. She won't quit that bastard, but that's okay with me. I don't love her, really, and I don't need to."

Dr. Krone rifled through the cabinet and discovered Parker's secret stash of bourbon.

"*Hey*," Parker yipped, double backing from the intruder, almost stumbling over his feet in shock. "How did you know where that was? And what the hell are you doing in my house? Do I know you? I'm gonna have to ask you to leave."

"I know everything in Craig's mind, and I know what's in yours too." The man poured a shot and threw it back. "*Grrr!* The mangy hair of the dog."

"What are you doing in my house?" Parker raised his voice, now standing tall. "I don't know you. Get out. I'll call the police. Right now, I want you out. This is trespassing."

"The line is dead," the doctor warned him, pointing at the phone broken in ten pieces on the floor. He had a romp of a time smashing it. "And there's no police here unless I want them to be here. Listen, I'm your friend. Let's talk."

Parker was shaken. He didn't trust him. The man didn't have a choice but to hear him out, too scared to be physical with the intruder.

"Calm down." Dr. Krone placed a hand on the man's shoulder. "I'm a friend. So tell me—and level with me, huh? Is Tina a good fuck? Does she enjoy missionary position? I guess any position with you is missionary."

Dr. Krone knew he could instruct the man to obey him. All he had to do was think it. Will it. And he did. Flexing his strength was one of his favorite pastimes.

Parker's face relaxed. He no longer distrusted him. He gave Dr. Krone a chiding expression.

"That's desperate pussy, man. She's so scared of Brandon. It's more passionate like that—you know, women in those situations. That's why I like her. I can avoid marriage and still enjoy that high-altitude fuck.

Women like Tina, they pretend they're in love with you, but it's exaggerated because of how shitty their romantic life has become. She even said she loves me. Isn't that funny? She whispered it in my ear. One fuck, and it's monumental to her."

"Her tits look great in that tube top." Dr. Krone poured a shot of bourbon for each of them. They toasted each other, swigging the warm bullets down. "I wish I could have a round with that head case. I know all about the emotionally abused. The insane are the best. You ever fuck a girl in a straightjacket? Fucking girls with dementia, it's the best time you'll ever have. The things they say and do, no ordinary woman would ever conceive it. I've been around *let—me—tell—you!*"

The doctor confided in him, now that they were good friends. "What would you do for another round with her, seriously?"

Parker stared out the kitchen window at Tina's house, weighing his options. "It's taking risks. We're next-door neighbors. It's been fun. And she's one hell of a woman. I'm afraid of Brandon, though. He'd smash my face in."

"Why not have more fun? It doesn't have to end. You don't have to be scared of him."

He shook his head, dismissing the notion. "Naw. It's for the best. She's married."

The doctor winked at him. "She told me she wanted otherwise. She wants to be with you, and only you."

Parker's eyebrow arched. "Oh. She said that?"

It was so fun to inject hope into people. It always worked to his advantage, the doctor thought.

"Yes, it's true, but we'll have to do something

about that husband of hers. You're right to be concerned about him." His tone demurred into a cretin's. "I'm sure Tina will be receptive to anything you suggest. *Anything.*"

picking up the tab

RAIg wAShed hIS hands in the bathroom at The Italian Garden Restaurant, having been sent to a new memory. In this part of his life, it was the night of his high school prom. He was on an arranged date with Janna Cunningham. Janna was dumped by Bobby Keaton, and Craig didn't have a date to begin with, so it worked out for the both of them. The majority of the kids with them tonight he wasn't familiar with except for Rose Farrow, and she was the one in his Biology class who had arranged his date with Janna. Senior year, and this was the final hoorah, aside from graduation. His powder-blue suit was purchased from the thrift store. His mother bought it for fifty bucks. The waistline was a tad too tight, and the extra tension made it feel like he was full of gas, but this was the big night.

Prom night.

Brandon's pep talk before he left the house went like this: "You're eighteen and graduating. Go attack the world. I'll help you get an apartment." *And you'll help me get the hell out of your house, right, Daddy?*

Why had he wanted to go to prom so badly? He didn't have that many friends, and his best friend, Alice, refused to attend. She detested it and wrote up anti-prom posters in the school cafeteria to promote her cause. Pictures of couples holding babies, facts about early teen pregnancy, the cost of raising children, and the statistics of condoms and birth control methods failing was her poster material. Alice had been sent to the principal's office, but beyond a talking to and a call to her parents, that was the extent of the reprimand. He didn't relish prom either, but that was before he had a shot at dating Janna Cunningham.

He'd taken a piss before the memory started, and now, he washed his hands and held them under the air dryer. Standing there, Craig realized something.

Damn it, I missed Parker's answer to my question. Dr. Krone, your timing is shit. The look on the priest's face was priceless. Caught. The man even blushed. That meant it was true. He was having fun with his mother between the sheets.

But now he had a new worry. This night was one of the most embarrassing in the history of Craig Horsy. He didn't want to leave the bathroom. He was stuck standing there, nailed to the floor in fear.

If this is your idea of therapy, Dr. Krone, then you suck.

"I have to leave sometime." He squeezed his fists together. "You won't let me go into the next memory until I do so, huh? Is that the catch?" Growing defiant, he shoved down his apprehensions and built himself up. "I'll be proactive. Fuck it."

He trudged out of the bathroom. Ahead of him, the restaurant was dimly lit. A semi-romantic Saturday evening at a high-priced restaurant. The walls were styled with columns like an Italian coliseum. Painted murals of vineyards decorated the walls, men and women in rough-neck clothing picking precious grapes from a vineyard. He saved money from working extra shifts at the Burger Barn for two months to afford this expensive evening, but his excitement and hard work was ill-fated.

The table in the back, his table, was empty. All eight seats. Janna was missing. The bill was propped intentionally in front of his seat. The bill was over three hundred dollars. It burned him so bad in that moment his pulse pounded and pounded. The guys at the table were jocks on the football team, and it was typical they'd play a joke on Craig Horsy, the unpopular and unknown kid. It was easy to pick on somebody without friends, he thought bitterly. And here he was, the helpless victim, fooled by his gullible good intentions.

He called his father for the cash that night, but Brandon immediately turned him down, saying, *"You let those kids bamboozle you, then you're going to fix your own mess, you idiot. I don't have the goddamn bread to pay for your friends' meals."*

No—wait! What am I thinking?

He skirted to the window, and he caught the group romping and bursting out in laughter in the parking lot. He did this the first time it happened, but he was too hurt and afraid to challenge them. Craig simply watched them carry on with the night.

They hadn't left the parking lot yet. He couldn't leave without committing mischief. What did he have to be afraid of? This was his mind, and he wouldn't be arrested. He wouldn't be grounded. The moment was truly his own to decide.

He ripped the fire extinguisher from the wall, cackling at the flurry of ideas spinning about in his head. He jacked open the window and crawled through, a new energy surging through him. It was well into May, the night air a brisk sixty degrees. He couldn't help cackling again at the prospect of revenge, even throwing his head back in delight. This is what he dreamed of all these years.

Revenge.

He recalled the owner, Rick Margolia, forcing him to wash dishes for a week to repay the debt. Prom didn't happen. He was stuck at the place until three in the morning that night.

Pacing faster toward them, he whispered, "*Oh, they're gonna get it now.*"

Janna noticed him first, catching the darting figure in the corner of her eye. Mark Stolburg was next to spy him. And then Jack Neilson, Bryce Johnson, and Alex Cartman stepped out of the car one after the other to challenge his challenge. They were the defensive line for the Theodore Roosevelt High School Bears. They went to state, but lost the championship. They wore matching black suits with bright red cummerbunds. This was the joke to commiserate the loss of the game.

The other girls wore pastel dresses. They screamed, knowing what was coming, and looking into Craig's diabolical face, they knew it was coming without mercy.

They're not yucking it up anymore! Yuppie bastard assholes.

Mark, the burly lineman, stepped up to intercept Craig, waving his hands to stop him. "It was a joke, man. We were coming back in." Forming his hand into a fist and punching his open hand, he threatened, "Seriously, put that down or else I'll beat your ass."

"That's why Janna's got the getaway car started, huh, you were coming back for me?" He lifted up the fire extinguisher. "Beat my ass after this!"

He sprayed the extinguisher at Mark's face, caking him in white foam. *Caaaaack!* Mark charged forward, slipping on the foam and crashing to the pavement with an audible collapse. "You fucker—!"

"Tackle that prick!" Jack lunged for him. "Get him!"

He showered the rest of the group in white, laughing in glee, unafraid of the group approaching him, knowing he'd ruin their precious prom night. They battled to avoid the flurries of whipped white, but they couldn't dodge it. "This one's for Craig Horsy, assholes!"

Janna's face looked like an opened container of whipped topping, the white staining the front of her dress and between her breasts.

He channeled his scorn into words. "Jokes on you, bitches!"

Alex Cartman swung a punch, being close enough to him now, but Craig rammed the butt end of the extinguisher into his stomach. "*Uggggh*!" He faltered to the curb on his knees, coughing and groaning in pain.

Craig challenged them, feeling on top of the world. "Who else wants some more? Anyone?"

Janna wept next to the car. Her real date was in the passenger seat, Hank Pinzer. He was pissed, he could see, but the expression was muddled by a dollop of white foam across his nose and lips.

"I have one last parting gift," Craig shouted. He hurled the extinguisher at the back windshield and shattered it. "Pay for that with your own money—

maybe you can wash dishes inside to pay it off, you dick lickers!"

"It looks like they screwed you over," Dr. Krone *tsk-tsk*ed. He was finishing his linguine and clams inside the restaurant, and when he was finally done, he wiped his lips clean with a burgundy napkin. "Ah, yes, the meal's free tonight. Compliments of Rick Margolia—and this wouldn't be the first time some kids ripped you off, is it?"

Dr. Krone stood up from his table to intercept the owner. "It's a terrible shame. Kids aren't grateful. Snot-nosed brats have no respect these days, do they?"

Rick's thick black eyebrows furrowed. He ran his hands down his white dress shirt and gray pinstripe pants, his Italian blood burning hot. "Those kids were trouble, especially that last one. He just leapt out the window. He wasn't afraid of me. I'd like to pound his ass. I'd send him to the hospital. I'm serious, I don't care how young that punk is, I'd smash his face in."

Dr. Krone downed the last of the glass of wine in one hearty gulp. "It's a real fine establishment to knock over, huh? Kids are so disrespectful. There's no getting through to them."

"No, there isn't." Rick spoke as if winded, "This isn't the first dine-and-dash in my restaurant. The other kid who did this, I had arrested. Nobody robs the Margolias, especially some punk kids. And this one thinks he'll get away with it."

The doctor patted his back. "What if I can bring one back to you? The one who stole your fire extinguisher and disrupted your fine establishment?"

"You could do that?" He brightened, imagining

the kid in his mind and mentally squashing him. "The things I could do to that kid, he'd know true pain."

The doctor heartily shook his hand. "It'd be my pleasure, sir."

the LAte CALL

CRAIg wAS ventuRIng from one extreme to the next, and the adrenaline rush didn't recede. Endorphins were replenished and burned and replenished again. His armpits were sopping wet and so was his back. He quivered in the wake of such an experience. It'd been years since he pictured and recreated the scenario in his mind, how he'd change the way that night had unfolded. He whooped, and hollered, and cheered. "Yeah! Fuck them. Fuck Janna in the ass. She's a slut. Nobody crosses Craig Horsy and gets away with it clean."

He was driving an '81 Fiesta now. The rust bucket struggled up the hill, the engine gasping and clunking. The evening air blew with a chill, and he shivered, being glazed in sweat. He read the dashboard clock, and it was 7:30. He was dressed in black jeans and a navy-blue sweater with a red stripe across the chest. Craig's hardhat and orange reflective vest were heaped on top of each other in the passenger seat. This was the brief spell he was working beside his father with the city. It lasted three months, and he vowed never to work alongside his father again patching roads and sidewalks. It was to pay rent, and that was it. But tonight had nothing to do with

Brandon or his job prospects. Alice Denny called him twenty minutes ago. She was desperate, and she wouldn't tell him what was wrong. He sped across town at Briar Ridge, which was about twenty miles from his original home. He lost touch with Alice post high school. She started dating a guy named Dylan Thomas, and like many friends, time had its way with them. It'd almost been a full year since he'd last spoken with her.

Alice lived with Dylan in an apartment downtown. He passed the Indiana Airport and Amtrak station. The main road turned into an avenue of fast food restaurants and low-rent hotels, and on the outskirts of that area stood the apartment building named Corner Square Commons. The buildings resembled four-story tall white houses. There were six huddles of them. Alice was located on the very end of the series in apartment 4C.

He dreaded the arrival. Alice wouldn't tell him why she wanted him there. Her voice was flat and without character, the throat stripped down to the barest of functions. "Please come over to my place, Craig. I need your help. Don't ask me anything. Just come here now." Weeping, "*Please.*"

Craig steadied the wheel and drove into a parking space. Getting out and stepping to the entrance of the apartments, the night had disguised the run-down façade of the building into a shadowy tower. Green shutters were broken. The rails of the stairs wobbled at the touch. The carpet over the stairs inside was faded and coming up at the edges. The walls had been punched with holes and poorly spackled.

He froze on the first level. "I don't want to do this, Dr. Krone." Turning back to the door, but freezing in place, he knew there was no turning back without facing the next thing. Craig waited, caught up in his indecision. Would the doctor show up and save him from the horrible memory, perhaps bring him to Lake Jacomo and have a chat? A blink, and he'd be there. That's how it kept happening. He wasn't allowed much reaction time to any of this, and it was exhausting. The last round would've been a wonderful finale, but there was so much else to accomplish, he sensed, before the treatment was over.

"What else do you have for me?" he asked the walls, the ceiling, the stairs, anybody who'd listen. "I need a break. Time out, okay? Where are you, Dr. Krone? Speak to me. Why are you hiding? You're watching, aren't you? Show yourself. Damn it, why are you treating me like this? If I'm your patient, why won't you see me?"

Dr. Krone wasn't coming. Five minutes passed. Ten minutes passed. The staircase was blank of human presence or the desperately needed answers he required.

This is supposed to make me feel better?

Fuck you, Dr. Krone. Fuck you.

Craig charged up the stairs, fired up for the wrong reasons. He couldn't avoid it. Dr. Krone ran the show. He was helpless to choose his next move because it had been provided for him.

"This is truly against my will. I've missed you, Alice, but I didn't want to see you like this. Not like *this.*"

He walked the stairs up to the second floor and completed the third. The final floor, the fourth, he read across the board—4A, 4B, and 4C—and he kept quivering, feeling his pulse rise, the heat on his back a beast of a blush. His instincts commanded him to turn around and forget the venture regardless of the consequences.

Just see it through. It might not happen the way you remember. It's worked out that way a few times.

Still uncomfortable, he was close enough to Alice's apartment that he could see her door was a fraction ajar. He opened it all the way and closed it behind him. He called in softly, "Alice, are you there?"

"Lock the door behind you," she managed through tears. "I'm in the bathroom."

"Where's Dylan?"

"He's gone." She wept harder. "I showed him what had happened, and he left me. He said, he said, *he said he loved me.*"

He carefully chose his next steps. The lights were off in the other half of the apartment. The thin crack of yellow light beckoned him from a short hallway.

He tried to dodge any surprises, "What's wrong, Alice?"

Now her voice was flat. "I want you to come in and help me."

"You said Dylan's gone?"

Alice was quiet. He stayed outside the bathroom door, afraid to open it. "I'm here, Alice. Tell me what's going on."

Under her breath, "*Just come inside.*"

Craig edged the door open with two fingers. Slowly, he entered, and then viewed Alice who was deathly pale, as white as the terrycloth bathrobe she had wrapped around herself. She sat on the edge of the shower, eyes affixed on the closed toilet. She didn't blink or look up when he entered. He wasn't sure what to say.

He noted the droplets of blood around the circumference of the toilet. Ruby-red drops. He eyed the blood, Alice, the blood, Alice, the blood. "W-what's this? What happened, Alice?"

He touched Alice's arm lovingly, lowering to her level. "Are you hurt?"

Alice's eyes pooled, wet and fat tears spilled down her cheeks. Her skin flushed a purple shade, like she'd been holding her breath for too long. "I told Dylan, and he left me. He said he didn't love me anymore. He doesn't understand. I didn't tell him because I was scared. He just doesn't understand." She eyed the closed toilet, mentally cursing it. "He'll be back. He's just scared."

"I don't understand what's wrong?"

She pointed at the toilet. "You have to . . . *look*."

He reached for the toilet rim, but he didn't lift it up yet. Alice watched him. She wanted him to see it. He didn't understand what possessed him to lift it—because he knew what it was, and that's what had him running the first time he'd done this in his life—but he did so now anyway. The water was blood red. Spattered.

The miscarriage.

He dialed 9-1-1 and demanded an ambulance. And after he belted out the information to the dispatcher, he hung up. He rushed out the door. Alice didn't call for him again. Down the stairs, he conquered the task of escaping, and once the night air struck him, he could breathe again. He was dizzy and plopped down onto the seat of his car. He couldn't stay with her, the bloody sight churning his stomach, forever branding his memory with a blot of horror. He wanted Alice to be of sound mind, but this was beyond his reach and beyond his experience. The dead half-formed baby sucked any fight he had left to change the past. Again.

LAKe jAcomo

CRAIg couLdn't be any happier to return to the frozen-over lake. The refuge appealed to him so much he ran straight for it. He pressed his back to the snow-covered ice and formed snow angels. Flakes dropped from the sky in light blankets, and he let them touch his tongue and melt.

He was free of Alice's tragedy. Guilt attached itself to his freedom. It was the same regret he experienced that exact night. He abandoned her. He failed to see her through the ordeal. But it was over now. The snow, the lake, the seclusion, it was easy to shove Alice back into his deepest memories and move on.

As he expected, Dr. Krone crunched across the snow, bounding down a set of long ice-covered stairs to reach the lake. Craig was about to verbalize a greeting when he caught the doctor's grim expression. He stopped three yards from the iced-over lake.

Dr. Krone accused, "*You.*"

The scowl continued to take shape, everything in his features curling and then hardening. The fat man's face was capable of many expressions despite its soft quality. "You're not going along with the program. You ran away from her. What kind of a friend are you? This was supposed to be a turning point for you. A big one, too. You were supposed to see her through her horrible time."

"I was scared," Craig argued, standing up from the ice and struggling not to slip on the way up. "I'm doing fucking fantastic, I think. It's hard going back in time and reliving your hardest memories. It's messing with me, so forgive me if I screw up. I've always had regrets about Alice. I have no idea if she'd ever forgive me for that night or if she hates me."

"You had no problem with that memory with Susan. Oh, and those kids who played the joke on you at the Italian restaurant, you embraced it. You have to take the good with the bad, Mr. Horsy. It's part of your treatment. You can't get better without complete participation. Give yourself over to the treatment." Now a whisper. "*Give yourself over to me.*"

Craig refused to accept the scolding without a fight. He charged at Dr. Krone and pushed him to the ground. He flopped backwards, legs lifting high, as he connected against the ice with a thud. "Fuck you, Doctor! Until you've run the gauntlet yourself, I suggest you settle down."

He glared up at Craig, offended. His face was cherry red and turning darker. Dr. Krone worked back to a standing position, and after a long struggle—even waving Craig off after he offered to help him despite his current sentiments—he moved in close to Craig, cocking his head to the side.

"Mr. Horsy, I've experienced my mind inside and out. I have 'run the gauntlet.' I'm perfectly happy with my past. And I've been in many heads—yours and maybe a thousand others. It's mesmerizing, and it's a dreadful shame you're not embracing the tragedies with the rewards. It offends me that you shirk in the face of perfection. Yes, you flinched. They all do. That's why I'm the doctor, and you're the patient. You need guidance. I give all my patients a chance to treat themselves, so to speak, but it sounds like you need my help as much as the rest." Eyes brimming with angry tears, he rasped, "*I guess I have to intervene.*"

Craig backed up, suddenly terrified of the man, the genius lunatic. He was the one in power, and the doctor wanted to use it. He was unsettled and knew he couldn't continue with this mysterious, cutting-edge treatment anymore. "Okay, let me go. Unhook me from the machine.

"This is finished. I don't trust you. If you're so genuine and honest, then I can leave when I want to, right? You forced me onto that machine against my will."

"It had to happen that way," the doctor said. "Nobody hands themselves over to treatment without sedatives and restraints. This happens in many treatments. You're no exception, Mr. Horsy."

"How did I get here? That letter, I was really supposed to be at Dr. Herbert's office. You did something to me. Tell me how I got here, and no more of your lies."

His eyes widened, their color as bright as wind-kissed embers in a fire pit. "Fine, I'll show you."

The blink happened.

Craig rose from his twin-sized bed and clutched his back. Every time he slept longer than eight hours, the kink in his back was razor sharp. It was the day of his psychiatrist's visit, and he dreaded it. Afterwards, he'd drive to the unemployment office and seek work. The first unemployment check hadn't shown up. His case was under review.

He stripped from his pajama bottoms and the faded Cinderella metal band T-shirt. He trudged to the bathroom, washing his face in the sink. When he lifted up his head from the first splash, Rachael, the receptionist, opened the bathroom door. He was seized by the neck, bent over, and a pinprick entered his back. His body went loose, and he flapped his arms against invisible waves of liquid, and drowning in them, he dropped to his knees. Then a black curtain fell, ushering him to sleep in the darkness, but first he seized Rachael by the leg, brought her down, and that's when she growled at him, and the weapon swiftly came down in a blur of metal. A quick refraction of silver in light, and the head of the hammer pounded into his skull.

The blink happened.

He returned to Lake Jacomo. The winter. The snow pelted him, the light curtains now firing down in blinding fury. The doctor was disguised by the curtain of snow and rain mixture. The man's secret was revealed, and he was prepared to explain why it happened.

"I kidnapped you. Yes, you were supposed to be at Dr. Herbert's, but I took the initiative to take you in as a patient. Nobody gives themselves completely over to any treatment. But like my father, I want to cure people through and through. I won't waste your time with expensive and pointless visits and introspection that fails to go anywhere. Talking does nothing. Dr. Herbert would've failed you. That's why I reference other doctors' patients in the area, and I get my hands on whoever I can, like you. Rachael's a master of breaking into facilities and stealing information. It'll benefit society in the long run. You'll see. I did this for the good of mankind. Sometimes bad things have to happen before something good can happen.

"Being in the moment heals, Mr. Horsy, like facing your fears, living your regrets, changing your past, that's how one copes with life. I've barely scratched the surface of your treatment, Mr. Horsy." He put his fingers together. "My father called this part of the treatment 'shock therapy.'"

He waved his hands to prevent Craig from speaking. "No, I won't send electrodes into your skull. That's along the lines of those false alternatives other doctors offer. I might as well resort to bloodletting or pouring ice-cold water over your body to shock the anger out of you. No, I'll do things to your mind you won't understand. It takes the threat of death to make one appreciate their lives and cope with their past. Yes, you can die during this treatment, Mr. Horsy. Clinically dead, Craig—I won't lie. Many do perish during these exercises. You're a danger to society, and the reasons are as volatile as the treatment. If you overcome my procedure, you'll be worthy of mixing with the world again."

"*I'm not a danger to society!*" Craig balled his hands into fists, appalled at the ludicrous explanation. "I made one mistake. Yes, my childhood was fucked up. I've joined the club, Dr. Krone. Willis was a mistake, my only mistake, you lunatic. I've listened to you, and you're the one who needs to take your own medicine, not me. You can't keep me here. I don't want to be here."

This was the defining moment he was waiting for, the actual truth. Dr. Krone had kidnapped him. He was hooked to a machine, in God-knows-where, under the control of this madman. Now the man admitted he could die. It came off as a promise. He wasn't safe. The gut feeling was correct. The man and his female assistant were criminals. He was helpless in his mind.

How could he escape a place without an exit?

Desperation sent him to his knees. He clutched a flap of the doctor's lab coat. "Just let me go, okay? I'll forget any of this happened. I'm sorry for what I did to Willis. It's a mistake. Send me to jail if that's what it takes. I can't take any more of this memory shit. It's too much." He threw his head back and unleashed a wild roar, "*Let me out of my mind!*"

Dr. Krone kneed him in the chest. The connection forced the air from his lungs, and it took him a moment to relearn how to breathe, sprawled out on the ice.

"What is it that you're after, really?" Craig gasped, the winter's cold suddenly setting in. Whatever protected him from the elements before had suddenly been lifted. "Why did you pick me?"

"I'm not allowed to practice legally," Dr. Krone confessed, shaking his head as if consoling himself. "My father wasn't either after his breakthrough. Stripped of his license, actually." He mulled the question over longer. "You interested me more than the rest in the stack of files. Your history, your potential, I couldn't resist treating you. There's nothing like being inside you, Mr. Horsy." He stared at him with big eyes. "I can fix you. My father wanted to cure people with this machine, as do I."

"This has nothing to do with treating me or some doctor's code of honor." Craig rose to his feet. "Your life isn't interesting enough so you have to become someone else, is that it?"

The doctor didn't refute the statement. The doctor was on the verge of many wild, ridiculous expressions. It chilled Craig to wonder what channeled through the man's head.

"Your machine's an excuse to be a voyeur. You watched Susan and me make love. You've been there the entire time while everything's happened."

"I've gotten to know your family and friends quite well too." The doctor kept on track with his own morbid agenda. "And they're not happy at all with you. Now, it's time for the *real* treatment."

hIghwAy 90

WintRy gu$t$ bAtted the parked '81 Chrysler station wagon. He shivered in the cold. The heater spat out lukewarm air, and now the hot air had stopped coming out altogether. He escaped Dr. Krone and the lake. No, Dr. Krone had released him. Nobody could help him. He was stuck in the moment, and the moment was soon to unfold. The highway in front of him was swallowed up by pelting snow. The car's engine rattled, and shortly after, the car conked out. He was stranded. Miles in both directions, white blanketed the horizon.

"Don't tell me the car broke down!" It was Katie. She was in the backseat sprawled out in the late stages of giving birth.

Oh God, not this.

Anything but this moment!

Katie's water had already broken, and her contractions were seconds apart. It wouldn't be long before the baby made its way into the world.

He dialed his cell phone, his fingers trembling. Craig couldn't get a signal. "Hey, I got a signal when this happened the first time."

He pounded the seat. *This isn't making sense.*

Katie voiced her confusion. "What are you talking

about the first time? You have a child with somebody else?"

He rubbed at his face, trying to regain his composure. "No, Katie. You won't understand."

Wait. What does she know? If she's a memory Dr. Krone's conjured up, who is she really?

"Who's my favorite baseball team?"

"The Atlanta Braves. Why the hell are you asking me that? Craig, I'm scared. If we can't get to the hospital, what are we going to do?"

He dialed the cell phone again. The buttons didn't work. The screen was blank. He wasn't sure what to make of her answer. She was correct, the Braves were his favorite team. Everybody from his past spoke on their own accord, and it fit their personalities.

How was it possible?

Craig flipped on the hazard lights next, and then he dialed the phone again. Nothing. "Goddamn it!"

This is about regrets, right? Do something different. She's in your mind. She's passed on. You can't lose the same baby twice. You can't lose Katie twice.

"I don't have much choice. I'll be quick. I'll call for help, and I'll come right back."

"I don't want to be alone," she begged him, her fingers digging into the seat, anticipating another contraction. "It hurts so much. I'm not ready for this. This isn't a good idea!"

He looked her over, splayed in the backseat so helpless. For a moment, he believed Katie was real again, but she wasn't. It was Dr. Krone's manipulations. He had to escape his mind.

How did one accomplish such a feat? Craig knew Dr. Krone wanted him to make changes and face the problems of his past, and that meant he'd have to play into the doctor's games for now.

"Keep my phone," he said, giving it to her. "I'll run as fast as I can. There's no choice. Help can't arrive unless they know we need it. Forgive me for leaving you."

"You bastard!"

He shut the door. Would this be another regret? *She's deceased, how could it get any worse?*

The wind battered him. He clutched the median to stay upright. The snow increased the longer he traveled, the winds literally working against him. He was ankle-deep in snow now, his legs burning, and his body weakening. He prayed there was a service station off the next exit.

Exit 30A was barely visible ahead. He walked downhill, careful not to fall down the exit. The service station had its lights on. The open sign was a faded beacon.

"Thank God."

He hurried to the destination, and finally arriving there, he threw open the door. An older man sat behind a desk watching television, a late night rerun of *Family Ties*. He sipped on a cup of coffee raucously, with an opened bag of potato chips on the counter. He wore a faded gray sweater and blue jeans, a shawl wrapped tightly around his neck to ward off the cold.

"Hey there, fella." The man was happy; he didn't have to suffer the weather alone anymore. "Come on inside and get warm. It's crazy out there."

He cut to the point. "Let me use your phone."

"Sure." He pointed at the phone near the chips rack. "But it's not working. The storm's knocked it out."

"Do you have a working vehicle I can use? It's an emergency. My wife's on the highway in labor. My car broke down. It's barely a mile out of the way. Please. She's alone."

The old man eyed him with skepticism. "What kind of a man would leave his pregnant wife alone on the highway, especially during a mean storm like this?"

"My phone won't get a signal. And she's so close to giving birth. What choice did I have? I had to do something."

Wait, why is he judging me? That never happened. I didn't come here.

"You're not going to help me then?"

The old man watched the television screen. "Yeah. You about got it."

Craig noticed a set of car keys behind the counter resting on a stool. He reached for them, bringing his body halfway over the counter. Swiping them, he ran out into the parking lot. There was only one car out there, the choice obvious.

Caught in headlights, he was suddenly blinded. Then a car screeched, plowing through the deep snow, and afterwards, the car fishtailed and slid on black ice. He leapt out of the car's direct path as the vehicle smashed through the front entrance with a great spray of glass and the give of steel beams. He landed on the pavement in a tailspin, looking up at the vehicle and discovering it was his station wagon. Navigating through the wreckage, he entered the gaping hole that used to be the entrance. He winced, discovering the cashier was pinned against the wall, the bumper flattening his rib cage.

The man was dead.

Craig stared at the car in horror. The lights were out, and it was pure darkness inside. Did Katie drive all this way? How could she in labor?

He mustered the words. "Katie? Are you okay?"

He feared walking to the station wagon. Was she hurt? What force impelled her to drive through the gas station? Was it an accident? The speed she was driving, he believed she was trying to plow into him.

The car windows were too much in shadow to view inside. Craig waited. Two pieces of glass fell from the broken entrance behind him. Minutes dragged on, and still, nothing happened. He was on the verge of calling out again when the driver's side door opened.

"Honey, what are you doing?"

Craig took a step closer. He couldn't look into the window. Everything was abyss black.

"Please, say something."

He failed to make out the profile of Katie inside. She had to be at the driver's seat, perhaps slumped over.

Unless someone stole the car.

"Is that you, Katie?"

The old man's leg jittered in an after-death twitch.

Craig didn't want to look into the car. She was inside, but it wasn't her. It was Dr. Krone's version of her. He couldn't trust his surroundings or even the ones he loved.

He scanned the wrecked shelves of snack foods and broken bottles of soda for a light source. He finally discovered a flashlight in the mess. It didn't have batteries.

"Shit."

Craig lowered to his haunches and sorted through a pile of Snickers bars and a deflated bag of Doritos for a pack of D batteries. He inserted them and aimed the yellow beam toward the car.

Crab-walking backwards in an instantaneous reaction, he shouted in shock, "Katie, Katie—no!"

Blood dribbled from her mouth in a continuous flow. She was hunched in the seat, her belly wedged against the steering wheel. And when she jerked awake, an alien sound escaped from his throat, one of stone-cold terror. Katie stomped out of the car, moving her damaged body at a slow, determined pace.

He took it all in. Her face was corpse blue. The left eye was all white, no pupil, the eye slowly sinking into the back of her socket. Blood issued from a set of broken front teeth. Grimy red streamed down her legs in heavy black crimson trails. It drip, drip, dripped from between her legs with each new step she took. Her bathrobe hung loosely from her body in dirty flaps and folds.

She hissed, "*You . . . left . . . me . . . alone.*"

"I had to, honey. I didn't leave you. My phone, you know it wasn't working. The car broke down. What could I do? I had to get help. You know I was coming back—you know it!"

"You don't know how to drive a *fah-king* car." She coughed up blood and spat it to the side. "I got it to run fine. What's the matter with you? You were always a pitiful failure. You can't even hold down a descent job. Why did I marry you?"

He suffered a vicious bout of tremors. "I-I love you. I'm sorry it happened like this. I panicked. Please understand."

She didn't explain why she tried to run him over outside or why she smashed through the gas station.

And there was the other dilemma. She was dead in pallor, dead for real, he thought, especially when her right eye was completely sucked up into the socket and pink tissue replaced the orb.

He wept, overwhelmed by surreal emotion. "H-honey, you're . . . *you're dead.*"

She screeched so loud, offended by his observation. "*My baby is dead because of you!*"

Katie stomped after him, her decision to inflict pain upon him decided. He froze, unable to comprehend that this was an attack. She wasn't limber, but she was powerful. She reached him in seconds, her hands digging into his shoulders. Claiming hold of him, she launched him against the bathroom door. His shoulder cracked the surface, absorbing the impact, and his bone radiated with white-hot burning pain. He prayed he hadn't dislocated the shoulder blade or unhinged a rotator cup. Thrown to the floor, he cradled his shoulder, moaning softly, rocking himself to combat the agony.

Dead vocal cords threatened, "I will wash you in the blood of our dead child."

"What are you saying?" He couldn't hold back the torment of watching his dead wife skulk about the room, bleeding from the face and legs. "Don't talk like that. It wasn't my fault. The situation was out of my control. I never wanted any of this to happen."

"I'm still dead regardless of your feelings." She turned direction, then threw open a back door and entered it. "*Dead forever.*"

Clop. Clop. Clop.

She was barefoot and skulking about the station, seeking something, and what, he failed to imagine. He wasn't going anywhere, experiencing so much pain.

123

After many moments, she returned, coming in closer. He gazed up at her. She was a ghoul drooling blood and broken bits of teeth. Her robe came undone, her sagging breasts spattered in red, the distended belly blackening from the middle, the rot slowly spreading to other vital places. She kicked up a horrendous smell.

"W-what are you doing, Katie?" He managed to speak through a tight throat. "Stop this insanity." He raised his voice. "Dr. Krone, where are you hiding—where are you? Stop this, stop this now! You know me, Katie. I wouldn't intentionally hurt you."

He scanned the room. There was nothing outside the windows except snow for miles. He was trapped with his dead vengeful wife.

Out of nowhere, she dropped a steel bucket onto the floor with a rusty clang. She propped it between her legs, and droplets of blood pinged inside. The flow increased once the bucket was in position. He stared in horror. The pain was abating in his shoulder, but the shock of the scene kept him still. Deathly afraid.

What is she doing with the bucket?

"What's Dr. Krone doing to you, Katie? He's doing something to you. You must tell me what it is."

Katie's smile wasn't natural, and it wasn't hers. It curled too much at the sides, and it spread out so long; the lips couldn't possibly stretch that far. Again, she was a ghoul, so pale and dead. This wasn't his wife. Dr. Krone's imagination was at work, distorting and darkening reality.

"I warned you, you could die." She watched the blood fill the bucket. "Face your fears. You said you wanted to get well. But you get so violent. You're a danger to society. Do you want to be locked up, Mr. Horsy?"

"You bastard!"

She cackled in delight. Her belly shriveled audibly. She clapped her hands once, looking down. "Oh, the bucket's full now."

Craig used the wall to work up to a standing position. He hobbled for the entrance, but he was driven back to the ground, tackled by the shoulders, and yanked back to where he came from. Her stink washed over him in the form of blood and bile as he was sent crashing beside the bucket. He reached out to tip it over, but he was too late. Seized by the neck, kicked between the shoulders, head lifted, hair yanked, neck forced forward, he was dunked into the steaming bucket of crimson.

"*Gahwk!*"

He closed his eyes. Sticky blood filled his ear canals and nostrils. It was so hot, unnaturally warm, it burned his face at a scalding temperature. Gobs of flesh were mixed in. Placenta. After-birth.

Muffled hysterics. "*Drown in your child's blood!*"

He was doing just that. His head swelled and filled with pressure. He refused to open his mouth. He couldn't call it blood, it was disgusting and not of a human. It was red. It was black. It was animal's blood. It was rancid blood. It was the blood rendered from tainted meat.

He thrashed, but Katie sat on his back like an anchor. He frantically scanned the floor with his hands, searching for a weapon. What he found was an electrical cord. He played with it, tugging and jerking it back and forth. Desperate for air, his skull tightening against his brain, his mouth threatening to open and scream and taste the vile contents of the bucket, he tossed up the cord. The first attempt was lame, landing uselessly to her left. He collected it again, each bend of the cord another second closer to drowning. The next attempt, the cord whipped her back, and she laughed out loud, amused by his fight.

"You have to do more than that, Mr. Horsy, to stop me!"

Angry and fueled by the wicked sensations crawling up and down his spinal cord and bursting into his skull, he threw up the cord and somehow it wrapped around Katie's throat. He tightened the slack and jerked it forward. She cawed in shock and faltered from his back. He lifted his head up, gasping for air. Gel-thick fluid dripped down his face and clotted his hair. The berating laughter at his impending death ceased.

He cleaned his eyes with the tips of his fingers and faltered against the check-out counter, weak and panting. "Katie, you don't have to do this. Please, you're killing me. Let's talk about this."

She was facedown on the floor. Motionless. Her chest didn't move to breathe. "Katie?"

Craig crept to her. He didn't trust her. This wasn't his wife.

Fresh blood circled her head. She'd cracked her nose against the floor. He touched her with his foot. "Katie, are you alive?"

She remained still.

And that's when he caught Dr. Krone watching through the back window. It was frosted over, his features two eyes and a nose. He darted away once he was caught.

"No you don't!"

Craig sprinted across the shop and threw open the back door in pursuit. The doctor disappeared into the storm, well hidden. Running outside, he sucked in the below-freezing cold and accepted the mean gusts that smacked into his body.

"*Stay out of my mind!*" He belted it out once more, this time falling to his knees. "*Stay out of my mind, you demented asshole!*"

The winter sucked him up and trapped him, the snow piling all around him until he was buried.

***

The device resembled a giant corkscrew connected to a man's head. Leather straps down the man's cheeks and buckles clamped firmly at his chin. The man wore a straightjacket, and he was sedated. The drool and glassy eyes revealed that much.

Craig watched the tip of the corkscrew puncture into the man's skull with a drawn-out squish and brittle cracking. He also wore a steel rim around his forehead, the bottom part of a crown. Blood rivulets streamed from puncture wounds around the circumference of the head.

Ka-chunk.

The corkscrew dug deeper, the entry twisting meat, hair, and rendering fat spurts of blood. The man working the device wore a white lab coat. He used all of his strength to grind the device farther into the victim's head. His back was turned, and Craig couldn't see his face.

Ka-chunk.

The room stank of death. Wet leather and copper. He observed in the darkened shadows the outline of other corpses. They were strewn in piles five high, twenty bodies thick. They were all wrapped in straightjackets. Blood stained the floor and gurgled and belched down a drain.

Ka-chunk.

"I've got another one!" the man cheered. "Another brain for the pile, Danny-boy. We have to work faster. There's not nearly enough of them for our studies."

The operator wrenched back the giant screw and the skull cap and half of the man's head was uprooted. He twisted the steel cork back, rung by rung, until the brain slithered from the metal coils and into a plastic receptacle.

Craig's view was obscured, and all he could watch was a gloved hand—a hand that was caked in blood well above the wrist and up to the elbow—touch and caress and poke at the row of buckets that each harbored wet slithery brains.

The man whispered, "Just a few more is all we need . . . only a few more, son, and the machine will be ready."

edith miLLeR

CRAIG'S ShouLdeR continued to ache. He didn't think he had dislocated it, but he couldn't be certain. He was no doctor. He wasn't cold anymore, the snow that had buried him missing. The air was dry and stale. There was little ventilation. Katie's blood had dried on his face, and hands, and shirt. What had he just witnessed? A man's brain was removed. It had to be Dr. Krone's work. The bastard was up to more than Craig could ever imagine, and this was the beginning of finding out.

Was it on purpose he witnessed the snippet of a memory, or was he somehow connected to Dr. Krone's mind? The scene itself was disturbing. Stacks of bodies. Buckets of freshly removed brains. And did the man call out to his son? Craig was confused and realized it was best he cover his ass instead of evaluating a vision he didn't understand.

He stopped walking.

He had no memory of this place.

Craig roamed the halls of a mausoleum. Green marble walls, gray marble floors, he eyed the brass plates without recognition. The names were unfamiliar. How he wound up here, Dr. Krone would only know.

He scratched at his face. The blood was drying and itching him. He was exhausted and wanted to close his eyes, and sleep, and quit being the victim for a change. But there were so many corners that anything could pop out from and attack, no moment was safe. The place was turn after long hall, turn after long hall.

Craig listened after catching a muffled startle ahead. Footsteps scuffed the tiles and then suddenly stopped, alerted by something. "Is that you, Dr. Krone? I can hear you. Show yourself. Just me and you this time, okay? No more tricks. Let's talk man to man."

Silence.

He refused to break down. He wouldn't grovel to Dr. Krone like he did on the ice. This was a fight to escape his mind, and only Dr. Krone could provide the way out.

"I heard someone down there. Step out and show me your face."

His patience was depleted, so he bounded forward and rounded the next corner, catching another person anticipating his arrival. She charged the opposite way from him. The person was unfamiliar. The mausoleum wasn't triggering any memories either. This was his adult body. He didn't revert back to a child or a teenager.

He pursued the stranger. "Hey—stop!"

The woman yipped at the command, startled that what she'd seen was real. She was five feet tall. Dirty blonde hair in strings and matted strands about her head. She harbored a black eye and a long gash across her cheek, perhaps inflicted by a claw. She wore a pair of torn-up jeans and a gray sweater. The stranger was stained in blood, especially at the shoulder area. The woman was worn down, the kind that'd seen a lot of eighty-hour work weeks.

"I won't hurt you." Craig softened his tone and slowed his advances. "Who are you? Did Dr. Krone do this to you?"

She stopped and sneered at him. The woman confronted him, taking fast strides, suddenly struck by a surge of courage. It was Craig's turn to be startled. The woman clutched his shirt and drew him close. Her breath stank of cottonmouth and cigarettes. "He's after you too, isn't he?"

He sucked in a thick breath to steady his words. "Did he hook you up to that dreadful machine?"

"What do you know about it? Tell me who you are."

She looked even older at a closer view. Late forties, early fifties. Her black eye made it difficult to maintain eye contact.

"I'm Craig Horsy," he explained nervously. "I-I don't know much about Dr. Krone. I was supposed to visit a psychiatrist, and I ended up here. They injected me with drugs, and I woke hooked up to a machine. Needles punctured my eyes and skull, and there's so much of that bright fucking light, it scorched my retinas. And then I'm reliving my memories. Dr. Krone said it's supposed to be therapeutic. But he's insane. He somehow made it so my dead wife attacked me. That's why I'm covered in blood. He won't let me out of my mind."

"That's where we are," she said. "But it's all of our minds. We're hooked into the same machine."

"Then how come I'm here with you? Do I know you?"

"Does the name Edith Miller sound familiar?"

131

He thought hard. "No. And why am I here in a mausoleum? I've actually never stepped foot into one before."

"Have you seen any of the doctor's memories yet?" She picked at the scab on her cheek, lessening her defenses. "That's why we're here. Sometimes we happen upon the doctor's memories on accident. This is why we're here. This is his father's resting place."

She pointed at the wall, specifically at the bronze marker that read—

Bruce Denning
1899-1985

He was confused. "Who's Bruce Denning?"

"Nobody important, but Bruce isn't alone in there. Dr. Krone's memory showed me what this place means. I saw Dr. Krone opening the slot and placing his father's corpse with Bruce's. He's kept his father's body in hiding. They're criminals. The name on the plate isn't accurate. There's two bodies sharing one slot."

"They're worse than criminals," Craig said. "They're lunatics with the means to break into our minds."

"He won't come here," Edith reassured him. "He doesn't want anything to do with the mausoleum. It's too painful to revisit for him. He stays outside, though. He knocks on the door sometimes and tries to talk me into coming out. Forget that idea." She shouted toward the east hall. "Fuck you, Dr. Krone!"

He traced his finger down Bruce Denning's marker. "I feel sorry for Bruce having to share a grave with the likes of a Krone."

"Do you know anything about Dr. Krone's father?"

He shook his head.

"He's the one who invented the machine. I keep seeing the number of bodies he's dissected and tested to create the device. The memories I see are quick flashes. It's like Dr. Krone lets his guard down and I see into him. I was lucky to learn of this place. I don't want to go back out there. It's not safe. It's never going to be safe."

Craig did catch a memory of Dr. Krone's, he realized. But it could've been his father he was watching turn that gigantic corkscrew device into that poor man's skull. The victim was in a straightjacket. Was the man taking subjects from sanitariums to complete his project? He didn't want to bring it up to Edith. She was visibly distraught.

"How long have you been in here hiding?"

Edith shrugged her shoulders. "A long time, I can't say exactly. It's all in the mind. It could be hours, days, weeks . . . "

They were both in the dark about many things. "I'm glad I found somebody who isn't from my past. But still, how did I get in here with you?"

"You resisted him. You refused to play into his game. It's all in the mind. You can fight back to an extent. What you did was probably involuntary."

"What do you mean by fight back?"

"Picture yourself somewhere, and you'll go there. You need a weapon, imagine it in your hand. When I saw Dr. Krone's memory of this place, and how he fled the scene once his father's body was buried in there, I decided to return. He seemed afraid of the mausoleum. He can't make me do anything if I resist. But it hurts. My head is a fucking migraine constantly. And I wasn't good at it at first. Dr. Krone kept winning."

Edith's eyebrows were always furrowed. She didn't blink either. She was focusing. However she did it, it was taking a toll on her. Her eyes were bloodshot red. Sweat glazed her features. Her skin was sheet white, her overall look malnourished.

"You can't go on like this," he insisted. "We can't hide from him. You're forgetting we're hooked up to a machine. He has us where he wants us."

"Then I'll die in here. I don't care. I've seen people and experienced shit that belongs in the past, and it should stay there. Dr. Krone's a deviant. My pain, it's his masturbation material. You do what you want, and I'll do as I want, and the world will move on with or without me. I don't care if he has us where he wants us. I never want to see him again. Bastard."

Thunck-thunck-thunck.

Knocking.

Then words were shouted, muffled by walls, "*I know you're in there!*"

The knocks against stone reverberated down the narrow hallway. Edith gasped. "That lunatic won't give up. I'm not coming out, so fuck off!"

"*I can wait forever, how about you? And you, Craig, would you like to make the mausoleum your new home?*"

Craig's tongue locked. He wanted to shout his defiance, but there wasn't any defiance left in him, only fatigue. He trembled, terrified of what the man was capable of accomplishing. He resurrected his wife only for her to attempt to drown him in his dead child's blood. What would come next? What other memories could the doctor use against him?

Edith glanced at him. "Ignore him. He'll go away eventually. He gets bored quick."

"*Your bodies will starve. I'll let you die if you don't come out soon. This is the final warning. Come out or starve to death. Your treatment is far from over for the both of you!*"

Dr. Krone's steps echoed against the marble steps outside, and he was gone. Edith rubbed at her eyes and blinked twice. She was weary. Ragged.

When he was convinced the doctor was gone, he asked her, "Hey, tell me how you got here? I mean how you came to be in Dr. Krone's office."

She frowned. "I was simply walking down the street, but it was late. I wanted a pack of cigarettes, so I was heading to a 7-11. It was a Friday night, so I was going to get piss-and-shit drunk. There's a stretch of lone road, trees at both sides of you, secluded, perfect for kidnapping. Dr. Krone came at me in the shadows, and I woke up hooked to the machine. He claimed he was a doctor cutting out my brain cancer, but I knew it was a lie. I have no health insurance. I'm broke. No doctor would go out of his way to save my ass. And the machine itself terrified me so much I knew he wasn't a real doctor."

This time Edith asked a question. "Do you have any kids?"

The question was a common one, and it always reminded him of Katie. "I was supposed to. My wife died in childbirth. We were stranded on the highway during a winter storm, we panicked, and help didn't arrive until she bled too much." He paused, taking in the horrible facts. "I lost them both."

Sympathy played out on her face. "That's awful."

"Dr. Krone brought her back a few times. Dead and alive."

"Some things we're not meant to experience again."

Edith squeezed her eyes hard. The action was so violent, her face flushed. Crow's feet formed deep trenches around the sockets. She squeezed her eyes harder. Her fists were clenched and trembling at her sides. She was grunting under her breath. Her face turned bright cherry red. She was growling when a pack of cigarettes popped into her hands. She removed a lighter from her pocket and lit a smoke. Edith offered him one, and he accepted it, taking in a luxurious puff.

"That's amazing how you did that."

"But now my head's on fire. It feels like razors are in my brain. And you can only do it so many times within a certain period of time, or else you'll faint. I've exhausted myself. I've produced guns, keys to escape rooms, you name it, and I'm still fighting for my sanity."

"Then talk about something pleasant." He thought hard. "Do you have kids?"

"I gave birth to three children. They're all two years apart with two different husbands. They're both bastards. Men are all shit, no offense. I can sure pick 'em, huh?" She rolled her eyes. "That's why I gave birth to all girls: Patricia, Claire, and Fiona. I miss them so much. The oldest will hit puberty soon. I'll be paying out as much for cigarettes as I do for tampons. And sex, oh God, I'll simply tell them the truth about men, and I'm sure it'll set them straight. They'll be lesbians by the time I'm through giving them their talks.

"I've survived with my sister. She has a little girl too. It's a Miller trait, I think. We're trying to rid the world of men, so we keep pumping out girls." She laughed softly. "Did I tell you both of my exes are in jail for evading child support? I've worked so many Merry Maid jobs and car washes and waitress gigs, I pray my kids can help me retire."

"We should fight our way out of here," Craig challenged her, once learning her motivation. "Do it for your girls. Dr. Krone wants us to be scared. You said it. He gets off on this shit. We're playing into his games."

"He wiped out my children in front of me." She stubbed out the cigarette and the cruelty of the statement played out on her face. "My sister, she's the one who did it. She drowned them in the bathtub one after the other, and I was helpless to watch."

"But they're not really dead."

She wept, picturing it happening again in her mind. "I know, but it was so real."

"My dead wife tried to drown me, how do you think I feel? I was scared. Terrified out of my mind. You have to be strong, and hiding isn't doing the trick."

"You're a typical man trying to take charge." Her steely eyes met his, and he backed down. "Leave me alone awhile. Back off, okay? Heart-to-heart talk is over."

He turned his back, disappointed, and feeling guilty and frustrated. She wouldn't fight back. Perhaps she'd been in here too long to conceive of another battle plan. Or she was exhausted. She'd been in here far longer than he'd been.

He continued down the opposite hall and stared at the walls, and soon, claustrophobia sank in. Craig couldn't stand it here. He paced, uncomfortable, restless, antsy, and without the answers to his questions. Then he sat down. Stood up. Sat down again. He walked more halls, but they were all the same drab marble and equally boring. *Couldn't they give the dead a livelier place to sleep for eternity?*

The doors were locked. He tried every set. Then, he eyed the front door. Through the cracks, a thin arc of light shined through, and he caught the outline of two feet.

Dr. Krone was waiting.

A whisper snuck through the door. "Mr. Horsy, you're restless in there. And I'm restless out here. Why not meet up?"

"I want off of that machine," he demanded, punching the door. "And I want you out of my mind. You don't belong there."

"There's so much malady deep inside you." His words were pinched. "And I want to bleed it from you. Only then can you be healed. To draw out the malady, you must create malady." Through gritted teeth he said, "I'm the professional, you're the patient."

"I'm a healthy, sane person!" He pounded the door harder. "You're the one with the malady. You're full of shit. You turned my wife into a monster. You're watching my every move. I don't want to be here anymore. This is against my will."

Dr. Krone stifled his amusement, although poorly, his chuckles and snickers as childish as they were demeaning. "Your mind turned your wife into a monster. The subconscious does strange things when untreated. It's not me."

"Your machine, your manipulations—it's you, you son of a bitch!"

"Oh, how can you be so sure I'm the bad guy?"

"Poor Edith, you haven't cured her. She knows about you, and so do I. And I've seen into your mind too, and it's not a pretty sight. You were removing the brains from mental patients. Is that treating your subconscious? Who's the monster, really? Maybe you should undergo your own treatment? What would your father say to that, or should I ask his corpse you've stashed in somebody else's grave? *May he not rest in peace.*"

This time Dr. Krone struck the door with his fist. "You know nothing about me! I'm the doctor, you're the patient. *Know—your—place!*"

"This machine you've created, do you really understand it? This treatment is bullshit. It isn't for me, it isn't for Edith. It's to fulfill your sick fantasies. My place, since you ask, is way the hell away from you." He said this knowing he was helpless. "But you won't let me."

"I'm the doctor," Dr. Krone repeated, flustered and out of breath, "and you're the patient."

Craig couldn't take any more conversation with the lunatic. He stormed down the hall and checked in on Edith. On his way there, Dr. Krone issued one final warning. "Come out, or I'm coming in after you."

AwAke In the mAusoLeum

edith hAd fALLen ASLeep. Was she really resting, he wondered. Could she in her own mind? He envied her if she was really asleep, the way she looked, so peaceful.

"*You poor thing.*"

He listened. The silence was reassuring. He stared at his hands. The blood crusted on his skin was now like orange rust. This was his baby's blood. Katie's blood. They were both gone. That would never change. Only here in this horrible place could they exist, and even then, it was tainted. It would be a beautiful thing if it was used for good. It started off that way, he recalled, with his moment in bed with Katie. He made love to Susan. He retaliated against his father who belittled his mother. He showed Janna and her friends in the parking lot what revenge was all about. He visited Alice, though she was still viable to him in real life. She could be reached again if he could escape his mind.

He could start fresh.

Craig was then attacked by a pain of self-loathing so strong he forced every thought from his mind to escape the reality of his regrets.

Edith's talk of fighting back interested him more. He tried to focus on Katie and home. He pictured taking a warm bath with her, perhaps a bottle of White Zinfandel to drink as they soaked. The idea was so pleasurable, but it wasn't possible. He held his eyes shut and thought hard. He strained so much he coughed and forced himself to breathe normally again. Maybe Edith did something else to accomplish the feat. Again, he tried. A sharp stab shot throughout his skull as he held his breath, focused, strained, clenched his fists, imagined it, and he still came up empty.

"Damn it."

He decided to let Edith sleep longer. She deserved a respite from this nightmare. He spent his time eyeing the inscriptions on the markers: names, and dates, and final commiserations. It messed with his mind to spend so long in a place of mourning.

Craig suddenly laughed, escaping the sense of impending doom with levity. *I guess I'm not missing work since I'm unemployed. I don't have to call in sick either.*

Someone would look for him soon. One person being his mother. She would call after his doctor's visit and ask how it went. Surely, she'd left a message and was concerned when he didn't call back. She was taking a sudden interest in his life after the court hearing, after Willis's assault. And his rent was due in two days. Carl Kenning would batter down his door for those five hundred dollars. He didn't attend his appointment with Dr. Richard Herbert either. The police would be dragged into it, and thank God, he thought, they would get to the bottom of his disappearance.

But how would they find him? He had no clue as to where he'd been kidnapped, so how would they? He had no real concept of where in the city he could be. The machine required electricity, so he couldn't be in the woods—or could he? There were abandoned buildings downtown, namely the burnt-out warehouses and the Carlton Hotel that went out of business. The property was two-years' condemned and unused. Or Dr. Krone could own private property under a false name. All of it was speculation. But why would Dr. Krone bury his father in someone else's grave? That would indicate the man was being sought, and if that was true, so was Dr. Krone. The victims were from the sanitarium. The Krones were murderers. But being in hiding and on the run, how could they invent such a bizarre machine?

Edith was still asleep. The sleeping-child expression made him jealous. He needed rest. *No, I can't. It's not safe for both of us to let our guards down.*

He rested his head against the wall, the cold marble soothing. He looked for the pack of cigarettes, but they had vanished.

They must've gone poof when she conked out.

Were the cigarettes they smoked a figment of their imagination? He could tear apart his brain to discover the answer, and he'd still be confused.

Slow steps sounded from outside, faded and from afar.

Edith shot up from her sleep, triggered awake. "*Uh!* Where is he?"

"It's okay, he's still outside."

"*Final warning, come out and visit with me, or you'll be sorry.*"

They huddled close together, depending on each other for comfort, and he was surprised and relieved when Edith hugged him. "Forgive me for earlier. I didn't mean to freak out at you. He really scares me."

"Ditto."

"*I guess I have to draw you out then. But first, let's have some fun.*"

Nothing happened. Five minutes passed, and his promises weren't delivered.

"He's full of shit," Edith muttered, throwing the corridor a middle finger. "He won't come in."

Uproarious laughter, a mad scientist's cackling, pierced the halls. "*Now it's time!*"

The bending of rails, the crack of marble, the splitting of concrete, the shifting of dust, a crunching noise, breaking wood, the twisting and removal of screws reverberated from all sides of them. The bronze markers rattled, shifting against concrete.

"What is he doing?" Edith unleashed the question in a shout. "You're not supposed to come in here. *You're not supposed to come in here!*"

"He's playing with us," Craig said, raising his voice above the strange cacophony. "If you have a magic trick up your sleeve to make yourself go somewhere else, now's the time to do it."

"And what about you?"

"I'll stand my ground."

"Big man," she scoffed. "I wish you the best with that."

The grave markers dropped onto the floor with a *broong* sound. Steel caskets fired out of their slots as if spring ejected, dozens at once. Edith clung to him, her nails digging into his body.

Coffins littered the ground, the wood splintering

down their length from the impact, dust rising into a brown smog, causing them to choke, and cough, and be blind.

Edith called out between fits of choking, "Do you see him coming?"

He squinted and covered his eyes with his hands. "I don't know. It hurts to look."

He stepped around the coffins, haphazardly tripping over them, struggling to form an escape route. Both of them going rigid, the columns of lights above them burnt out in a collective blackout, explosions of the fixtures repeating about the entirety of the mausoleum. Light by light, the way went dark. Crashes, the smashing and rendering of wood, the muffled punch and splinter of grain, their time to escape was now. A stench followed the ruckus—embalming fluid, putrefying organs, gangrene flesh, the wet leather smell of death, and the odd scent of mildew and coffin padding. Sheets and planks and pieces of wood rattled against the floor. The labored breathing surrounding them was a collective song—coughs from collapsed windpipes, whistles from throats riddled with holes, and pained moans issued with eerie acoustics.

Craig couldn't see anything except their profiles rise from their broken coffins. Then he heard the plop of feet against the floor, the click of exposed metatarsals and fancy shoes increasing in numbers.

He's brought the dead back to life.

Jesus Christ.

"What do we do now?" he cried out when he lost his grip on Edith's arm. She slipped free from his protective hold. "Where are you? *Goddamn it, where are you?*"

An arc of blue-and-white flames climbed upwards and spread into the shape of a corpse. The flesh was pure black, the skeleton caramelized beneath. The clothing had fossilized into the flesh. The rest of the hallway was lit up by the light of the burning corpse. Easily a hundred corpses stood in place, clogging up any avenue of escape.

They were trapped.

Craig grabbed Edith, finally spotting her, and they backed into the wall. Edith gasped, "I imagined a lighter in my hand, and I lit one on fire."

They faced the horde, and the horde acted accordingly. Arms outstretched—the very act tearing sinew and muscle, and breaking bone—and the ripe malodorous death stench corroded the air. Drips spattered the floor. Jellies splashed. Organs slithered from their cavities or hung in place. Bodies whose legs failed, the corpses crawled on the floor, their teeth clacking, their flesh slipping, and breaking, and contorting to express their eagerness to attack them.

Edith belted out a war cry, her voice cracking under the stress, "Stay the hell away from us!"

The corpse stood in place, burning. It couldn't understand what was happening to its body, so it stood confused and immobilized. Craig urged her to think of a plan, anything to survive. "We don't have much time. You have to think of something."

Edith squeezed her eyes, grunted, and thought so hard a stream of blood flowed out her nose. She couldn't pull it off. She was stunned, shaking off the pain in her head. Edith touched the blood that crossed her lips in abhorrence. "This is it. My tricks are used up."

Craig breathed in and thought hard. He suddenly

calmed down. Focused. A hand of bone clutched his collar. He choked on what smelled like sun baked raw meat. Blood stained and seeped through his shirt, fetid juices touching his skin. He thought harder. Focused again. Pictured it in his hands. Imagined every detail. Two more hands, this time newer dead flesh, choked him. Tighter still, he couldn't breathe. Hands clutched his legs. Then his ankles. His right hand. One tore the buttons from his shirt one by one. *Plick, plick, plick.*

Edith's next scream was muffled by a smothering hand, "*Naw—gaack!*"

Craig's hair was pulled.

He focused even harder.

Teeth clamped on his shoulder and bit in.

And then it happened.

His father's Browning pump-action shotgun materialized in his hands. He swung the stock into the dead man's jaw, breaking the porcelain-like bone into many shards.

"*Help me, Craig!*"

A group was dragging Edith into one of the wall slots. She kicked and thrashed, but she was viciously outnumbered. She'd been clawed and chewed up, her flesh glazed in red, the muscle tissue beneath raw and gleaming against the firelight. The meat of her arms was concave hollows in the shape of bites. White bone protruded where her wrists connected to the hands. Her ear-grinding fits and screeches faded, and she was gone.

"Let her go!"

Ba-boom!

Two of the corpses split in half, the bullets tearing through their soft, dead flesh, their torsos and legs landing in separate piles. He turned to the left, sizing up the threat, and pulled the trigger. *Ba-boom! Ba-boom!*

This is impossible.

He cleared a short path, shoving and kicking to where Edith had been taken, but he was thrown backwards, seized by the shoulders and legs, and brought down. He crashed against the marble. Craig fired upwards and regretted it. Blood and flesh splattered him in loads of macabre flotsam and jetsam, their fluids ice cold.

Craig refused to allow the dead to overtake him. Crawling to his feet, battering through them, he shoved himself through them to another hall. Three more shots, his ears ringing—the actual firing of a gun was three times louder than what one heard in movies—Craig arrived at a new hall. His clothes were in shreds, the skin beneath clawed and parted in sections. The pain kept his instincts finely tuned. He fired randomly and three heads went up filled to the brim with loose gray matter. Craig accidentally planted a foot into the stomach cavity of a woman in a purple dress, and it sank ankle-deep inside her belly. He tipped forward but didn't fall. He was unable to free his foot, somehow losing his weapon. The gun was kicked down the hall, useless to him, as more of the dead advanced closer to him.

Craig kicked upwards with all his force, driving his foot into the corpse woman's sternum, ripping through the skin and breaking marrow-less bones. He vaulted into the crowd. He used his shoulder as a battering ram. His elbow cracked faces, mere hollow bones breaking up into pottery pieces. His fists were soaked in black blood after punching a mandible loose with a solid blow. A nose was shattered and revealed maggots embedded in the sinus cavity.

The line wouldn't end. He couldn't fight them all. The hundreds had changed into thousands, and they were still gaining new numbers.

But that's impossible. There weren't that many coffins!

He raised his voice above the din of the dead to demand, "Dr. Krone, what do you want from me? What's the point of this fucked-up shit?"

The doorway out of the mausoleum was wide open. The dead filed in from the cemetery for miles out, their outlines dominating the horizon. The sky was thick with the lingering cloud of human decay, the night sky being impossibly black. There was no escape. Edith was lucky to be finished off so soon.

Three lunged on top of him from behind. Tackled, he was pinned to the floor by new hands. A blackened hand covered his mouth. The taste of soil and blood sullied his tongue. He couldn't breathe. So much rotten flesh surrounded and consumed him. His shirt was torn from his body in all directions, and next, it would be his flesh. Teeth clicked to render strips of flesh; small bites, but many were feeding at once. Blood spilled from fresh wounds. He was paralyzed. He'd be a pile of bones soon enough. The mastication of a city pounded throughout the corridor.

Just when he thought he understood something about Dr. Krone's work, everything changed. There was no way to hide like Edith had believed. No code existed to break the lock of his mind. Only death and suffering existed here, and his torment was overdue.

He closed his eyes in a last-ditch effort, and Craig imagined he was somewhere else.

first date

"**AAAAAAAAAAAAAAAh!**" he howled, abating the razor impressions of fingers and teeth gnawing into his flesh. Suddenly his clothing wasn't shredded. He wore a green polo top and blue jeans. The attackers were gone and so were the dead, though blood seeped through the shirt and the wounds were still gaping and fresh.

"What's wrong with you?" Katie asked from the passenger seat of the car. Her face was turned up to his, curious. She didn't notice he was bleeding. It was invisible to her. "I'm sorry I called you so late. I didn't know what else to do."

Craig remembered this moment, even while breathing in and out to battle the agony of his nerves. Katie was younger, about twenty-one, he imagined. She was stood up by Brice Adams that night. Brice was Craig's roommate at the time. He was supposed to meet Katie at Odyssey Cinema 30 to catch a chick flick, for a first date. Katie had called Craig in an emergency. She was dropped off at the theater by a friend, and she was stranded, and not being able to reach anyone on a Friday night, she got a hold of Craig. He arrived to pick her up, and it was only nine at night. He offered to take her to eat at a Japanese restaurant. Craig knew she loved sushi, and he consoled her ruined evening by saying, "Might as well make the most of this night. Call it a friendly date. Brice is a jackass. He's only my roommate because I can't afford rent right now. When I change jobs, I'll kick his ass the hell out."

Katie was still in date mode in this moment. She was grateful for his kindness, and Katie was beautiful. Her hair was curled at the ends, fresh from the salon. She wore a moderate amount of makeup, but it was the glow about her that interested him the most. Alive. Happy. Energetic. They were qualities he wished he owned and wanted to soak up. They had hit it off that night. Sushi. Dancing on retro disco night at Shakes. They stayed out until four in the morning and made out in the car before saying good night.

That was the beginning of their relationship, and he wanted so badly to enjoy it. The loss hurt him as much as his bleeding wounds. He couldn't shake the dead playing with his body, touching him, violating him, devouring him. His polo shirt was sodden through, and Craig had no choice but to pull the car over.

"You're so sweet to pick me up like this," she reiterated. Katie still had no idea he was bleeding. They'd just finished sushi before he entered the memory. "Craig, you're a nice guy. My dating life sucks. Let's do something else tonight. Do you like to dance?"

"Yes," he said, refusing to lose this moment, speaking through gritted teeth. He touched her cheek with his palm just as he did when he was twenty-two. "I like you. You're nice, Katie."

He winced. The blood dripped from his shirt onto

the steering column. It stained the seat too, colored his jeans, and now, Katie's cheek.

Craig gave in. He needed comfort, and he kissed her on the mouth softly. "I love you, Katie. I can't stop missing you. It's not fair you're gone. I'm sorry it ended the way it did. I think about it every day. I made so many mistakes."

Katie pushed him off. "What are you saying? Are you some kind of weirdo?"

The memory was gone as he knew it. Katie eyed him, infuriated. The blood on her demonized her. She still didn't wipe it off, oblivious to it.

Craig continued talking, despite her confusion. "I'm sorry for how you died, for whatever that counts for . . . "

Katie changed blink-fast. She was a blip, the transformation ending with a series of demeaning laughs. *"Being sorry doesn't count for much, Craig. It doesn't count for shit."*

She vanished in a split second, and then Dr. Krone seized his neck. "Whatever that bitch told you in the mausoleum, you can't fight me. You're not strong enough. You have no concept of what your brain is capable of!"

Craig drove again, slamming the gas, gasping for breath, the doctor's hands wrapped so tight around his throat. He clutched the wheel and battled to steady it as the man smothered his life.

"Yes, you can see within me. But I see much, much deeper inside of you, Mr. Horsy."

"Graaah!" he gasped, white-and-purple blotches filling his vision. Pinpricks stabbed at his head and body. Desperate to avoid death, Craig swung the vehicle off the road, swerving hard to the right.

The car barreled down a short hill, bouncing twice, the shocks bending, the back bumper ripped off. They were seconds from crashing into the trunk of a hulking tree. Gaining speed, Dr. Krone relaxed in the backseat and announced without an inkling of fear, "Now let's proceed with the treatment!"

hALf-tIme

heRe wAS SImpLy no escaping Dr. Krone. Craig barely had any concept of how to retaliate or survive, and even Edith's suggestions couldn't save him. He was eaten alive by the dead—hordes upon hordes of them. Then Katie watched him bleed in the car without any regard to his health. And now he was here at Willis's sports bar Half-Time, the blink and change of scene occurring seconds before the car slammed into the trees.

Dr. Krone showed no signs of slowing down the treatment. *Treatment.* That was the word he kept using. What did the man have to gain from this? Not even Edith knew the answer to that question.

His wounds had miraculously scabbed over. The shape of teeth and jagged marks were caked brown, as if aged. Forced to move on from the observation, he looked on at Half-Time, a bustling pub. Dart boards, pool tables, a twelve-piece arcade room, foosball, and eleven screens playing professional sports and independent events like logging championships and lady football kept the place hopping. The blink delivered him onto a stool, sitting at the bar. The KU versus K-State basketball game was in its second half. Random cheers and fists slammed onto the counters, the game was tied and would stay that way up until the final seconds.

He sipped on the frosty mug of ale. It tasted real and exactly the way it did when he assaulted Willis. A wave of nausea crept up his esophagus. He hadn't eaten in hours or days; he wasn't certain exactly how long it had been, but he was ravenous with hunger. Dr. Krone had strapped him in that machine for longer than twenty-four hours, he was certain. Maybe days. The thought made him dizzy and weak.

Craig peered at the exit, combing his mind for what could possibly happen. It didn't take long to realize what Dr. Krone had planned, and in moments, he'd learn just how wrong he was.

Just run.

You can go anywhere. Think. Imagine it.

Willis wasn't behind the counter. That's the only thing about the scene that had changed so far. As it happened that night, anger boiled under Craig's skin. This anger was focused on Willis. The moment Willis revealed he didn't have a job for him must've already happened, Craig realized, and now he was plotting how to channel his fury.

I won't be mad. It was wrong. I won't assault him again.

Willis returned from the back room. He was a young bartender, a fresh and upbeat face despite the hard-luck bullshit he absorbed on a daily basis. But he wasn't himself today. His face was solemn. The apologetic frown he wore months ago for Craig vanished and was replaced by an emotion he couldn't place, though it inspired a gut-churning pain in his abdomen to witness it.

Run for the door. Get the hell out of here.

Craig lunged for the exit, trusting his newly minted intuition. He knocked down the cardboard cutout of four Victoria's Secret Angels posed with footballs. The specials chalkboard smashed onto the floor. The crowd was roused from their fantasy cave of sports at the man suddenly running for his life. They were evil in his peripheral. Sneering. Scowling. Demonic. And now, calling out to him—

"Grab him!"

"Willis wants a word with you."

"You haven't received your free drink."

"I'll buy."

"No, allow me."

"You got next, I said I'd buy him one first."

"I owe him from last week."

"Scotch and soda."

"Seven and seven."

"He likes it on the rocks."

"I thought he'd enjoy a finger of scotch?"

"He likes a shot of anything that burns."

The door slowly grew farther and farther out of reach, like an optical illusion, and his fight grew weak as did his limbs. He was swarmed and surrounded by everybody in the bar, pulled back to where he was from the beginning and forced onto the stool. Then his arms were forced behind him. Grain alcohol exuded from his accuser's mouth—an accuser he couldn't see—so thick he could light a match and set the man's mouth aflame.

"You like alcohol, don't you? Oh yes, you're a booze hound. It's high time, Craig. Willis said you wanted the bar." A single snigger escaped the man's ragged throat, *"Well, he's giving it to you."*

Thirty men and women formed a circle around

him in a barrier, stealing his air, creating a film of sweat on his body. Rope bound his arms, legs, and torso, his body secured in minutes. The neon signs blurred as his processes raced to interpret the fate that would befall him. Instincts craned to full blast, he sensed every twitch and movement, each whisper and rant in the room, and then he caught Willis again. His face was chalky white, his lips blue-black. He could pass for a corpse. Purple saucers hardened his eyes, stealing what used to be a naturally friendly face.

"You wish to bust me up, huh?" Willis challenged him. "After everything I've done for you, Craig? Free booze, I loaned you money, you shit in my ear on a daily basis about unemployment and your dead bitch wife, I let you sleep on the futon in my one-bedroom apartment, and then for all my trouble, you smash a barstool over my head." He cranked out a sideways smile. "That's not the friendly thing to do, now is it?"

The damage played out on Willis's face without anything hitting him. An invisible bludgeon shattered his collarbone and dented his jaw, the effect as awe-inspiring as it was horrid. He spat out a row of teeth and a blood-spit combo, the mess dribbling down his mouth and chin and staining his brown cashmere shirt. He smiled to display the knocked-out teeth, the gums oozing red.

"You always wanted to become a bartender?" He raised his hands so those around him would cheer. "*Hoorah! Hoorah!* Let's have you drink up, then. Earn your stripes."

They stole the air—and his ability to breathe—with the scents of wheat, and barley hops, and grain alcohol. The room wavered like heat deflecting off the road. The room was combustible. Craig's eyes dried out. His skin ached as if paper cuts were inflicted upon every inch of him. Willis's ice-cold hands jerked his head up by his hair. "I'll give you what you always wanted, you fucking lush."

Joey, Willis's younger brother, sauntered from the back room after Willis said that. Uproarious cheers—clapping and carrying on three times that of the Kansas State and Kansas University basketball game—dominated the room. Joey clutched an oversized steel funnel. It was larger than the ones used to place coolant into a Mac truck.

"Drink up, Craig."

Three hands pried his mouth open. Craig threw his face back and forth and cried out when fingernails tore into his lips. Hands intruded, fists causing his jaw to open wide, and then the funnel was jammed into his mouth with a wet *thuck*.

"*Naaawgh!*"

"Yes!" Willis shouted, throwing his head back. "Let's hear it. What'll it be, partner? Hard on your luck, asshole? Your woman leave you—no wait, did your woman die during childbirth? Oh wait, you lost both of them. That's right. Both of them are dead."

"How so?"

"Was it gruesome?"

"Did the baby's head poke out of the womb or did it die inside her?"

"Did she bleed to death?"

Willis waved them down. "No, this asshole's car breaks down on the highway. He's so broke ass, he can't afford a car that runs. He uses this piece of shit during a snowstorm. What a fuck up."

You son of a bitch, how dare you say that?

This wasn't Willis. The man would never speak

like this in real life. The crowd wouldn't team up against him either. The people in the room were in lynch mode. He couldn't slip the restraints. He was surrounded, regardless of his ability to escape.

He called out again, his mouth obstructed by plastic. "*Stawp! Graaaagh!*"

"He's ready," Joey declared. He tipped a bottle of High Noon whiskey into his mouth. "I think this is a good start. It was always Craig's drink of choice."

He tipped the bottle into the opening of the funnel. Craig wasn't used to downing the shots with his mouth wide open. The fluid splashed the back of his throat, burning hot and chemical. "*Gaaack!*"

Craig struggled to swallow without gagging. He hiccupped. He aspirated on the whiskey and forced it back down, fearing he'd choke if it didn't go down.

"Hair of the dog," Willis announced like the referee of the sporting event. "First round is always the hardest. Now you're warmed up. Let's make this interesting. You ever enjoy a Molotov Fire Dog?"

He snapped his fingers, and Joey went to work. The man poured half a can of soda into a beer glass. Then he added Rumple Minze and Hot Damn. Next, he squeezed lime, lemon, and orange juice into the mix. Joey poured it into the funnel and struck a match simultaneously. *Whup-whoosh!*

Fire exploded out the funnel the size of a basketball. The flames trailed like dragon's breath into the air, but the tendrils were exaggerated, spraying across the room, and random patrons were set afire. They didn't scream or panic. Laughter ensued, the kind so awkward and wrong it churned Craig's stomach. The left wall burst into flames with the crackle and jarring splinter of wood. The ceiling was clotted with gray smoke. The barmaid poured a Guinness on tap, but half her face was busy with flames, the fat boiling on her cheeks dribbling into the glass. Another patron was hunched over the Simpsons' pinball machine, engrossed in the game, fire eating into his back. Singed and cooking flesh stank up the room. Many others enjoyed buffalo wings and a new round while their flesh sizzled and evaporated. Joey's left arm and midsection brimmed with fire and gobs of flesh slopped onto Craig's body, searing hot.

He shook his head, begging to be released before the fire consumed him. "*Naaawgh!*"

Fire danced at his feet. The air continued to reignite itself, every square inch of space flammable. *Whup-whoosh! Whup-whoosh! Whup-whoosh!*

Willis's skin slithered from his face in one piece, a slick skeletal face berating Craig, "Hair of the dog, hair of the dog—*hah, hah, hah, hah, hah, hah!*"

The eyes of the patron tossing darts suddenly burst from the flames' pressure, and then his torso broke down the center, spewing brighter fire and sparks like a disturbed log at the bottom of a bonfire. The man called out to Craig before he collapsed, "Another round on me, pal!"

A pair of hands laid down ten dollars on the counter. The money went up in smoke before Willis accepted it—not that he cared. It was Susan from their singles club, but her clothes were missing, her naked body surrounded by acrid orange-and-red flames. "How about a double shot on the rocks, sexy?"

The effects of the alcohol were setting in, and for Craig, the room was a spinning top, tilting upside down, right-side-up, and pivoting like he was inside of a moving mirrored ball. Craig used his tongue to shove out the funnel, but Willis shoved it back down into place, like a stake into the earth.

"This one's all mine," a seductive voice carried over to him, shoving aside Willis. It was Katie this time. She wasn't pale, or dead, or on fire, but alive, actual flesh and blood. "This drink's from me to you."

She swiped a bottle of vodka from the counter. Katie poured it down her arm and poised her hand above the funnel. It trickled down her arm, then her fingers, and into the opening. The gesture would've been arousing in any other scenario, but now, it was brutal and mean. The alcohol was like gasoline filling his mouth. Noxious. Stomach acids crawled up his throat. His throat rejected it outright, but Willis pinched his nose and squeezed his throat until he had no choice but to swallow it back again or suffocate.

Katie bent over him, the bottle of vodka poised above the funnel. "Let me pour you another, cowboy."

This isn't Katie. This isn't Katie. This isn't Katie. This isn't Katie.

The mantra did nothing to calm him. His heart thrummed twice as fast and loud by the power of alcohol. He closed his eyes, his head spinning, far beyond drunk. Craig was at the helm of a careening single-engine plane amid a jolting wind storm. He affixed his eyes on the smoke climbing to the ceiling, trying to hatch an escape plan and failing miserably.

"Swallow this for me, baby," Katie teased. Her eyes glowed with a demented fervor, tears running down her eyes, so gripped by hateful emotions, her grin boasted of sadistic pleasures created and fulfilled. He suddenly wanted her as far away from him as possible. Her touch wasn't Katie's. Nobody in this room was who they were supposed to be.

"Drink it down," she sniggered, her hair suddenly lit up by flames, burning bright and burning fast. "You'll feel so good!"

This isn't Katie!

Craig summoned the courage to fight back, and knowing this wasn't his wife, he head-butted her. Her nose popped. The flames on her head carried down to the rest of her body, and every inch of her was animated with fire. The entire room was engulfed. Bodies lay in blackened piles, still shifting, trying to survive. Joey stole shots from bottles from the bar as he too was turning into a blackened crisp. Willis towered above him, covered in red, and orange, and yellow arches. His cashmere shirt melted into his liquid flesh and tangles of his black hair were embedded into the mudslide of his face. He was about to seize Craig by the throat when his legs buckled beneath him, and he landed in a burning pile at Craig's feet.

He wasn't out of harm's way, though, as the fires raged. Now Craig's legs burned. The rope loosened under the flames, and using his strength, he pulled and snapped the binds free. The legs of the chair broke when he pivoted. He worked to his feet, not giving up on escaping the inferno. The room was curtain upon curtain of flame. Skeletons were twisted and mangled along the floor, and the room was becoming an oven. Craig struggled to walk a straight line, so drunk. Vomit lurched up his throat.

Just run.

Keep moving.

Craig lost it. There was no relief afterwards. The

alcohol was still absorbing into his system, and it would stay with him. Wherever he escaped, he would surely be at a disadvantage, and that was one thing he didn't need against Dr. Krone.

He stormed the exit of the bar, throwing himself through the doors, awaiting the blink, the next moment of horror.

Nothing could prepare him for what he stepped into next.

beggARS cAn't be chooseRS

The bLInk hAppened without him realizing it. He was too drunk to notice. Craig clutched the wall for balance. He lost it again, retching and buckling to his knees. Booze and stomach acids burned his throat and corrupted his mouth. First-degree burns played down his legs up to the knees. His khakis were blackened and parts of his shirt were singed. He curled into a ball and attempted to sober up. The amount of alcohol he'd ingested, he would be under the effects for hours.

Willis, and Joey, and Katie were villains in familiar masks. They wanted him dead. The torture wouldn't have stopped at alcohol poisoning. He would've been a charred corpse. Then what would happen to him? Would he die sitting against the machine? Was he covered in burns and throwing up on himself in the room for real?

"They wouldn't hurt me," he whispered, shaking his head, the dooming thoughts intensified by his condition. "Not for real."

The hall was pitch-black. The kind of darkness where there were no windows to let in the moonlight or the sun. Soft mewls played throughout the hallways in varying levels of echoes. Complaints. Fear. Roused suspicion. The tripwires of this place were set off. Bedsprings groaned. Bare feet pattered the floor and paced back and forth—*clop, clop, clop, clop*. Steel doors were shook, pounded, and kicked. Toilets were flushed repeatedly. Arms reached through the square set of bars in each door for attention. Monkey jeers blasted through the chorus of noises—

"The doctor's in! The doctor's in! The doctor's in!" "Baaah! Baaah! Baaah!" "No more therapy." "It's *my* brain. *You* can't have it!" "Check my pulse, Doctor. Do I have a pulse? Do I have a heart? How can it beat if I don't have a heart?" "Don't take my brain. *It's mine! Mine!*"

"Silence!"

The thick guttural command down the hallway did the trick.

The hall went silent.

"I'll take all of you with me if you're not quiet."

The speaker was distinguished. Professional. The man could make serious things happen, and the patients in this asylum—that's what it had to be—understood his capabilities. Craig followed the echo of the voices up the hall and made two turns. The event worked to sober him up enough to walk a straight line. A beam of light panned from one iron door to the next. Faces shirked from the light, frightened.

"You can't hide from me," the man boasted, hidden in shadow. "I know who each and every one of you are. Some of you have visitors weekly, sometimes monthly, and some of you," he cackled, "*don't have visitors at all*. You don't exist. I can shred your documents and have my way with you. Most of you

164

are so far gone you wouldn't even know anything's different, dead or alive."

The speaker was familiar. He wore winter garb: a black stocking cap, thick wool overcoat, and black leather boots. But there was another person with him. He was a teenager dressed in a blue polyester and cotton overcoat, clothing for a winter hiking expedition. The boy was glued to the older man's side.

That's Dr. Krone and his father.

Jesus, I'm in his head again.

The last memory reoccurred to him. The man wrenching the brains out of straight jacketed individuals with an oversized corkscrew, it had to be Dr. Krone's father doing the messy work. Now, they were exploring the sanitarium after hours for the best pickings. And it made sense what Dr. Krone's father said moments ago. There were many people who'd given up on the criminally insane. How many people had been blasted with shock treatment and narcotics to the point they resembled nothing of their former selves? Nobody cared what happened to these people, he thought. How did they break into the sanitarium, Craig wondered, and why wasn't security here?

Craig poised himself, ready to hide if they walked too close to him. The two were slow and precise about their choices, and he listened and waited.

"Danny," Dr. Krone's father whispered to the boy. "Here's Jamie Henderson. She's a looker. Only nineteen, and wow, she's a knockout. She's an orphan too. Strangled four people on the streets for their money. She was already experiencing the early signs of dementia when the police booked her. Smeared her shit on the holding cell walls. She's calmed down with the help of Thorazine and Deranal. We can clean her up and use her. You can do it this time, son. I'll let you complete the process from start to finish. Would you like that?"

"I've been waiting for you to say that, Dad," a soft and hesitant voice replied. "Jamie's the perfect choice. I like her. I like her a lot. She's pretty."

Dr. Krone's father fished out an oversized pair of jailor's keys and unlocked the door. He loaded a syringe and entered the room. "She's staring at the walls again. I'm surprised the world doesn't care about what these people are thinking. They are curable. Drugs aren't the answer. Drugs numb the beast, but the brain harbors it. Nurtures it. If I can find that beast and snuff it out, I can save these people from permanent isolation. Padded walls and institutionalized food would drive any disturbed individual further into the abyss."

Is that how you validate butchering the infirm? Looks like your son has taken the next step by kidnapping innocent people from the streets and removing their so-called "beasts."

A woman in a straightjacket with greasy black hair was dragged from the room. She was unconscious, but her eyes were wide open. The way the flashlight beam struck them, they shined like a goldfish's scales. Permanently affixed to nothing, she was gone. Perhaps the notion itself of combing the mind for the malady rang of scientific purpose, but taking out the brain completely was a different science altogether.

"Wouldn't you ask the girl on a date if she went to your school, Danny?"

The young Dr. Krone looked her up and down. "Yes. Because she's pretty."

"She has potential, but it's wasted here." An

expression of self-loathing warped the man's face. "I own six clinics, boy. I'm the root of the problem. I support this grand failure. But not forever, son. I'll end this once and for all. All I have to do is conquer the mind. If I could get in there, then that'd be a credible feat. I could cure the insane."

His son approached him, leaving the dazed woman sprawled on the floor. A conviction unknown to such a young face played out on his features. "I see the point of your work. I understand why your colleagues wouldn't because they're cowards. It's revolutionary. Nobody else has the guts to try it, but you do. It's not pretty. It's messy. Humanitarians would burn you at the stake, but so what? Nuclear war and nuclear capabilities caused cancer and Down's Syndrome and gene deficiencies and nobody goes on a witch hunt on the White House lawn. Improvements don't come without a cost. You're looking for a cure, not a place to shove the infirm into a room and throw away the key. Some of these people have been buried under the facility. The families don't care about them. This is the only way to make improvements, Dad."

The man was astounded at his son's prolific speech. "You're right. You're starting to sound like a scholar. I'm proud of you, boy. So young and so articulate." He focused on the girl. "Okay, the night's burning fast. Let's move out."

Together, father and son carried the patient by the arms and legs. The patient didn't budge or resist, her being drugged. Craig pursued them from a distance, keeping low. He caught the faces of those within the rooms peek out. Dozens of watching eyes drove shudders through Craig. How often did they suffer this fear of being chosen?

The fire exit was opened farther down the hall. A wash of light chased away the dark, and Craig raced forward so the door wouldn't close before he could cross. He accomplished his goal, and the door closed behind him. He watched them turn at the bend of the stairs below.

He tiptoed down the staircase. Another door opened below, and he launched down after he caught the young Dr. Krone pass through another door's threshold. Catching up, out of breath, a burst of wintry air shot across him and irritated his burn wounds. Gritting his teeth, moaning under his breath, he fought the pain and was distracted when he heard the door close.

Shit.

It wasn't the door. The patient had been dropped. The door struck her head and was wedged in place. Her eyes leered up at him. The whites were the same as those in the hall. Wide. Glowing. Burning with a secret and begging for help. Terror was a thought process even the infirm could understand. Snowflakes dusted her face. If she was kept there long enough, she'd be buried in white.

I can't help you.

Forgive me.

What were the two doing now? They left their stolen prize. Five minutes, and she was left on the ground. The girl watched the walls, the stairs, and then she studied him again. She didn't panic or speak. She enjoyed the fresh air and being free of the padded cell.

Take her and run. Save her from these psychos. You're in Dr. Krone's mind. Maybe he can hurt you here. But maybe you can hurt him too.

The notion brought so much pleasure that he smiled. Craig kicked open the door and lifted the woman out of its way, softly placing her on the side of the steps. Dr. Krone's father had lifted up the hood of a Bronco truck—a model from the seventies—and was inspecting the engine. The teenager was throwing rocks at the barbed perimeter. This was a prison. The darkness turned the proximity into a concentration camp. He couldn't carry the woman without knowing where he was going first.

"Hey—who are you? What the hell are you doing with that woman?"

Dr. Krone's father raced toward him, a shambling effort in the snow. Craig rushed toward the doctor in retaliation. The man wasn't accustomed to anybody fighting back, and he cowered at the last moment. Craig swung a good punch to his jaw, and the doctor was sent backwards onto the pavement.

Whump.

A metallic ring jarred his back. Craig landed on all fours, and he turned to fight back, but the shadows disguised the next blow.

Whump.

The back of his neck radiated with agony. He looked up at the teen. He was thin, maybe one hundred and thirty pounds. He wasn't anything like the man he'd become later on. There was no recognition on the teen's face. Craig had simply traipsed into the man's mind without him knowing it, and this was what he found.

The teen raised the crowbar again, but Craig retreated along the perimeter of the building, crawling at first, then working up to his feet and sprinting. He kept running and sucking in the below-freezing air. Craig shivered. His skin was attacked by gooseflesh, splitting his skin. He wasn't dressed for the elements. Soon, his retreat was a feeble walk. He tripped over the dips in the grass. The snowstorm was building momentum. The snow was already ankle-deep. The darkness was so thick, he wasn't sure if he was running to or from them.

"I can hear him."

"He's not getting far—you beat him good, Danny. Good boy! I'd like to get my licks in next."

He slipped on ice and was pitched forward, scuffing his palms and knees. He curled up against the concrete wall, needing a break, hunkering into himself for warmth. The winds pounded him head-on. The snow collected over him in a shroud, and soon, he'd be buried.

He closed his eyes tight, squeezing himself harder. "I won't die like this. I won't . . . d-die . . . "

"He's whimpering. I can hear him. He's yards away."

His eyelids froze shut. "I won't die like this."

"I see him. He's on the ground. He won't run anymore. Ah yes, another brain we can use. *Another mind.*"

Throwing his head back, using his brain, he pictured a better reality, and he shouted, "*I won't die like this!*"

The darkness turned blacker, and the cold finally receded.

dEAd cønfedeRAteS

ISpLAced At A nanosecond's speed, Craig was suddenly hunkered against a stone wall. The rustle of wind and dirt breached the silence—a silence that seemed wrong in his predicament. He hadn't opened his eyes yet. Nothing about the dry and searing-hot weather and the smells in the air—raw black gunpowder, iron, blood, and the not-so-subtle hint of recent death—was reassuring. He was losing courage, battling fatigue and the knowing that something horrible would be coming his way soon. He was far removed from the happy memories of necking with Susan and loving Katie in bed.

The silence must've occurred recently, Craig thought, as mewling voices and weak conversation broke out throughout the area. He opened his eyes and studied the dead bodies along a stone wall, some of them unmoving, and bloody, and shot to pieces, and others on the verge of death. The ground was rock-hard dirt. Craig focused on the bodies strewn about the way. They wore strange uniforms. They weren't navy, marines, or army. Shell jackets, frock coats, forage caps, cravats, and suspenders were the components of the wardrobe, each a powder-gray color.

My God, these are confederate soldiers.

Dust blew in his face, attaching to the streaming sweat on his face and limbs. Many of the living wounded soldiers clutched their muskets to their bodies in fear of another attack. It was too quiet, he kept telling himself. A gunfire battle had recently ceased, and each side was waiting for either a retreat or a counterattack.

One of the soldiers seized Craig's leg. "Who are you? You're not one of Lee's men. No, you can't be. Whose side are you on?"

"I-I I don't know," he replied, overwhelmed looking at the soldier's face caked in blood. He'd taken two shots to the stomach and one had blown off his ear. "The good side."

The solider didn't seem to hear Craig. "Our pumpkin slingers couldn't hold 'em off. Hooker doesn't know how to fight. Bastard got us all killed."

"What year is it?"

The soldier laughed, coughing up blood and clutching his chest in raging pain. "It's 1863. Suppose you don't know where we're at either?"

Craig shrugged his shoulders. "I don't."

"Fredericksburg, Virginia, boy, and I'm a Confederate until my dying day!"

The man's eyes rolled into the back of his head, but they didn't close, the marbles forever trained in a strange moment of glory.

He heard drumming and commands issued in the far distance. The rest of the Confederates had retreated, he guessed, and the dead and critically wounded had been left behind. Craig scavenged for a way out, though he still didn't know why he was here during the Civil War. He crossed soldiers cut in half, missing arms and legs, and otherwise shot to pieces.

"*Hmmm* . . . the head's already opened, but the brains are ruined."

Who was that?

Craig lowered onto all fours. Farther down the stone wall built into a hill, he heard somebody stir.

"Oh no, it's worthless. Ruined. I can't use him. Pitiful and a bloody mess. Putrid magpie waste of human flesh. I'll never get anything accomplished at this rate."

The speaker wasn't familiar. It wasn't Dr. Krone or anybody he'd known from his past. The man kept marching forward, concerned and curious. Sifting.Searching. Desperate.

Maybe he'd been sent to this memory on accident, he supposed. This had to be another person's life, another person's account of the past because it certainly wasn't Dr. Krone's or Craig's to recount.

"No—*naaaawwwgghhhh!*"

Craig bolted ahead, and a quick sprint later, he caught a man hunched over a soldier reaching out to fend off the man over him. The victim's defense quickly faltered, dying and finally dead. The attacker wasn't a soldier on either side of the war, though he wore a pair of Confederate trousers and suspenders without a top. He clutched a sizeable blade and hammer.

The man caught Craig behind him. "Oh, someone's watching me, I see. Well, you might as well enjoy the presentation. It's about to get messy!"

Craig was flabbergasted, catching a mouthful of dust and choking on it.

"I'm saving this man's life—no, not his life, he's dead. In fact, he's been shot four times. No, not saving him. His lungs have pooled up with blood. *A dead son of a bitch*. Heart might've taken a hit. Ah, another casualty, but his soul can be saved. Maybe. I just need one thing."

And what would that be?

The extraction was crude and performed with careless precision. The man propped the tip of a blade—what was actually a socket bayonet without the rifle—and hammered it through his skull. The man playfully struck and chiseled at the skull around the circumference of the man's head. Blood burst with each strike, the skin in ribbons, the skull in brittle pieces.

"And here it is . . . *the soul*."

Craig fixated on the man. He was rotund, fat beefy fingers, double chin, eyes slightly crossed, and his spectacles magnified his stare. He had to ask, "You wouldn't happen to be a part of the Krone family?"

The man jerked from his work, disturbed, clutching an empty skull cap and admiring the glistening brain he excavated. "Who told you? How do you know me? You speak up."

"I'm a friend," he lied. "I'm not a threat." He needed a better explanation to appease the man. "I'm interested in your work. Your work is important. Worthwhile. Genius."

The man was breathing hard, his mouth slightly open in a soft pant. Then he loosened up and traced his dirty hands along each crevice and lobe of the brain. "Nobody appreciates my work. That's why I was so happy the war began. I could take my subjects without scrutiny. I used to be a doctor. Dead cadavers were all I could use, but they caught me, banned me from practice, and the bastards, they tried to lynch me. They'll see I can save the soul even after death. Nobody has to be a casualty of war."

The knife carved around the circumference of the brain with wet sloshes and gushing blood, and then Krone clutched the brain in one hand. "It's magnificent. So much potential and we still barely know the human brain."

He stuffed the brain into a blood-sodden knapsack. "So you're interested in my work? I can't share it. You being here has put me at risk. They'd hang me, shove sawdust into my eyes, and execute me. Southern boys are as adamant about slavery as they are about their punishments for treason. You're not going anywhere, friend. In fact, I can use you. You want life after death? I can grant it. You enjoy me and my work," a sly grin, "why don't you become a part of it?"

Craig snarled, with hands and arms poised to fight back. "You stay the hell away from me."

"A willing test subject," he laughed, albeit bitterly, "is too good to be true. You'll talk to anybody who'll listen, and they will listen to your tale and someone will believe you."

He clutched the knife. "Now come here. *Give me that brain!*"

Craig raced back the way he came, stamping on dead bodies, kicking at broken muskets, and trudging through puddles of blood spread out on the killing ground.

Did the Krones have a killing gene, he wondered, every generation as sick and twisted and deranged in the name of science as the next?

He ducked, the socket bayonet hurled at him and sticking into the ground. Craig picked up the weapon, claiming it as his own. "And how about your brain? How would you like it if I took it from you?"

"What exactly do you know of my work?"

"You want to steal memories, don't you?"

"Oh, that's an interesting idea," Krone said, placing his finger on his lip introspectively. "No, no, I'm after the soul. I want to retrieve the person out of the organ. Maybe the memory would be a good avenue to study. Do you want to combine ideas? You sound as interested as I do. Let's talk about our ideas over a bottle of whiskey." He winked at Craig. "Interested?"

"Hardly," he spat at him, wielding the knife. "I'm not a murderer, and I'm certainly not a madman like the rest of your fucked-up gene pool."

"Gene pool?" The man was confused and rightfully so. "Just who are you? You're not a soldier from either side. I haven't seen anybody in such strange clothing before. How did you arrive here?"

"I'm not sure," he admitted. "And it doesn't matter. You stay where you are, and I'll stay where I'm at."

Ka-boom! Ka-boom! Ka-boom!

Krone was shot three times, his chest blooming red. Landing on his back, the man pointed at Craig with his blood-caked hands, curled up in excruciating agony. "He's a traitor! I caught him cutting up the dead. He's stealing their brains! He's got dozens of them. Check that knapsack. Execute him. Behead him. He did it. It was him!"

That son of a bitch.

Craig ducked, numerous muskets aimed in his general direction. The shots rattled and pinged at the stone wall, followed up by a gray fog that obscured the gap between him and the Union soldiers standing above the wall. He had a temporary shield to hide behind, but it wouldn't be long before the smoke dissipated and a clear shot could be made.

"Shit!"

He launched in the opposite direction, praying he didn't catch buckshot or whatever the hell they used to unload their muskets into his back.

I can't stay here much longer. I'll be a dead corpse baking in the sun in no time. Damn you, Krone, even your family is trying to murder me.

His options were low. The wall was near an ending point, the hill continuing on to an open field. Many more soldiers were strewn about in death poses by the hundreds along the green pastures. The Union soldiers would surround him soon if they didn't already have him in their sights.

He decided on one last option. He lifted up a series of bodies and buried himself underneath them. Blood soaked into his clothes. Flies buzzed, landed, and tested his body and were displeased he wasn't ripe and covered in open wounds.

The pounding of boots surrounded the wall, and he waited, listened, and prayed that he'd hidden successfully.

the SecRet bASement

he wAIt ended soon enough. He was safe from the musket fire, but not from what was in the room. Studying the area, Craig wasn't chained up like the rest of them in the concrete cinder-block room. He counted nine individuals in chains, wearing institutionalized garb. He shivered, perplexed and relieved all at once. The room was half dark, with lights on farther down in the corridor, but where he was now, he was shrouded in darkness. The room leaked from the foundation, the stink of stagnant and earthy-smelling water filling up the area. Then there were the smells of feces and urine hanging in the air.

"Where the hell am I *now*?" he whispered to himself. "This shit is unending."

"Silence back there—I'll rip your tongue out if you speak again! I thought I sedated all of you. It will be your turn soon enough. Your wait won't be much longer."

The speaker was a woman. He thought back to when he was walking the halls of a sanitarium. The walls here were also institutionalized and characterless. *You'd think when trying to cure the mentally ill, you'd give the place a bit of pep. I wonder if the paint color is named Clinical Depression?*

The joke left his mind immediately once his eyes adjusted to the darkness. The mental patients were all in straightjackets. Leather belts were wrapped tightly around their eyes. Hands and feet were shackled to the walls. Water dripped from the ceiling and gargled and belched down the drain feet from where he stood, the trickle slow but steady. Farther down the room was the reason why their eyes were blocked by belts. His mouth unhinged at the sight.

First, he took in the strange device—homemade in appearance and craftsmanship. The guillotine was crafted from two planks of wood with a hole cut out for the head, the blade a piece of sheet metal sharpened to slice. Chains were connected to the wood to keep the hands in place behind the back. The device stood on a metal pushcart for easy transportation.

A guillotine on wheels, how original.

Shuck!

Another's head was removed. The woman collected it from the bucket. Then, she shoved the head into a vice on a nearby table. She placed a metal crown onto the skull and spun a handle until the gradual cracking turned into one loud and sharp *crick* noise. The woman removed the head device—a crown with razors, he guessed—and the top section of the skull was detached. She plunged her fingers in and retrieved the brain with practiced skill.

The body finally went still, all nerve pulses killed. The woman dumped the brain into a plastic case brimming with clear fluid. She sealed it, labeled it by name, and was moving toward the room with the other patients in-waiting when she caught Craig hiding.

"Who are you and why aren't you in restraints?"

Craig tightened his fists. "I'm not one of the patients you're exploiting. You take another step, and I'll hurt you."

She smiled, tickled by his defense. "You will do no such thing."

"Let me guess, you're another Krone. And you're crazy too. Another crazy Krone."

"Excuse me? How do you know me?"

"You're extracting brains. All of you do that. Every Krone is obsessed with brains, and memories, and whatever else you people do. And let me guess, we're in one of his facilities. You're killing patients and nobody cares to find out about it. You're doing research."

"I'm helping my husband complete his work. You don't belong here, do you? Come here. Let's straighten this out."

"You don't take another step toward me." He eyed the space behind her work area. Five headless bodies were heaped in a laundry basket on wheels. "I'm not ending up like them, and you're not hurting another one of these people."

"I only want to cure them of their minds," she explained, her intensity revealed by her widening, globular eyes. "I work alongside my husband. His work is essential. These people take their meds, shit their diapers, suffer manic fits, and they stay here locked up in these depressing quarters. Our facilities offer no cure for these people. Families leave them behind, heartbroken and fed up. We have to physically extract the maladies they contain. And it'll take a practiced physician to actually enter their minds, their memories, and their thoughts to save them." She tightened her fists. "Can't you see this is crucial work?"

"Do you have anybody's consent to do this?"

She scoffed, shaking her head, and feigned resignation. "This is work taken with a leap of faith. Our hearts are in the right place, and more importantly, so are our minds. Breakthroughs aren't made by the books. All will be forgiven when these patients walk out of here sane, cured, and able to live meaningful lives. I'm preserving our patients' minds. Their souls are very much still alive, and they will be forever."

"How do you know this? You can't, really. Nobody's been cured."

He caught the row of brains on a shelf hooked to electrodes, and the EEG machine spitting out readings. Two bodies were placed standing on an upright stretcher. Their brains were exposed, another EEG machine charting brain waves.

"You see those two bodies," she explained. "I switched their brains, and they still live! It's amazing. Imagine if I can get them to return to consciousness what they might say."

Craig yelled with every muscle of his throat, "What the hell is the point of this work?"

"I'm going to cure them of their maladies!" she shrieked and aimed a pistol at him, which had been tucked under her belt. "Look, I don't know how or why you're here. Now I can either shoot you, or I can drug you. Regardless, that brain of yours is all mine."

"Wait!" He battled to create a diversion from her shooting him. "You see, I'm a part of your husband's work. He's created a machine. This machine can play my memories on a TV screen. He can also enter my mind and my thoughts."

She was stumped. "My husband showed me the machine, but he hasn't gotten it to work. Is he keeping secrets from me?" She raised the gun so it was face level. "Tell me how you know about this right now, or I'll kill you."

"I'm one of his patients," he pleaded, then realized he was talking to Dr. Krone Sr.'s wife. "Look, I'm actually one of your son's patients. And he's in my mind playing games with me. He's not curing anybody. He's enjoying himself, the sick fuck."

She trained the pistol at his head. "No, you lie. *You're not making any sense! You're just another one of these lunatics.*"

The patients mumbled collectively, ball gags stuffed into their mouths. Many drooled and their muffled laughter distracted the woman long enough for him to launch over to her. He landed a stiff punch to her stomach, swinging hard. He pushed her to the ground, forcing the gun from her grip after stepping on her wrist. Craig raced to pick up the gun, and he couldn't believe what he witnessed in the back of the room.

Dr. Krone Sr. stood confused and frightened. The doctor helped his wife to her feet. Craig raised the gun and kept them where they stood. This was his chance to observe the rest of the room.

Heads without eyes were stored in formaldehyde jars. Hundreds of brains floated in preservatives. More bodies were also wrapped up in blankets and heaped in laundry carts.

"What do you do with the bodies, Krone?"

Dr. Krone Sr.'s brow sweated and he clutched onto his wife, shaken from his daily routine. "I don't have to tell you anything." He turned to the woman. "Are you okay, Hillary?"

She nodded, still out of sorts.

Craig insisted, "Where are we right now?"

"You don't know where we are?" Hillary was stumped by his naivety. "Why don't you know? Isn't it obvious?"

He raised the gun. "Spell it out for me, or I shoot you both. I'm in my brain. I guess it's not murder."

"You're in one of my sanitariums," Dr. Krone Sr. enumerated, sharpening his eyes, penetrating Craig. "And what do you mean by 'I'm in my brain'?"

"You hooked me to a machine. You, no, wait, your son, Dr. Krone, he did it. That fat bastard roams my memories and thoughts. He's manipulating my past. Treating me, that's what he calls it. Tormenting me is a better word. I guess in the future, he fucked up and decided to have fun instead. He's a sadistic voyeur. He's nothing more than a criminal."

"My son brought you here by the machine?"

Dr. Krone Sr. almost fell backwards, the revelation so powerful. Hillary propped him up straight, making sure he wouldn't tip over again. "This is . . . well, staggering. The machine works. I haven't hooked a living patient up to it yet. I wanted to commit to more research first, but if what you're saying is true, I'm launching into it right now."

He pointed the gun between Dr. Krone Sr.'s eyes. "You'll do no such thing. This ends now!"

He pulled the trigger.

The gun blast was rudely abbreviated by the blink. Dr. Krone Sr. was in sight, the bullet shattered his skull, and then the doctor was gone. A shout involuntarily slipped from Craig, high-pitched and from his sternum. He forced himself quiet and stood in place. The darkness was blinding, and Craig was forced to rely on a different set of senses to survive, namely his nose. Something wet and ice cold was seeping through his shoes. The stench became a film on his skin. Pneumonia strong. He coughed, and coughed, and coughed to breathe. Death consumed the room. He could smell blood and spoiled human carcasses en masse.

He feared stepping another inch. The room, whatever box he was now in, was silent. No crazies babbling in their padded rooms or victims mewling in torment. From above, a series of light bulbs flickered on. Rust light provided red and orange hues to the damnable room. He didn't hear anybody's approach yet, and it gave him an opportunity—though it nearly claimed his wits to do so—to study the horrifying box.

The institutional appearance made Craig believe he was still in an asylum. The walls were tiled, the floor concrete. He counted fifteen steel gurneys haphazardly strewn side by side, discarded and piled up, with bloodless corpses on them. Their skullcaps had been removed, the brains pilfered. Many of the bodies had begun to putrefy into greens and browns. Faces reflected waxen, bodies sunken and soft in the middle, and they were leaking their bodily fluids, the brackish substance dripping from the edge of gurneys in thick caramel consistencies. Sets of tools on carts ranged from scalpels, pinch claps, bone saws, circular saws, and pliers. Hundreds of used surgeon gloves littered the floor.

The rusted light kept the room healthy in its supply of shadows. Somehow, Craig managed to decipher the bulky items positioned throughout the rest of the corridor—the very purpose of the room. They were prototypes, he believed, of the machine he was hooked up to, though he hadn't seen the damn thing yet. Craig compared many of them to the body of a tractor where the engine component was hidden. Steel doors were open from two sides of the machine, and within, nine brains were housed in a dark yellow fluid. Electrodes were inserted between hemispheres and lobes of the brain, though they were collecting green growths and far from fresh. From the back end of the machine, an industrial-sized plug-in trailed out. It was unplugged and discarded as a failure.

Across the room, four men in straightjackets were sitting with their backs to each other in chairs. Their mummified heads were reared back with a silver bowl placed over each of their skulls. A long steel rod extended out the bowls and connected to a black box with circuits and projection lights. The victims' mouths were wide in an eternal scream.

The stink hit a crescendo, and Craig covered his mouth and held his breath. A glass box the size of a hatchback's trunk contained hundreds of deflated, cut-up, and otherwise ruined brains. They stank and stewed in a yellow fluid. Whatever preservative it had been, it had lost its potency.

He then inched toward a wall, curious at what was taped up on display. He counted twenty, thirty, forty, and many more blueprint sketches of the machine throughout the various stages of its development. Each had the steel box as the core. The power source ranged from mechanical hinges and lawnmower engines, to car engines and a wheel-and-pulley system—an Amish version of Dr. Krone's machine, he thought. Ropes and circuits, steel wires and bared wire were used interchangeably. Car batteries, nuts, bolts, copper wire, computer keyboards, steel gears, and rods were among many of the pieces scattered about the floor.

Disturbed from his investigation, he heard the confident stride of footsteps enter the corridor. Ducking behind a wooden crate, he looked out and found it was father and son Krone. He caught their shadows come closer, and Craig couldn't stand to be in the wretched cesspool room a moment longer.

He closed his eyes and thought of a happier place.

bAcheLoR pAd

RAIg wAS AgAIn moved to a new place, guided by the blink, the shift and placement influenced by his thoughts. He studied his surroundings, taking in the danger level. The darkness was the only factor that remained a constant. The sliver of light, a square, was the only indication he was far away from the sanitarium and the two Krones. The musical humming urged him into an erect position. His back, shoulders, and head bumped into boxes. Dust was disturbed, and he coughed on it.

The humming stopped.

He froze.

And then the humming started again. A wet *schick* followed the return of the humming.

Shick-shick-shick-shick-shick.

The sound was rhythmic, on time.

He gathered the courage to move again, having to know what was happening. He peered at the line of light in the corner. He couldn't see anything yet.

Wait.

This is the crawlspace.

The humming wasn't from Brandon. His father wasn't the type to hum or sing. Maybe to get laid he'd

187

do it. That meant his mom was out there. He craved her comfort. The warmth of her hug, and the humming, the ability to soothe was a motherly instinct she could wield to perfection.

He worked his way out of the boxes, pushing them aside, and barged through the door. He stopped before revealing himself to his mother.

This is too easy.

"Where are you, Dr. Krone?"

Did the doctor know he had trespassed into his mind? And if he did, what form of retribution would he take?

If I die here, what happens to me in that room? Will I decay like those other bodies?

The door was thrown open from the other side before he could work out a solution. "Oh, there you are, kiddo."

Tina grabbed him by the arms and dragged him out. He was a child again. He couldn't have been older than ten. He issued a high-pitched scream. Tina held his lips shut. The tang of blood met his nose, and Craig gasped, looking at her face and the red pasted on it. Blood clung to her shirt and painted her body like she'd bathed in it. Her hair was standing on end in sections and was pasted to her scalp in others. Tina's eyes were wide, her mouth drawn in a straight line but it quivered. She contained her amusement, a secret pleasure. Something brewed inside of her that had yet to be released.

The source of the blood was still a mystery, but the blood itself was well utilized. Large red X's crossed out Brandon's super model and playmate posters. The thick slashes dribbled onto the floor, fresh. Brandon's Budweiser can fridge was knocked onto the ground, the cans inside littering the floor.

"This is my room now," she shouted out with the zest of a seven-year-old. "I'm the decorator. What do you think, Craig? I'll let you come down whenever you like. I had to make some changes first. Brandon let me . . . *after we talked*. Parker guided me through it. He told me what to do with your father. We can be together now. No more secrecy and Parker will love you like a son." Under her breath, "*For the first time you'll feel a father's love.*"

Tina's hands squished within his. It wasn't only blood. Gobs of flesh were tangled between the notches of her fingers. The adult statement was foreign through the mouth of a child. "Mom . . . what have you done to Dad? What did Parker tell you to do?"

The thrill continued to sparkle in her eyes. "Parker said God would look the other way, and God did." She was whispering now. "Parker knows God's feelings. And now I know God too. You should get to know God. I've brought Dad directly to God, and God can deal with him."

Under the green fixture that shone onto the pool table—the only source of light on in the entire room— was Brandon's body. His throat had been gouged through numerous times. Brandon's eyes were affixed on nothing, wide open. The eyes screamed terror and agony but the rest of his face was limp. He'd turned blue and pale, losing much blood. A seven-inch steak knife was laid out on the green carpet alongside Brandon's straight razor. Strips of flesh similar to the thin slices of a carrot peeler were taken from Brandon's naked back.

Craig curled into himself, repulsed. Tina tightened her grip on his hand to the point his bones protested. "Ah, you're hurting me!"

Tina shrieked, triggered by his reaction, "And your father hurt me! He tore my heart out. I caught him sticking his dick in a random stranger. I was walking to the grocery store, and I noticed our car parked outside a hotel. I fought my way inside, and there was the slut spent and ready to go home. Cum and wash bitch, that whore, that slut, that fucking diseased bitch, only my husband could find something attractive about her. I acted like I'd forgiven him. I brought us home. Then I remembered what Parker said about bringing Brandon to God." She paused, licking her dried lips. "That's when I stabbed him in the throat."

She looked to him for acceptance and understanding. "This was what you wanted for me, Craig. Remember? Don't you remember? You said he didn't deserve me. You were right. Now he can't have me. I can be happy now."

Tina snarled and returned to the pool table. She picked up the straight razor and began flensing strips of skin from Brandon's spine and between his shoulder blades, the blade clicking against bone with each swipe. "He's slept with so many women. He's dirty. I'm sure he's passed something on to me. He didn't make love to me with real passion. But Parker, he's a real man. I'm his one and only."

She shaved down the back of Brandon's head and removed a long cut of meat. Craig abhorred the sight, internally shrinking from it. Tina expressed more joy than he'd ever seen, and it disgusted him. "Dr. Krone taught me this trick."

Both his fists tightened at his name. "What did he say to you? When did he talk to you, Mom?" He closed in, grabbing her by both arms to steal her attention. "Christ, speak up—tell me right now!"

Tina's eyes, Tina's smile, Tina's brow, everything about her face went crooked. The shadows gnarled the blood stains on her face. It looked like she'd been the one who was bleeding. "He said simply stabbing him in the throat wasn't good enough. I'd regret not torturing him more—even though he's already dead. Parting the skin, I'm shaving him clean. He'll be a good man when there's nothing left of him. The doctor said that's the only way for a devious man to make a fresh start. Clean. Pure. Without sin—oh wait, the sin part was Parker's talk, not the doctor's."

She glared at him, her joy suddenly draining, her smile fading into a frown. She growled, "I see your father in you. You'll be just like him soon, Craig." A whimper of fear, her eyes shirked from him, and then they returned, staring at him like he was stranger, someone to harm. "I can't let you go, Craig. You'll break another girl's heart." She tightened her stare. "Poor Katie. You were supposed to be a man. You let her bleed to death. It's your fault your wife and baby died."

She cast her head down, mourning his ineptitudes. "But your mistakes hurt others, Craig. You could potentially harm another girl that may come into your life." The next words caused the hairs on the nape of his neck to stand. "I must save you. Cleanse you like I cleansed your daddy."

The motherly role was distorted. She had consoled him when Katie died in real life. She was the major factor in moving on versus wallowing in self-pity and guilt, and now, she was taking back that gift.

Shick-shick-shick-shick-shick.

Brandon's scalp was bared to the skull, Tina carving the straight razor with precision and determination. She slapped the skin onto the floor, wringing her hands of the flesh.

Unable to speak, forcing himself to act, his body weighing double what it used to, his limbs cooperating only because he demanded his nerves to respond, Craig launched across the basement to escape. Tina leapt over the pool table, posing like a crawling spider on all fours, and landed onto his back, tackling him from behind. On the way down, the straight razor sliced across the back of his neck, and the skin parted audibly, punctuated by the heavy flow of warm blood.

"*I know what you did*," she accused, shrieking at alarming octaves. "Of the things you'd do in your mind, you slept with Susan. Wouldn't you rather sleep with your wife? Or no, that's right. You're just like your father. Can't keep his dick to himself."

Craig whipped around, turning from his side, and seizing the arm poised to slice him again, he shoved her backwards by the jaw, her body flopping onto the floor. "Dr. Krone's putting you up to this. It's not you, Mom!"

"Your mind is the greatest place to venture," she said, her words spittle-heavy, her eyes slanted and flickering with unreal emotion. "You want to throw this opportunity away on bullshit fantasies. You don't really want to cure yourself of your anger."

"You're the one who's deciding the outcomes, not me. You put me in those situations." Craig clenched his fists, bent to fight off his mother at the first indication of another attack. "I want out of my mind and back into my body. I'm done, you hear me, Doctor, *I'm finished!*"

The Browning shotgun materialized in his hands. He gripped it tight so as not to drop it, the weapon heavy and real. He was an adult again too, all in a blink's time. She admired him with distaste, her desire to cut him up realized once again. "All I see is your father in you. You're not my child. Not if his blood is in your veins."

She raised the straight razor, posed to swipe it across his throat.

He raised the gun, reminding himself this wasn't his real mother. She was alive somewhere else and out of harm's way. "Stay back or I'll shoot!"

Inching closer, her legs became springs, ejecting her forward, a wild *shaleeeeeh* escaping her lungs as her voice matched her animal mentality to maim.

Ba-boom!

Knowing he wasn't harming a real person, pulling the trigger was easy, but the effect was too real. The impact rendered her face inside out, the bullet spray chewing away any familiarity of his mother.

She wasn't deterred from the attack. Tina had one eye she could view him through beneath a blackened and bleeding pulp for a face. The other eye was pink socket tissue and smashed retina and orb. Her lips had disintegrated, both rows of teeth shattered or fractured and bared. She swallowed the remains of her tongue in a thick gulp. Pointing the straight razor at him again, Craig picked up his feet and bounded up the stairs, knowing if the shotgun blast didn't deter her, nothing could.

Tina chased him down, her steps thundering behind him in pursuit. The words about Katie still burned him, and true or not, his mother had spoken them, and he'd taken them in. There wasn't time to think about it, his neck bleeding down his shirt and turning cold. Afternoon sunlight poured through the windows of his childhood home. The beacon of safety, his haven, was demurred. His guts churned at the noises coming from outside. Screams and unrelenting rounds of torture played out in the front yard. He couldn't stop now, despite his reservations. Tina charged behind him, forcing him to retreat into the living room, still at his heels, slashing the air, spilling blood onto the floor with each effort. Craig had no choice but to throw open the front door and flee outside.

Sinner

CRAIG unlocked the bolt and launched through the front door. He hopped over the three front steps and landed in the yard, but the sight ahead halted him. Parker Stevens wore a white ceremonial robe the likes of the Pope's. A blood cross was painted on his forehead. It bled down his face to his chin, gelling at the apex. Life-sized crosses were erected as tall as nine feet, each carved out of an unknown wood. Brandon was impaled on one. He was stripped to only a loincloth. His hands and legs were nailed to the cross by four nails—nails the size of railroad spikes. Willis and Joey were hanging from the other two beside his father. Down the street, his neighbors were impaled on the crosses, even Margaret and Ray Highland, who were in their mid-eighties. The sun was baking them, turning them red. They'd die of exposure, but they'd surely bleed to death first. The persons on the cross chanted, *"For I have sinned, for I have sinned, for I have sinned . . . "*

Parker closed his Bible at the sight of Craig. "Erect another cross. We have another sinner. He can be saved, if he's willing. I tried to bless him, but, Lord, I failed. He needs divine intervention. Let him bear the weight of your sacrifices to mankind, and then we'll see if he's ready to live a life in your image."

Blood spilled from so many bodies, it trickled in a stream into the streets and gutters. Robed individuals paraded up and down the block, each from Parker's congregation. Tina threatened to take Craig down again, and angling after him, she was bent on her haunches and about to jump onto his back, but he turned, aimed, prayed to God—the real God, not who Parker Stevens' congregation was praying to—and unloaded another barrage of shells. Blasting through her stomach, the pieces firing out between her shoulder blades, she kept resisting her damage, and then he blew out her legs beneath her with another shot, the dismantled body finally collapsing onto the lawn.

His mother was alive, but immobilized. He aimed the gun at Parker next, anticipating a new round of pursuit. "You stay away from me. Nobody else gets hurt. You're not hanging me on a cross." He cocked the shotgun. "You can shove your fire-and-brimstone bullshit up your ass."

The pulpit, self-righteousness tone resonated in Parker's words. "You've gunned down your own mother. She created you. Now two of God's creations are ruined . . . *mother and son*."

His mother coughed up more blood and looked on at Parker in admiration, disturbing because she had only a fraction of her face.

"Did you see what she did to my father? She was shaving his skin."

He peered up at Brandon writhing on the cross. "How, how did he get up there?" Craig studied the lawns and the twitching bodies on the crosses.

"Where are you, Dr. Krone? Show yourself. You coward, where are you?"

Parker paid no attention to what he said and focused on his mission. "Come willingly to God, Craig."

Brandon's hands slipped through the spikes, splitting two fingers apart. The spikes through his ankles did the same, and he flopped onto the ground. Willis and Joey slithered free next. The entire block, one by one, was released from the crosses, breaking their flesh and breaking bone to do so. They teetered in place, difficult to walk with torn ankles.

"*Come willingly to God,*" they chanted. "*Come to Him.*"

Craig was cornered, and from every angle they approached. He dashed forward to the Corolla parked in Mr. Davidson's lawn. The car door was unlocked, but he didn't have the keys.

"*Come willingly to God . . . come to Him.*"

He locked the doors once he hunkered in. Parker Stevens leapt on top of the Corolla's hood with an aluminum pop. "Bring him to the cross. Salvation is his if we can bring him to the cross!"

They chanted, "*Come willingly to God . . . come to Him.*"

The back window was smashed. Fists pounded the driver and passenger side windows in unison. Sweat smears turned to blood as faces pressed up against glass and fists continued to mash the breakable barrier. Tina worked up to the hood as a torso with arms. The skin on her face slipped down and stuck to the hood, the slick muscle-tissue face speaking nonsense without a tongue.

"*Come willingly to God . . . come to Him.*"

The passenger side window was shattered next. Tina and the others turned the front windshield into a spider web of fractures with their blows. Brian Gwinn, a neighbor, crawled through the broken window and reached for his neck. "Come willing to God—come to Him!"

Craig slammed Brian's face into the dashboard. The man wasn't fazed, reaching up, hands squeezing his neck, fingers bending in deep. He couldn't breathe. He had no leverage to batter the man aside, the space too small to fight back. He closed his eyes, taking desperate measures.

Picture the keys.

This is your mind.

Make it happen.

The driver's side window shattered, the shards raining upon him as several fists performed the job at once.

"*Come willing to God . . . come to Him.*"

Picture it!

White blotches ruined his vision. He was growing dizzy. He'd been without air for nearly two minutes. Bodies worked their way into the backseat through the windshield. New hands would serve to snuff him dead in moments. The stomping above him was rekindled. Brian's fingers squeezed tighter. "*Gaack!*" He thought the man's grip would collapse his trachea.

Picture it.

His hair was tugged backwards. Two different hands spread blood into his eyes, and he was blinded.

"*Come willing to God . . . come to Him.*"

His lungs tightened and convulsed, the organ trying to force him to breathe, but it was impossible.

Picture it before you die!

Then the keys materialized. He shoved the key into the ignition. Stomping on the gas, screeching and spinning his tires, a cloud of smoke surrounded them, burying his adversaries in a palpable fog. The Corolla gained speed, and those on the outside began faltering, the car racing from thirty to sixty miles an hour.

The hand in his mouth and the hands around his throat had somehow stayed in place. Not much longer, he'd be dead. Would he become a vegetable in the real world? Was he already one in his physical body?

"Come willingly to God . . . come to Him."

His eyelids were stuck together with drying blood.

He stomped on the gas pedal. He sharply turned right, the wheel wobbling from the force, the shocks grinding, the brakes failing, and the car turned over when it hit the curb. The vehicle flipped and kept spinning across the street in wild circles. The car absorbed each crash and jolt as steel crunched. When the car finally stopped, the hands over his throat were absent.

fInAL hAVen

CRAIg CRAwLeD thRough the broken driver's side window, cutting his palms of the glittering fragments of glass. Getting up to his feet and forcing himself onwards, he completed three blocks in a desperate sprint. He soon spotted the congregation of naked bodies with Parker in the lead three yards behind him and fast approaching.

He shouted, "Can't you people leave me be?"

He knew the answer to that. They would stalk him to the very end of his sanity. Dr. Krone was here somewhere, orchestrating this masquerade. He looked in every direction for the man and came up empty.

How much farther could he run to avoid them? He wasn't up for the task. He'd slammed his head against the steering wheel earlier. He suffered a wicked migraine from the near strangulation. His wounds bogging him down, knowing he had little endurance left, he stumbled onto the lawn of a nearby house to seek refuge.

Craig thought about the car keys he produced with his mind. He'd pictured them and screamed for his life. Extreme emotion. The only times he'd conjured things up was when he was on the brink of death.

"End this treatment, Dr. Krone," he whimpered, feeling the extent of his injuries creep up on him again. "I can't take any more. This isn't a cure. This is murder."

The house loomed before him, an easy beacon. He had no choice but to enter the unknown haven, an unassuming two-story colonial house. He closed the door behind him. He dead bolted it. Craig prayed what he thought would happen did. He parted the curtain. Outside, the street was empty. But he wasn't in a house anymore. He overlooked a parking lot. It was dark enough to be late evening. The room was familiar, but vaguely. A black leather couch and cherry oak table took up most of the living room. A pale face hovered in the shadows of the unlit hallway to his left. The face looked at him. Studied him. The person couldn't decide how to approach him.

"No more," he begged, recognizing her. "I can't take any more punishment. You stay where you are. Please, leave me alone."

She seethed, "I'm not the one you need to apologize to this time."

Katie stepped out of the darkness. She was corpse blue. Her body had suffered further deterioration. The skeleton was visible underneath the thin, translucent skin. The bones could tear free of their flesh packaging any moment, he thought. Black and green patches of fungus played at the sides of her neck and her clavicle. She stank of putrefying organs. The eyes were saturated in fluids. They weren't round anymore, but instead sagged in the center and lent the orbs a wrinkled look. Her belly was round, but it too had caved in. Blood had caked the insides of her thighs in so many layers.

She spoke with a delay, the deep lull of collapsed vocal cords. "There's somebody else you should say sorry to, and she's here."

"Oh, God," he wept, feeling a part of him collapse. "I-I was scared. Alice, I'm so sorry. You have to understand I didn't know what to do. It's not an excuse or a validation for my actions. I got scared, and I acted like a coward."

Katie shook her head, ligaments and bones popping. She opened her mouth and revealed her purple-white tongue. "*Ah-ah-ah.* I'm not Alice. She's waiting for you down the hallway, Craig. Don't talk to me. Talk to her."

"What if I refuse?" Not waiting for a reply, he rushed for the front door. It wouldn't open, the door not having real function. It was only an image. He tried the windows, but they were painted shut. Katie sauntered over to him, confident he couldn't evade her. "You can't leave. He won't let you."

He whispered the name as a curse. "*Dr. Krone.*" He surveyed the kitchen and the hallway, searching for him. "Is he here?"

The dead earthworm lips created a hideous smile. "He's always been here."

Craig wedged himself into the farthest corner away from the hallway. "I can't do this. Terminate the session. The treatment is over, Dr. Krone. You've made your fucking point. Yes, I get it. My mother cheated on my father with Parker. She was the one abused, not me. My dad fucked around behind her back, and she knew about it and she didn't quit the marriage for me. But she cheated too. She empowered herself, didn't she? I should've done something to help her. I could've talked her up. And I screwed up royally with Katie. I should've ordered a cab or called the ambulance to our house. I'm responsible for her death. I can deny it and attempt to live it down, but it's true. It's my mistake. It's my biggest regret.

"What else do you want me to say? Okay, I shouldn't have bashed a barstool over Willis. I was drunk and pissed off. Hey, it's no excuse. I'll do the time. I'll perform community service. I'll give blood to those people when they call every time. I'll donate to charity. Take your pick, the Salvation Army, Goodwill, whatever, I can change my life. The treatment has scared the shit out of me." He pointed at the shadowy corner. "You don't have to send me down that hallway. *I—am—begging—you.*"

Katie's purple and dehydrated face attempted an amused expression, but it was mostly wet shifting without anything taking shape. "You still owe her an apology. You didn't stay. She needed you. You abandoned her."

"Alice," he pleaded to her, though she wasn't in the room. "Forgive me. I can't handle my emotions. I'm a scared wreck. We've established that, Dr. Krone. Is this what you wanted to see? I'm falling apart, you happy? You want me dead. I know because I've been in your head too, Dr. Krone. I've watched your father remove the brains of those infirm victims you nabbed from the sanitarium. You're not so innocent. The blood is on your hands, and you don't even bother to wash it away. This is your sick show. What's the point in treating somebody if you can't accept it when the patient's cured?"

"You're not better," Katie advised. "And the treatment is far from over."

Katie throttled him by the throat with both hands,

closing in with ghostly speed, the putrescence causing him to stagger in shock. She shoved him into the hallway, utilizing surprising strength. She stomped on his back and pinned him down outside the bathroom door. "Squirm all you want, Craig. Alice's ready for your apology. And I'm taking you right to her."

He couldn't apologize to her in words. Dr. Krone wouldn't allow that. That would be too easy. And Craig already anticipated where Katie would deliver him. The crack of light under the door, it was just like the door at Alice's apartment. And tonight was that horrible night he fled from years ago.

Katie's breath reeked of expired internal organs, and with every word, her tongue flicked cold turpentine fluid onto him. "You can't avoid this. Submit to his treatment."

Rage overwhelmed him, and he channeled fear, desperation, and regret into a sweeping kick under her legs. Katie's leg unhinged from the knee socket joint with a jarring pop. She tumbled to the floor, losing balance.

Craig spoke desperately, "I'm trapped in my mind without a way out. Dr. Krone, you're in control—okay? I absolutely have no choice but to do what you want me to do."

He prayed he could bargain with Alice. Craig was genuinely sorry for what he did to her. He left her alone at the apartment in her moment of crisis. He was terrified, and he could only guess to understand how she felt then.

Craig challenged the dark, walking to the door with his head up. This was his moment to receive forgiveness. He sucked in a final breath before entering. He didn't knock. Alice knew he was coming.

He closed the door behind him, locking it. Katie could enter, and he couldn't handle the two at once. He stopped shortly after entering. Alice was bathing. She was naked, and the bath water was pink. He wasn't embarrassed at her nakedness. He was too busy reading her glazed eyes. The stare was affixed on the wall ahead of her. She was in a trance. Alice had confined herself to her own mind.

Alice noticed him moments later. Her lips were stuck together, and the adhesive skin broke when she spoke. "Katie didn't have to drag you in here."

He was stumped for a response, so he kept it simple. "No, she didn't."

Bloody footprints stained the beige shag rug. The sink was also colored red. The white porcelain was stained in handprints, the floor stained in spatters and footprints.

He broke the silence. "How do I apologize to you?"

Alice scoffed. Her eyes were now locked on the toilet bowl. The lid was closed. "How do you apologize? You can't truly apologize. But I can forgive you."

"Really?" His hopes were raised. He didn't forget Dr. Krone was somewhere close by, and this wouldn't pan out so easily. "Please tell me how."

After pausing for ten seconds, Alice said, "I want you to see it."

His stomach sank. "Excuse me?"

He understood what she had requested, but refused to accept it. Alice made eye contact. She was ghostly white. Deadly serious. "I want you to look at my baby. See what you left me alone with. You were supposed to be my friend and be there for me through anything. So be there for me now. *Look at my baby.*"

Craig eyed the toilet bowl. Blood trailed down two sides of the lid. He couldn't decide what to do. "That's the apology you want?"

He was startled when Alice stood up. Water spilled from the sides in generous waves. He couldn't trust his eyes. Was this Alice naked? How did Dr. Krone know how she looked naked? Craig had no memory of it. And how would Dr. Krone know Alice wanted to be his blood brother on Halloween night? It was impossible, yet there was a part of him that couldn't deny it. Somehow, Dr. Krone discovered the truth, and the machine had everything to do with it.

She touched his chin, caressing him. She barely spoke, Craig having to read her lips. "*Look at my baby.*"

He shook his head, a surge of fear working up his spine and bursting into his brain. "What will that prove? You know I'm sorry. I am sorry."

Her words came off as a pouting child's. "You won't look at my baby?"

Crash.

The bathroom door exploded into four pieces, the unreal strength followed by an unreal attack. Katie seized hold of him, the rotten stink of dried-up meat swarmed him, crippling him. He was driven onto his knees, her form performing actions he couldn't take in, she was so fast.

On the ground, Alice clutched his hair and reared his head back. Spittle foamed at her lips and sprayed him with each syllable, "*You will look at my* baby!"

She reached for the toilet lid, trying to lift it up. He broke one hand free and forced it back down. "No—you're not yourselves! This is Dr. Krone. Don't listen to him. Shut him out. You have your own personalities, even if you're just in my head. I should be able to control you, not him!"

Alice reared back his hair again. "This is what I want, Craig, nothing else."

Katie smothered his mouth with her hand to prevent him from speaking. "I won't let go until you do. If you're sorry, you know what I want you to do . . . "

Alice wedged his hand from the toilet. She clutched the rim and raised it. He closed his eyes. Alice's fingers poked at his eyelids, and she dug her fingernails to pry them back open.

"Look inside, Craig. Say you're sorry. Open those eyes. *Open them!*"

The nails worked against his soft orbs. Craig shouted his horror. The toilet was open. He didn't want to see what was inside. He couldn't take it. He lost his own child. He refused to have the impression of Alice's lost baby ingrained in his mind as well. This wasn't the real Alice. This wasn't the real Katie. And it wouldn't be Alice's real baby. What it would turn out to be was the scariest thing, and he collected every ounce of strength in his failing body to fight them.

He needed air, but Katie's hand blocked his nostrils and mouth. Alice wedged open one eye, but the toilet seat clapped shut, falling due to gravity.

"Open your eyes!"

Katie removed her hands and dug into the razor-blade slash Tina had delivered in his neck. "*Aaaaaaaah!*"

Alice opened the toilet seat. He turned his head again to the side and avoided the sight. That's when the blink happened. An electric flash. Static electricity played on his skin and raised his hairs. He smelled burnt skin. It was ten degrees hotter, his flesh stinging and burning.

He was sitting upright now.

The metallic *ticking* was a loud, piercing rhythm.

Then as quickly as it began, there was silence.

AwAke

The Agony brewing at his eyes and skull touched nerves that forced his body to twitch. Spittle had dried on his lips and chin into a crusty film. The wounds on his neck, the jolt from the car wreck, and the strangulation attempts were no longer bothering him. Those sensations had passed. The wounds no longer existed.

Wuuuuuuuuuuum.

The soft mechanical hum lasted thirty seconds. He was burning hot. His clothes were glued to his body by sweat. He couldn't speak, but the swatch of tape at his lips was puckering at the edges. The darkness was so thick he wouldn't be able to see his hand in front of his face.

The motor's groan kicked up anew, though it was strained. Static electricity crackled up and down his arms, each jolt a pinch of flesh and a visible blue spark. *Zzzzt—crick!*

A generator kicked on from another room with a muffled stomp. *Da-dump*. The overhead lights flickered on. The noises at his back increased. The steel prong laced with circuits and steel wires retracted from his face. Craig's head was jerked back. The weight pressing on his skull was lifted, and he was free of the machine and the needles.

He had a split second to react.

Ca-clunk.

The needles shot back down into place, the machine revving back up, but he pivoted his head to the side to avoid them.

"Shit!"

He couldn't move from the seat, posed awkwardly. The leather bands around his chest and legs bound him in place. He couldn't budge his neck or head or else he'd touch the prong attached with the needles. The needles themselves were wet and glazed with clear fluids. Drugs.

Craig had escaped viewing what waited inside the toilet, Alice's dead child. It couldn't have been so simple. Nothing in Dr. Krone's treatment was innocent. Would he be coming soon to tend after him? He assumed there were numerous machines. He still couldn't visualize the contraption. He imagined a creation out of a Tim Burton film.

And Edith was another victim. Where was she? Did she survive the attack at the mausoleum? The battle wounds vanished once he awoke. She had to be alive. But if one died in their mind, did their body cease to function as well? It was a question he couldn't answer. Dr. Krone led him to believe he could die for real, but was that really the case?

He shifted and attempted to worm from the leather belts, but there was no slack. If he didn't escape now, he feared the opportunity would pass.

The stained cherry oak door remained closed. Any moment, it would fly open and Dr. Krone would hook him back up to the machine. And Dr. Krone's assistant, Rachael, what happened to her? Craig feared she was lurking around the place somewhere.

His neck ached from the angle it was bent. He couldn't move. He feared coming in contact with any part of the machine.

He was burning up. Dehydrated. His stomach growled from days of going unfed. How long had he been hooked up to the machine?

Craig had plenty of time to mull over the question.

He wasn't going anywhere.

behInd the wALL

WAS theRe A term for the anxiety of being hooked up to experimental machines? If so, Craig suffered this malady. He couldn't steady his breathing, hyperventilating. He eyed the door without flinching.

Just breathe. One breath at a time.

Soft steps tamped the carpet nearby, then the sharp crick of a floorboard resounded.

"Who's there?" he demanded.

The movements abruptly halted. It was difficult to listen over the drone of the machine. Maybe he imagined it?

No, you heard it. Somebody's out there.

Dr. Krone wouldn't sneak around. He was in charge and in control of the situation. Who would walk about quietly?

He called out, "Is that you, Edith?"

The immediate reply was, "Is that you, Craig?"

Hearing it was her, he begged and pleaded to her, "You have to help me. I'm behind this door. I can't move. I'm strapped down to the machine. I'm not hooked up to it. Please help me. Dr. Krone could be coming any second. Watch your back. Rachael's around here too somewhere."

The knob rattled. "Damn, it's locked. I can pick it. Let me run to the kitchen. Sit tight."

"God, hurry," he mewled, though he didn't mean to. He was desperate, run through and chased out of hell. "And be careful."

"I'm a tough bitch, Craig, don't you worry about me."

On that note, she skulked back down the way she came from, and he waited. The burn in his neck continued to worsen. His spine was twisted at a bad angle and his legs tingled.

Come on, Edith. I'm dying here.

He refocused his thoughts. There were a few pleasing memories he'd relived in his head. The bastard started him easy, buttering him up, before turning his loved ones against him. He spooned Katie in bed, playing his hands around their baby. It was a moment he cherished. He couldn't have been more comfortable with a person. And Susan was a strong fantasy he kept tucked in the back of his head. It was both shameful and pleasurable. He was a child again in Alice's company. He missed her. If he survived this, he was determined to apologize to her. And how could he not appreciate telling off his dad for cheating on his mother? But that was strange. Tina was sleeping with Parker Stevens, but was it really true? He couldn't be sure.

Edith hadn't returned.

Forced not to think about her, he focused on what had happened again while hooked up to the machine. One memory stuck out among the rest under the machine's control. He was kidnapped in his home and brought here by Rachael. His initial instinct after his consultation with Dr. Krone was foul play, but he distrusted himself. Now, he was certain, and he'd been a fool to consider otherwise. This was completely against his will.

He had no idea where he'd been taken. The research itself was also troubling. If Dr. Krone's goal was to allow the patient to relive the past and reconcile the issues that plagued them in the present, why did he turn the memories against him later on?

Craig stiffened upon hearing new steps.

Then the lock jangled.

"Edith?"

The mechanism shook. The knob jangled.

The lock came undone, and the door swung open.

fRee of the mAchIne

edith unbuckled his straps, and one by one, they came loose. She worked at the restraints at his feet. Craig was so caught up in his escape that he forgot he was hooked up to a catheter and IV fluids. Urine filled half the plastic bag. Edith turned away and let him unhook himself. "Don't be embarrassed. I was hooked up like that too."

After freeing himself, he tried to stand, and when he did, he unleashed an abbreviated shout. "Ah, God!" His legs were assaulted by pins and needles. He rubbed at them to force circulation. He rotated his neck and twisted his back. He'd been sitting in the same position for essentially days. He grinded his teeth and cursed and cursed under his breath. Craig laid flat on his back, and then he returned to his feet and used the wall for support.

Edith hugged him, clinging to him for relief.

"It's okay, you can cry," he encouraged her. "This is worth crying over."

She wept. "I-I just want to see my children again. I want out of this damnable place. The windows are boarded up. Every door is locked. There's no way out of here."

215

The news soured his excitement of being free of the machine. He turned to the device. Craig didn't mean to laugh. The device was a metallic box the size of a refrigerator tilted to its side with a chair bolted to one end. Metal legs propped it four feet high. A computer screen and keyboard were crafted into the side, but the monitor was black. A trail of wires, thick as rope, exited one end and continued through a hole in the wall.

Edith was confused. "What's so funny?"

"This machine, it's so . . . so simple. I expected Dr. Frankenstein's lab. This is all it takes to open up a person's memory and play it on a movie screen and to place the person back into their memories?"

He walked to the machine and dared to touch it. Maybe there was something inside the steel box. He traced the edges and the thin line where he thought the box would come open. The edge wouldn't budge. It was locked by a series of three keyhole entries.

More secrets, great.

"Whatever's in there," he speculated, "is what's fucking with our minds."

He touched the cords trailing out the back. He tugged, ripped, and yanked to unplug the machine. No luck. The wires held strong. The device was homemade. Soldering lines and different shades of metal lent it a rough prototype look. *I'm sure this was independently funded. No university in their right mind would allow this to happen. The testing alone, and the trial research.*

It doesn't matter.

Just get the hell out of here.

"Let's find a way out of this place."

He was careful leaving the room. Edith was glued

to his side. "Listen, I couldn't find an exit. Like I said, everything's sealed up. A mouse couldn't get in or out."

Craig challenged the hallway. The wallpaper was a floral print and stained with water spots. Pieces of plaster showed through the wall and littered the floor in powdery circles.

"The maid's on strike," Craig joked.

The narrow corridor went on for a series of rooms. Edith's room was three ahead of his. The same machine was positioned in an otherwise empty room. The electrical cords also trailed into the wall.

"Where do those cords lead to?"

Edith shook her head. "It beats me. You have to see the living room and kitchen. This is somebody's home."

"Wait," he said, making her stop. "How did we escape the machine?"

Edith had the answer. "The power went out. It flickered back on five minutes later. The needles in my eyes and my skull were removed, and I slipped from the restraints." She smiled, flexing her eyebrows. "I'm flexible."

"But if that's true, how come nobody's coming after us?"

She pointed to the end of the hall. "Forget it. Help me find an escape before they do find us."

They rushed forward and stopped at a living room where they found cherry-finished wood floors, mauve drapes over the windows, a three-piece furniture set, and an Egyptian rug that covered the majority of the room's surface area. She was correct, this was somebody's home. Craig rushed to the windows. There were wrought iron bars preventing their escape. The front door had no doorknob.

"Step back."

He rammed the door with his shoulder.

Big mistake.

"*Shit, shit, shit.*"

Craig grasped his shoulder, which was covered in wild blinding pain. "It's like a concrete wall."

He rapped on the door with his knuckle. "Yep, it's concrete."

Edith was devastated, and she failed to reserve her emotions. She bounded into the kitchen, weeping. The room was well-furnished—pizza oven, overhead pots and pans rack, modern oven and stove, and a refrigerator with a television installed on the door. The room was perfectly clean. Edith had been in the room before. She quickly located a bottle of scotch in the cupboard and tilted her head back to enjoy a swig.

"Easy," he advised, checking the room over again. "I don't need you drunk. They could be watching us. Dr. Krone or that nurse, whoever she is, might be skulking about."

He observed the stairwell that twisted up to the second floor. There was another set that led to the basement. "We should check upstairs and down next."

Edith nursed the bottle in her hands, standing in the kitchen. Craig eyed the refrigerator. He was starving. He wrenched the doors open and scavenged for something. The insides were bare except for sandwich meat, wine, and cheese. He located a loaf of Wonder Bread on the counter and slapped a wad of turkey between the bread. Craig ate, watching every direction for anyone. He feared this was the bait inside a trap.

He finished the sandwich, and with his belly

satisfied, Craig thought about the stairwells. Where did they lead? Edith's glassy eyes were in a trance. She was defeated, broken-hoped.

Craig studied her arms, and legs, and body. "Dr. Krone's a liar."

Her reply was delayed. "Huh?"

"I was attacked numerous times when I was hooked up to that machine, but I don't have a scratch on me now, except from those needles on that metal crown we wore on our heads."

"No. I guess you're right. It was all in our minds."

"I say we comb over this place. Those electrical cords channel somewhere. Perhaps there's a power source we can knock out." He pointed at the kitchen window armed with iron bars. The windows were tinted, and he couldn't view outside. "We still don't know where we are. It's a mansion, sure, but where is it? They don't have us contained in our minds anymore." He sighed. "Those were horrible memories."

"But there were good memories too." She enjoyed a short pull from the bottle. "It was beautiful, at first. The moment after giving birth to your first child, when the pain has finished, and there's an endorphin kick, and then a slow release of tension, and you have this little child in your arms. It's yours, and this person is the only thing you can really call yours. It came from you, you know what I mean? Trent was there with me. He still loved me then, my first husband. I had a decent job. I worked at a print shop, making copies for businesses. Trent was a truck driver. We both had money and what we needed to be happy.

"But it quickly went to shit. Dr. Krone would

manipulate the situation. Trent would steal my children. He'd hold them hostage. I would be at home, and I'd receive pieces of them in the mail. Fingers, toes, and locks of hair, and before I woke from Dr. Krone's machine, he sent me a head. I couldn't recognize it, it was so mutilated." She winced, shutting her eyes, banishing the image from her mind. "I can still feel the blood on my fingers."

He wrapped his arms around her, sensing her emotional fatigue. Their memories had something in common. Heartbreak and violence.

Edith continued her story, living down the tears. "Trent really did kidnap Fiona when she was three. The cops arrested him, but I didn't press charges. Fiona wasn't hurt. She was gone for two days. But in the machine, all my children were kidnapped, and each was murdered. They also came back as . . . as monsters to hurt me. Snarling demons with red eyes and demented claws. And then I'm behind Dr. Krone in the mausoleum. He's removing a coffin, that Bruce Denning guy. I see desiccated bones. He unfolds another body in a towel and buries him there. Dr. Krone said a prayer over his father's body, and he fled the cemetery after returning the coffin into the wall. He was crying, really upset. That's why I stayed inside the place. I thought he was terrified to enter the mausoleum."

Craig pondered the memory he had of Dr. Krone, the doctor working with his wife in the asylum, and the numerous contraptions and early prototypes of the machine. He explained the details to Edith, and she was astounded.

"So the Krones own insane asylums, and they were stealing victims as test subjects?"

"I'm not sure how they were used, but I also had a shorter glimpse of another memory. I believe I was watching Dr. Krone's father twisting out the brains from his patients. There were dead bodies in that room strewn all over the place."

Edith bit her lip, puzzled. But then her eyes lit up. "It makes you wonder why our memories are so terrible. Our past is twisted against us, and we're attacked by our friends and loved ones. Who would wish that on anybody?"

Craig smiled. "Someone who's obviously criminally insane would enjoy that kind of shit."

She was snapped out her pitiful victim stance. "Dr. Krone is watching all of this. He has control, yes, but maybe he's losing that control himself."

"Or he's influenced by his victims." He strained to think, parting the gray curtain over the facts. "Consider it. He's had too many visions of insanity or he's lived in the heads of the criminally insane one too many times. That's who he's been dissecting. If he's lived in our heads like that, he's done it with the straightjackets too. But we're missing a big piece of information. How he uses the machine and the mental patients, we still don't know. This is merely speculation on our part. That's why we should check out the place. This machine is obviously dangerous, and I want to destroy it."

Edith's jaw clenched. "He kidnapped us against our will. It's obvious his bullshit about treating us for our problems is a hoax. He said I had a case of depression and alcohol addiction." She eyed the scotch in her hands. "And maybe so, but none of this is for the bettering of me." She tipped the bottle into her mouth again. "I'm obviously not cured."

"I agree," he sighed, experiencing the same vexing thoughts. "I was originally going to visit a psychiatrist. I was court ordered to do so." He cleared his throat and lowered his eyes. "I, um, slammed a barstool over my best friend's body. I was drunk, unemployed, and desperate . . . "

She touched his shoulder. "We've all been there. You're sorry, I can tell." She injected him with encouraging words. "Let's escape so we can make up for lost time. It's been at least two days. We'll have a wild time, me and you—fast friends."

He laughed. "No shit. This'll make for a great story, for anybody that'll believe us. If we escape, we're having the biggest party ever."

She stole another swig from the bottle to acknowledge the idea. And then her eyes skirted to the wall, and she placed the bottle on the counter, moving to the magnetic kitchen strip and taking the five-inch kitchen knife. He was disappointed the other knives were gone—perhaps other people had escaped the machine and taken them—and after rooting through the drawers himself, he came upon the best option: a rolling pin. He studied the upstairs and then the bottom stairs. He believed the cords from the machine traveled down, not up, but it was merely a guess.

"I say we check out the basement first. The cords should lead there. I really want to bash the shit out of whatever makes that machine tick."

She sprinted down the hallway, impelled by an idea she didn't share with him. Craig chased after her, growing paranoid with each step. There were closed doors and any one of them could harbor Dr. Krone and Rachael. Edith was already in the room she came from, where she was held captive to the machine. She tried to saw through the cords around the box, but the effort was wasted. They were impenetrable. Craig bashed the steel box. The connections didn't even dent or harm the surface.

Edith was frustrated. "This is bullshit!"

Craig cut her off. "Let's search the place out. This isn't getting us anywhere. This thing has a power source. We can destroy it."

She was the first out of the room, finally embracing the idea, and Craig was fast at her heels.

The Krone mansion tour began.

the bASement

he bASement StAIRweLL was the same cherry oak color as the floors upstairs, but a rubber mat was placed over each step. The rubber was dented and scraped, a lot of heavy objects lifted up and down these stairs. The mother-of-pearl walls were marked up as well, black scuffs, and dents, and minor scrapes. The stairs winded down for two stories. There was no light source so far down, and they were descending into pitch. He grew stiff, anticipating somebody grabbing him. The shadows played tricks on his eyes, and he pictured forms bending and walking toward him. He held fast to the rail for support, steadfast and braced for an attack.

"You still there, Craig?"

Edith was beside him, practically hip to hip.

A hollow breath. "Yeah."

Their words echoed, traveling down a far-reaching corridor. The air turned colder. It also contained substance. The air was heavy. The smell was faint, and his nostrils worked overtime to identify it. Iron. Copper. Expired meat.

"It smells dead," she complained. "Should we be going down here?"

"Whatever or whoever's down here will come after

us eventually, whether we're hanging out in the kitchen or coming after them upstairs. Besides, I don't hear anything."

The stairs ended. Craig almost tripped, overcompensating his last step. He touched a bare wall. It was ice cold like metal.

Edith reached out to him, clamping her hand on his forearm so hard it almost pushed him up against the wall. "I don't like it here."

"Just relax. I'm here. It's best to keep your ears open. Listen."

He was convinced the walls were steel. Condensation formed on sections. The bad smell increased in potency. Edith was correct. It smelled dead. Death was near, and none if it was imaginary.

The corridor was long and continuing. He kept walking. He was now in pure darkness, the color of moonless woods. He realized how exhausted he was. His eyelids wanted to close. It was an effort to force them open. The drumming of his heart, the climbing of his pulse, and the break of sweat and the cooling of that sweat kept his fatigue at bay. The sandwich he ate digested painfully in his stomach.

Craig regretted not taking a drink of the scotch.

Edith bickered, "How long does this fucking hall go on for?"

"I'm not sure. *Shhh*. Keep listening."

Was the corridor long, or were they just taking short strides? She reached out for him again. She breathed loud through her mouth, panting. She was panicking.

Then she suddenly fled the other way. "I can't do this—I'll wait upstairs!"

He reached out for her and missed. "Wait!"

There was no stopping her. Her steps were tinny against the floor. They faded softer and softer until they were gone altogether. He was alone in the dark. Craig reached out for the wall, his only compass. And that's when his finger graced a light switch.

Craig turned it on, an instinct. The corridor was flooded with white light. It reflected off the stainless steel walls so white it was purple, and he was temporarily blinded. He shielded his face and waited. Moments later, he adjusted to the harsh beams. There was one long fluorescent panel channeling down the hall's ceiling. Underfoot, the floor was still the same wood with that strip of rubber.

"What in the hell is this place?"

"Who in God's name knows?" A hand touched his back.

"Ah—Jesus Christ!" He backed against the wall, raising the rolling pin. "Stay back—back!"

Edith yipped, shielding her head in case the weapon came down to bash her. "Oh, I'm sorry—sorry!"

Craig's pulse pounded so hard he clasped his neck to subdue his racing nerves. He sucked in breaths and kneeled down to allow the blood to rush to his head. Edith patted his back. "I'm so sorry, Craig."

He replied, "You—scared—the—poop—out—of—me."

"I noticed the lights came on, and I waited at the edge of the stairs for you. I got so excited, I didn't think about warning you I was coming."

His breathing calmed. He started the search again. Down the hallway, two steel doors looked back at them. Craig didn't hesitate. He ran to them, praying they would open. He wanted answers about the machine as much as he wanted the damn thing pummeled.

He reached out for the door and pressed his hands against the steel bar to open it.

Edith gasped and shielded her eyes.

Craig kept his stare glued ahead of him.

UPSTAIRS

edith pounded her fists against the doors. "You're kidding me."

The door wouldn't budge. There was no window or peephole to see through to the other side. They were locked out of the room.

She huffed. "The smell's coming from that room. Surely there's something important behind there."

He slammed his wooden roller against the door, releasing his disappointment. The attempt was as ridiculous as it was fruitless. "Maybe the locks are automated. I don't see a keyhole anywhere. This place is secure."

She shrugged her shoulders. "So what do we do now?"

"Upstairs. It's the next best option. We could still find a way out. Perhaps there's a window without bars. It'd be a jump. I'm guessing it's a two-story drop. You could turn an ankle or break a leg. The risks aren't worse than staying here. We're in agreement, I'm sure."

Edith nodded. Her mouth was slightly open, on the verge of words. She wanted a better plan. Craig considered it lucky Dr. Krone or Rachael hadn't located them. There wasn't a bend of a wooden beam or even the house settling. He hated the deep silence, being so quiet he could hear his ears ring. Edith wore a disgruntled face. The place loomed around them like a prison ward.

"The machine turned our best memories into nightmares," he began to speak for the sake of talking. "It reiterated the fact my dad was a huge asshole to my mom. He cheated on her on a regular basis. Perhaps there's a disease for chronic libido. My dad would be the poster child. I didn't really bond with him either. The closest he ever got was when I joined the Boy Scouts. Two weeks into attending meetings, we went on a weekend campout. My dad ended up punching out the scout master. I guess the man made an off-the-cuff remark about how he slept around on my mom, and he bloodied his nose. No charges were pressed, but my days as a Boy Scout were over."

Edith narrowed her eyes and busted out laughing. "Your dad sounds like the assholes I've dated. Over-macho and dicks ready for discharge."

She leaned into his shoulder and muffled her amusement. "Let me put it like this, I've punched a lot of men in the private area in my time. I know it hurts, so damn it, I take advantage. I guess God figured men were assholes, and they needed an off switch."

He laughed so hard it hurt. "Are we sure we want back out there? I'm unemployed. I'll have to look for a job. Jesus, I've been a snowplow man, I've worked performing oil changes at a Jiffy Lube, I've been a fucking janitor mopping up kids' puke with kitty litter and a dustpan, and I was most recently a garbage man. I was fired for singing on the job—literally. My coworkers didn't like the song 'Born in the USA.' I guess being drunk and missing half the garbage on my routes had nothing to do with it. I puked on my boss's desk when he fired me. That bastard won't forget Craig Horsy."

She gave him a high-five. "Good for you. But you're a lightweight. I worked in a coalmine when I was sixteen. I put up with old men looking at my ass and shaping my tits through my uniform. And I was actually a security guard for a time, guarding storage units for overstocked retail stores. I broke into one of the compartments, stealing cigarettes and beer—oh, and a television and boom box. Of course, I was fired. Oh, I've cleaned the floors of a hospital. I sanitized patient rooms and washed dirty linens. That was a shitty job. But I'd do anything for those three girls. They're everything. I could wade knee-deep in shit for eight dollars an hour, and it wouldn't matter."

"I'm changing a few things when I escape this place," he said, pouring his heart out to her. "I seriously have to have a chat with my mom. I have to know if she cheated on Dad—and if so, good for her. She deserves happiness. And Alice . . . "

"Who's Alice?"

"She's an old friend. The machine put her in the mix. I'll put it this way, I left her at a time when she needed me the most. There are so many things I wanted to say to her, but it's been years. I didn't have the guts to apologize to her, but now . . . "

"You don't have to tell me. We've both experienced enough heartache." She stepped forward, continuing to search the mansion for an escape. "Let's go upstairs, like you said. We'll find something, and if not, we'll watch our asses and figure out a better plan."

He led the two-person expedition. The trek was easier now that the corridor was lit. Craig peered behind them again into the basement, checking for anything that could come out at them. The double doors were still shut. The barriers contained secrets, but for now, it was best to move on. The authorities could dismantle the property and the machine. He wanted nothing to do with it now that he was free of the damned machine.

Edith extended the knife, ready to plunge it into a throat. He clutched the rolling pin. His stance was absent of the promise of violence. A blunt object had little sway over the unknown, especially in Dr. Krone's mansion.

They walked up the stairs, the rubber mat absorbing the impact of their steps. Upstairs, the kitchen and the living area were still unoccupied. He kept his eyes on the upstairs staircase. Each stair was draped in darkness. The lights were off upstairs. He sighed, frustrated he would be walking down a blind alley.

"This is it," he said. "Are you okay with this?"

"We have to do it, but I don't have to like it."

"That's the spirit."

She was eager to complete the staircase, and he lagged behind, having to double his strides to keep up. He didn't want to be alone in this place. The darkness hid Edith, but her general outline was visible.

The upstairs area was set up in a large square. The window on the end of the hall revealed it was nighttime. He also noticed the steel bars over the window.

"Fucked again," Edith spat. "We can't catch a break."

That left them one choice. "We have to hunt the two of them down before they find us."

"Are we the only two victims in this mansion? Maybe there are more of us here. Why would there only be two of us?"

He reached for the nearest door, curious by what she said. "Then let's open these doors and find out."

The nearest door was unlocked. Opening it, he stared into a black box. He traced the wall with his hand for the switch. Once it flickered on, he recognized the room.

the wAItIng Room

he **WAS ACROSS** from the door painted into the wall. The fake door in the waiting room. Dr. Krone's study was wide open, but it was missing the man himself. The fish tank's aeration device hummed, the cichlids oblivious to the things happening around them. He kicked open the receptionist's door.

Inside, there was simply a chair, a small refrigerator, and a pile of *Cosmopolitan*, *Elle*, and *People* magazines. The room stated the obvious—this wasn't a psychiatrist's office. How many people had slept on that plastic-covered couch unknowing of what demise was in store for them?

Craig kicked the coffee table over. "How long has this been going on? I know Dr. Krone and his dad kidnapped victims from the asylum, but what about random people on the streets? I relived it on the machine. He kidnapped me from my apartment. I was so confused, I played into his scenario."

"It's not your fault. We're victims, and they're the criminals. Anybody could wind up here. This was definitely well planned."

"That it was!"

Gun smoke clouded the room. The pound of the

bullet was deafening, and Craig swore he thought his heart stopped a full three seconds before ticking again. Edith was shot in the chest. She landed on the floor, losing her stance, and she cupped the blood that spilled from her chest wound. It glowed a violent neon, the bleeding red hole a bubbling geyser.

Rachael clutched onto a smoking Desert Eagle pistol. She wielded it like a practiced gunner. "Stay where you are, Mr. Horsy."

He kneeled down to Edith and cradled her in his arms. She gurgled on blood. Her lungs were filling up. Draining whiter and whiter, the life in her flesh was seeping out the bullet hole. Desperate eyes froze on him. Fix it, they begged, make the bleeding stop.

She edged him close to her lips, holding him by the collar. The whisper was barely audible, like a tickle to the skin. "*Find Alice and make it up to her . . . whatever it is you did wrong . . . make it up to her.*"

Her eyes rolled into the back of her head. One final breath expelled, her body sagged into itself, and she was dead. Dead for real. Dead for good.

Rachael took over the situation, motioning with the pistol. "Stand up and step away from the body. The bitch doesn't matter now." Her eyes narrowed on the corpse. "We can still use her brain."

He stiffened at the image of Edith's head being opened and her brain removed by Dr. Krone. "Why do you need her brain?"

She raised the gun to the level of his head. "You have no use for that information." A crooked smile wormed across her lips. Whatever she was thinking, it involved him. "It won't be long before this place is bustling with activity. You're a danger to us, Craig, and I'm glad I caught you in time. Our imaginations run wild, and yours will too. The doctor will be pleased. He wanted you alive."

"And why not Edith? She's a good person, and you fucking shot her."

"She's pitiful," Rachael said with disappointment drawn across her face. "Edith's another sob story. Too many children, not enough money, too much drugs and alcohol, who gives a shit? Her memories aren't entertaining, but Dr. Krone did appreciate the time in her life where she gave blowjobs for twenty bucks. She was nineteen at the time. He saved that memory." She shook her head, though she enjoyed the thought. "Pervert."

"Saved that memory, what do you mean?"

"You don't know shit, and it'll stay that way." She was irritated. He'd disturbed their plans for tonight—whatever their "imaginations running wild" meant. "I'm hooking you back up to the machine."

"Where's Dr. Krone?"

"He's resting." She muttered it in annoyance. "Fat ass wears out after so many hours on the machine. He's asleep. He can't wake up, he's that zonked out. The machine overheats. That's why the power shorted. Now, the device is recharging, and once it's recharged, the party begins." Her eyes were wide. "All the work pays off. It only happens once a week. We've collected so many memories. Only the best ones we keep."

Craig's skull ached. He was exhausted. The machine tasked the body and the mind and left both depleted. But he didn't have the luxury of sleep or relief. Blood stained his hands, and Edith was a corpse at his feet. That'd be three children without a mother.

"Now come with me," Rachael instructed, keeping one hand extended with the gun. She fished out a filled syringe from her white smock with her free hand. "It's easy. I poke you with this, and that's all you have to do."

"You're not a real nurse, you bitch." His blood pressure boiled. His skin flushed red. Rachael was startled by the looks he cast her. "You want to steal my memories, huh? It's great Dr. Krone finds my mind worthwhile to excavate. Then what? He'll steal my brain and leave me for dead? Why do you want our brains? Are you afraid to tell me?"

"It's dangerous for you to know too much." Fear weighed her words. "You have no idea what risks we're taking with you up and walking around. Stop asking questions. You can't possibly comprehend our work, so stop trying."

"You won't shoot me." It burst out of him in an explosion of words. "I have something to live for and you won't take that away from me!"

She was shaken by the outburst and backed up three steps, her confidence vanishing. She dropped the gun and waved her hands in defeat, begging him, "No—don't, Craig. I'm sorry. Put it down, okay? I'll let you go—listen to me!"

He was confused until his anger subsided enough to notice that he was clutching his father's Browning shotgun.

There was no decision-making process.

He pulled the trigger.

Rachael's feet lifted from the floor, thrown like a weightless doll into the wall behind her. Her torso was rendered into upturned clothing and flesh. Through the lifting haze of smoke, she coughed and belched.

She peered up at him, her eyes half slits. Blood streamed down both sides of her lips. "You'll never escape. You're a fool." She sneered hard. *"Soon you'll be dead . . . but it'll be much worse than death . . . "*

He was frightened at the amount of blood that spilled from her torso. She lived only ten more seconds, then she was dead, as limp as Edith's corpse. He stood in a room with two corpses. And before he realized it, the Browning had vanished.

the Room

he Refused to hold up in the waiting room a moment longer. He couldn't stand so much death. Real death. He murdered somebody, and though it was in self-defense, he'd still ended a life.

You had to, he reasoned to himself, hurrying through the doorway that led back into the darkened hallway. *Edith's dead and that could've been you. This is beyond a compromising situation. You've got memories coming to life, your wife coming back from the dead, and you've escaped certain death by a thread. Consider yourself lucky to be alive at all.*

Rachael's guarded explanation disturbed him, mentioning the machine overheating and how it was recharging. Once it was charged, she said a party would begin, and he couldn't help but think aloud, "'Only the best memories' . . . what the hell is she talking about?"

He finally stepped into the hallway, getting nowhere with ruminations about a machine he knew so little about. Entering the narrow hall, he checked every shadow for a looming person or persons. Surely Dr. Krone had heard the shotgun blast.

"All the work pays off. It only happens once a

week. We've collected so many memories . . . only the best ones . . . "

He rushed the nearest window and yanked back on the steel bars, attacked by a surge of panic. They wouldn't budge. Shaking in fear, pondering what the real Dr. Krone would do to him—in all probability, the doctor would strap him back onto the machine and further raid his mind—he slid down the wall onto his butt, losing all sensation in his body, overwhelmed by the fact he had no idea where to turn next.

Moments dragged on, and he stared down the darkened hallway. The eventless minutes served to ease his nerves, and he recollected himself. Getting up off the ground, forcing himself to walk in a silent skulking mode, he became proactive. Perhaps one of the doors was a way out, he thought, and began checking. After two, each of them being locked, he arrived at the final door on this side of the house. He kept listening for movement, failing to drop his guard. Dr. Krone was hidden in the mansion somewhere, he kept repeating to himself.

"The door," he whispered, focusing on the barrier again. "Just check it."

He turned the cold brass knob, and opening it inch by inch, darkness greeted him on the other side. He listened. Craig searched for a light switch, and after two seconds of laborious ticking, the overhead fluorescent bulbs blinked on. He closed and locked the door behind him, happy to create another barrier between him and the doctor.

The room itself was a conference room. His eyes roamed the room and found a long pine table and five leather rolling chairs on each side. A screen was pulled down at the opposite wall and a video projector on a cart stood right next to him. Five file cabinets were lined at the wall to the left of him. The object that caught his eye and reeled him in was the shelf of VHS tapes.

"This man can't keep up with the times. Hasn't this guy heard of DVD?"

Labels were slapped on the sides with people's names, hundreds of names. They were victims of the machine, his educated guess. The scope of Dr. Krone's work was staggering. He checked the shelf for his name, but thinking clearly, it was too soon for him to be catalogued. Rachael said they weren't finished with him yet. In five days, she'd said, and the machine recorded the best memories.

Edith's name wasn't on the shelf either. Their escape put them behind schedule, he supposed.

The bottom of the shelf, that row of tapes weren't labeled. He picked one up, sizing it up for content. Would he be watching the equivalent of a snuff film or somebody's innermost thoughts?

"You have to know," he muttered, blowing out a breath of pensive air. "How else can I understand? You didn't perform these sick procedures. You don't get off on this shit."

He slid the VHS from its sleeve, making his decision. The inside was also absent of a label except for the number 3/10/81 scrawled in magic marker.

"1981," he whispered. "The Krones have been at this for decades."

He guided the tape into the player, hitting play, and then turning on the projector device, he backed up a number of steps. A blue box formed on the screen, and then the image played out. It was Dr.

Krone's father. He was half the weight of his son, and he wore a more determined face.

"Somehow, the machine can deliver light through the retinas," he explained, sitting on a stool in front of the camera. "The needles through the skull stimulate nerve pulses called 'action potentials.' These action potentials stimulate ion channels and transporters. These carry an electric charge to command the brain. I've manipulated these channels to tap into the mind, memories, and thought processes. Once I deliver light through the eyes, we should see an image. I can use the computer to command the brain to play a specific memory. The brain has databanks of information, and I shall reference them like a library catalogue."

The camera pivoted around, and he caught a man for a blink's duration who Craig assumed was Dr. Krone.

Craig muttered, "The doctor was using his son as his assistant."

A man was strapped to the machine, an exact replica of the one Craig was on earlier. But this time a different device was strapped to his head. The crown of needles was fixed on his skull. The crown was suspended in the air by steel prongs attached to the ceiling. The crown was a rough prototype.

Craig studied the man's eyes, and it took him moments to really see what had been done to them. The eyes themselves had been removed. The sockets were hollow and surrounded by pink orbital tissue, scooped clean. The lens of a camera was inserted into each eye. It was fixed in place by thinly cut swatches of duct tape along the edges of the sockets. The victim's mouth was also sealed with duct tape. The man's head had been shaved down to the scalp, the patient sweating in thick beads and moaning in terror, but it was low and defeated, the victim strung out for so long that voicing his survival was futile.

"I have attached a camera's lens in each eye," Dr. Krone's father explained. "I'll flip on the switch, and I plan for an image to play out onto the wall. Daniel, flip off the light switch and turn on the lens. We'll see his thoughts. Keep your fingers crossed, boy."

Steps resounded in the background. The lights went out. Another switch was flicked and sparks issued in the background. The lens brightened inside the man's eyes. For a split second, Craig could view the inside of his brain through the lens, the gray mass magnified. The piece of meat constricted, glistening and wet.

"The machine opens up ion channels in the brain and increases the electrical impulses delivered to the brain. Memories come alive this way. It's happened before for the past fifty years. This is nothing new. Now that I've fixed it and tweaked the beast, it'll do more than replicate memories for those who get hooked up to it. It'll make memories flesh and blood. Flip the switch, Daniel!"

The patient grunted, though his mouth was covered. His face was lit up with intense white light, like bolts of lightning, the golden rays of heaven Craig experienced days ago. Moments later, the man went limp, the machine surging to its fullest potential, but the images Dr. Krone Sr. promised failed to play on the screen.

"Damn it, this didn't work! I fixed it. This is the six hundredth time I've tried this!"

And then Dr. Krone Sr. froze, and Dr. Krone

turned the camera, gasping, his hands trembling at the sight he captured. There stood the man from the machine. He was wearing a red polo shirt and chino pants. He also had long flowing brown hair and a quickly fading smile. The man had been beaming before he looked around confused. "*W-where am I?*"

Dr. Krone Sr. shook his head in disbelief. "He's real." Stepping closer to him, he said to his child, "You're recording this, right?"

"Yes, of course."

The background slowly came into better focus, the camera operator an amateur. Bodies were lined up along the wall side by side dressed in straightjackets, sitting in a position where their legs were spread out on the floor, their backs against the wall. They were wrapped in plastic, see-through body bags. Rotten, fetid faces matched the freshly dead.

Craig thought, *The stink downstairs. Christ, this happened in the basement. No wonder the door was locked.*

The man absorbed the room in horror, and he kept turning slowly in place, finding something else new to be disgusted by during each passing moment. "Who are you people?"

Dr. Krone Sr. touched the man's face, and the man jerked away, horrified at his presence. "How do you feel?"

The man blasted at him, "I'm fine—other than the fact I'm here! What the fuck is wrong with you people? Who killed these people? It wasn't you, was it?"

"Take note," Dr. Krone Sr. dictated, pointing at the patient. "Patient is flesh and blood. He's nothing of his former self. This is Gregory Camp before his mental illness. Now, I can dissect his mind for the cause. He can be cured and become a healthy member of society."

"I'm not mentally ill." Gregory raised his voice. "I want to leave. Where's the way out? And don't touch me again. I want nothing to do with you sick people."

Gregory bound across the room, quickly putting it together that they wouldn't let him leave. He dodged the bodies on the wall, tripping, dodging, and crying out whenever he touched one. Craig counted three dozen corpses, and that was just one corner of the room. The man frantically tried the doors and none of them worked. "You can't keep me h—!"

Bam!

The gunshot struck the man's head, his nose caving in the middle, and a fat bloom of gore sprayed the intricate damage against the wall. Thrown back, smacking the wall, and landing over the other dead bodies, the man lay silent and oozing blood.

Dr. Krone Sr. met the camera with a smoking pistol loosely in his clutches. "Note that the patient still sits in that chair. This other body bleeds on the floor. He's flesh and blood, but now watch this . . . "

The camera followed Dr. Krone Sr. to the actual machine. He punched the keys on the computer monitor on the side compartment of the machine. The device shut down with a gradual diminishing *whuuuuuuuuuuuum*. The lens in the patient's eyes went dark, and then the room went dark as well. Dr. Krone Sr. flipped on the overhead lights, and Gregory's body on the floor was missing, including the blood that spattered the walls.

"This is miraculous." His face lost its vigor and turned solemn. "I can bring back Mom, Daniel. She can be alive again. I'll find a way for me to be safely strapped into the machine. All I have to do is perfect the ocular lenses, and it's a sure win."

Craig turned away from the screen. He needed a breath. The information was swarming him at once. So much he'd seen, and there wasn't a soul to properly explain it to him. He stared at the shelf and counted the blank VHS tapes. "There's no way in hell I'm watching twenty tapes of this twisted shit."

The VHS tape was stopped, and the screen went blank. Craig whipped around, his body clenching, his legs ready to run, his mouth ready to plead with whoever might attack him next, but the intruder beat him to the punch.

"I'll explain everything to you, Mr. Horsy."

Dr. Krone's father stood behind the video projector.

Craig backed up to the other side of the room, creating more space between him and the strange man. He was the same person in the video—lab coat, red fingerprint stains caked along the front, faded beige pants, and a determined and hungry face. Murderously intelligent.

He couldn't speak. The doctor's presence robbed him of words. He simply shook his head and mouthed, "No . . . "

"This is reality, Mr. Horsy, and I am flesh and blood." Dr. Krone Sr. raised his arms and took a slow spin around. "I'm a body, and I've been dead for many years. Amazing, don't you think?"

Craig spat it out, "What the fuck are you talking about? This is murder you've participated in, not a scientific breakthrough."

"But it is a scientific breakthrough. Ah, I've

skipped ahead of the explanation. Forgive me." He walked to the corner with a metal pushcart stocked with glass bottles of booze. He poured himself one and raised an empty glass at Craig. "You want a drink?"

He shook his head, refusing to believe this conversation was happening, but what choice did he have?

"You're persistent—you and that woman, what's her name? She broke free of the restraints on her own. She's the first to escape, besides you." His face hardened. "You see, the machine turns itself off before it overloads. The power goes out, and the patient usually can't move or doesn't move. But that lady, she's one tough bitch. We only have three machines. I don't think the house can support anymore electricity use. The rest of the mansion usually sits in the dark to conserve. You're the first to ever escape for this long."

"Hurray for me," Craig snapped. "You realize you're a murderer, right? I've seen you in action. You steal mental patients from the asylum, and now you're kidnapping innocent people from the streets. I take it nobody walks out of here alive either, or cured."

Dr. Krone Sr. poured himself a scotch and drank it straight up. He was more concerned about the drink than Craig's accusations. "This is the first thing I do when I wake. It's the best way to come out of death. A good stiff drink down the hatch."

He was confused. "Wake up from death?"

Dr. Krone Sr. was enjoying the Q&A session. He sipped the scotch contentedly. Patting his belly, he sighed, "Ah, that's better. Yes, I'm dead—remember?

But the brain is a powerful vessel. It doesn't have to die. It has many abilities the human race has yet to decode. My great, great grandfather discovered a special feature of the brain. I've simply harnessed it. Turned it into something worth exploring. My son discovered the soul is in the brain. The soul itself is the electrical charge that occurs when nerve impulses called 'action potentials' command the body to function—to remember, to move, to act, to feel, to hate, to love, and so on. The soul is capable of anything if instructed, including returning to life after death. I am living once again."

He turned his head to the side, trying to read Craig. "I'm not completely alive, but once a week is better than never in eternity, I'll say."

Dr. Krone Sr. poured another drink, determined to catch a buzz. "Death is pitch-black. It's not sleep. There's nothing in death. Oblivion. Expansive black. I fear going back to it. I woke here after a long stay in death. My soul was commanded back to life by the machine, and I've returned once a week since I died of a stroke." With a creeping smile he said, "My son has seen to that."

"So you're essentially a walking corpse. But you're real now. Why not leave the house and experience the world if you're real? I'd go out, so why don't you?"

The doctor closed his eyes and rubbed them. "Ah, that's one feat we haven't mastered. The energy field can only reach so far, maybe half a mile from the house, if that. So I'm stuck here, Mr. Horsy. My son is working on fixing that issue. Once he dies, that's it. Somebody else will have to work the machine to keep me alive. It all hinges on 'action potentials.' You stimulate the right channels in the brain with electricity, the stronger the reaction you receive. "The machine is so powerful, it not only creates these electrical charges, it takes them from you and replicates them on a screen, replicates them in your mind, lets others like my son into others' minds." A malignant smile demurred his face. "The machine also mimics the memories in flesh and blood for a short period of time."

Unable to one-up the man, Craig turned his creation into a joke. "I bet your electricity bill is insane."

Dr. Krone Sr. was disappointed at Craig's lack of appreciation for the profound. "We don't get all of our power from the house. Electricity from nerve impulses, the soul itself, channels much of our power in this residence."

"How did you locate the soul?"

Dr. Krone Sr. rested on one of the leather swivel chairs, feeling tipsy. "The Krone family used to own ten asylums in the Midwest. My son finally sold off the businesses. Our goal originally was to cure insanity, dementia, and just about every mental disorder. I guess Dr. Larry Krone, the first to try in the late 1800s, already knew of the soul. He had forefathers before him who'd operated on fallen or near-dead soldiers during the Civil War and American Revolution. They discovered the nerve impulses and the electrical charges in the brain, the soul at work. The truth is the machine had already been built for decades. You see, other American asylums were very much interested in getting inside disturbed minds as well.

"The insane are the perfect guinea pigs. The families leave their loved ones behind once they're deemed incurable. Hundreds of thousands of victims of mental illness suffer this fate. Writing the *DSM*, shock therapy, drugs, none of it added up to shit as far as cures go. Treatments subdued the beast, but it didn't send the beast packing. We wanted the infirm to live a normal life. This is the price for that privilege. The machines were banned from use and destroyed, after, let's say, certain unwanted outcomes." He furrowed his eyebrows up and down. "But somehow, the Krones got ahold of the last prototypes. Three machines. I've had to spend years tweaking the machines to do as I wish. I got them to work again.

"At first, the machine simply projected images onto a screen. Memories. I wanted to physically enter the mind and encounter the mental illness myself. So many patients have been hooked up to the machine over the years, thousands, and it's added up to something miraculous. The databanks alone are so prolific. The electricity, the souls were collected in mass numbers up to the point the machine gained abilities of its own."

His booming voice shook Craig to the core, the news shouted from a confident maniac. "*How else do you think I'm flesh and blood after death?* This machine made it happen on its own. I'm real again. I was taken from death and put here. My soul was copied and is exactly as the original—it looks the same, thinks the same, deduces and reasons the same, but I'm not real. I am real, though." He waved his hand at Craig not to ask. "It's confusing. The living soul is not aware of itself, but the dead soul is free to venture into other places if it can be awakened and brought back to reality. The soul, the brain, it has so much potential yet to be discovered.

"That's why we've taken to kidnapping people from the streets. It's been difficult to obtain enough mental patients after my son sold the business. He's dedicated his time to locating people like you. People with rich minds to tap. Those troubled and on the verge of criminality. Admit it, you're amazed. What I'm telling you is revolutionary."

"Tell me something, Doctor. What success have you had?"

The question interrupted his proud reverie of success. "How do you figure?"

"You wanted to cure mental illness. Well, have you?"

The question lingered, and floated, and dissipated. Dr. Krone Sr. motioned to speak, but he stopped himself. The man was puzzled. Nobody had pointed out the flaws of his reasoning before. It also occurred to Craig their guinea pig picking pool was comprised of the insane. The souls charging this machine were disturbed, irrational, violent, and terrified.

"That's why my memories were turned against me," he said as a private revelation. "And that's how come your son is talking to my friends and loved ones and convincing them to conspire against me. That's why my dead wife tried to murder me. And the walking corpses at the mausoleum, it makes sense. You've allowed pandemonium to take over science."

Dr. Krone Sr. was clearly offended. He clutched his empty glass as if to chuck it at Craig. "Maybe you're right. But maybe it's because I don't want to share what we've found with the rest of the world. Nobody would understand. The machine would be trashed, and forgotten, and banned like it was half a century ago. I've made many friends, been to many foreign countries, have had sex with thousands of women, and I've experienced the world after death."

Pleased with the sound of his own words, his mouth quivered as if on the verge of weeping. "It's worth every drop of blood shed to reach this point. I've lived so many people's memories. Sadly, the patient does die after the fifth day strapped to the machine. The soul is completely removed and turned to energy for the machine. Each soul is catalogued into a computer database. I can type the dead up, and they can be flesh and blood again once a week, *if I so chose*. Once the machine has enough soul energy built up, it can do anything.

"Once a week that machine rests. It takes stock of the new souls, and when it comes back on—and you'll hear it—for twelve hours, my son can program that computer hooked to the device to play out any memories he wants. Flesh-and-blood memories, Mr. Horsy. Your memories. Anything in your mind can be recreated by the machine. You've been strapped in for three days. That's long enough for the machine to know an awful lot about you."

His smile was threatening. "And the memories in your head were harsh. We've tweaked your past a bit. Since you escaped, it's the least we could do to send you off according to the trouble you've been to us. But I have a feeling I won't bring you back to life again once you're dead. Your soul will be lost forever." He pretended he had Craig's soul in his hand, and he dropped it, looking around, and he couldn't find it. "You'll be oblivious in oblivion."

The glimmer in his eyes shined like a diamond. "We like to have fun. Being strapped to the machine for so long, we can hear your family and friends cry for you. They have things they want to share with you. Unfinished business. Why not let them have their way with you? It'll be therapeutic."

"Wait, my memories will come to life?" Craig was confused, watching the walls, the doors, and listening hard for what the man was talking about, what could come out and attack him at any moment. "No, you can't do that. Don't do this to me. Don't bring them back. What can I do to convince you to stop this?"

Dr. Krone Sr. stole the scotch bottle. He exited the room, content with what he shared with Craig, but before the door closed, he whispered, *"You'll have visitors soon, and I'll be watching."*

Lake Jacomo

The blink occurred shortly after the door closed. Craig was wrapped up in below-freezing winds that flanked him in all directions like a whirlwind of sharp stabbing ice. He was standing on Lake Jacomo's surface, but he was soon thrown off balance, landing on his palms and knees. Standing up, he scanned the area, though the air was hazy white with moving snow. The distance was impossible to penetrate by the naked eye.

He shouted over the wintry din, "Where are you, Krone?"

The son of Dr. Krone was suddenly behind him. He stood unaffected by the weather. Dr. Krone was covered in beads of sweat, his expression radiant despite the fact his eyes were heavy with purple bags.

"Why am I here?" Craig demanded over the winds. He reached out to seize the man's collar, but the burst of snow between them thwarted the attempt. "Tell me right now!"

Dr. Krone's boisterous laughter echoed throughout the empty lake and cut into his eardrums. "I know my father has spoken with you. He gave you a bit of a history lesson. But I wanted to let you know firsthand that I control who comes out of the machine and who doesn't. I've been hooked up to the machine so long, I'm aligned with it. *We are one.*"

He recalled the incident inside the fake waiting room. Rachael was dead. "You know I can kill you."

"Are you referring to Rachael?" He shrugged his shoulders, easily dismissing the loss. "You did me a favor. She's a stupid bitch who I used to need to help me run my affairs. She enjoyed the machine so much, she wasn't afraid of it. Rachael was captivated by it. She didn't care anymore that we'd kidnapped her. She was a hitchhiker, actually. I picked her up on a back road. It turns out she was fired from a decent job. She was a radiologist. She also had a nasty Demerol habit. She'd steal it from the pharmacy wing of the hospital. Of course she was caught, and she had nowhere to go after that—rent due, boyfriend abusive without his Demerol habit quenched, and one thing comes to another, she ran away from her problems and I found her. But now she's dead. I can run my own affairs just fine."

Dr. Krone studied him for a moment, doubling his voice over the battling winds. "You used to think I was an amazing man. I showed you old memories. You loved seeing Katie. You got to sleep with Susan. You told off your father. And your mother, you found out about her extra-marital affair with Parker Stevens. This machine is magnificent, are you not convinced?"

"I won't answer your questions!" Craig adjusted his footing so he wouldn't tip over onto the ice again. "This is your pleasure machine. You live through others because your life is so boring. It's an awful excuse for murder. And if I hadn't escaped, you would've killed me already. This is all for your entertainment. Your soul machine is corrupt. You've filled it with the criminally insane, and you don't even realize it."

Dr. Krone's eyes held no understanding of what Craig had said. Like father, like son, he thought. They were both controlled by the demented souls of the machine. They exploited minds, lived through other people's memories, and enjoyed tearing people's lives apart.

"The machine's recharging, right? How come your father visited me? How come you're visiting me like this in one of my memories?"

"I am asleep," Dr. Krone replied, blinking snow out of his eyes, "and the machine is on a sort of hibernation mode. My father is always the first to awake. And I'm always awake in some form or another."

The hairs on Craig's arms rose. Static electricity. The doctor harnessed souls within himself. He was electrically charged. He had the power of the machine in his body. What other powers did this man wield?

He sensed Krone wasn't completely at the helm. The souls were numerous and powerful. He'd been overtaken by them in some fashion.

"You're not all there in the head," Craig said, reiterating his thoughts. "You're influenced, controlled by other people."

Dr. Krone's smile was a lashing against his back. "*Yes.*"

"You don't have a soul of your own, do you?"

"No—*I have thousands!*"

"You've had too much of that electricity run through you." He berated the man, though he was terrified of him. "So this is it? You're going to release my memories against me in flesh and blood? I still don't understand why."

"We do this every week. Our favorites places, our favorite people, our favorite memories, I type them out on the computer, and it happens. But this week, since nobody like you has escaped before for this long, we're going to watch what happens to you in the flesh. That's not to say I won't participate.

"You are dangerous." The doctor gave Craig a mean glance. "You've used your mind to aid you. Edith did too. The machine grants special abilities once you've been hooked up to it so long. The machine enhances your mental abilities. You just have to know how to harness that ability. Keep in mind, you may have that ability—and this will make your death truly interesting—but I have so much more I can use against you. You'll never survive."

Craig stared into Dr. Krone's eyes, and he sensed thousand of eyes glaring back at him, sizing him up, each set planning his demise in their own special way.

The doctor issued a simple warning, "Listen for the machine . . . "

bRAndøn hoRSy

hIS body RetuRned to the conference room. He moved about the room, locking the two doors, and then barricading the chairs against them; he prayed they would hold. There were no windows in the room. He was as safe as he could be in Dr. Krone's mansion.

Listen for the machine.

He expected a grumble and then a mechanical hissing. Then what? Would he be visited by Katie, who tried to drown him in his dead child's blood?

Craig did his best to shrug the thoughts and relax. Impossible, but he tried for the sake of his heart not exploding in his chest.

Dr. Krone standing there on Lake Jacomo, it wasn't the same man he witnessed before. Even Dr. Krone's father wasn't there in the head. Their main objective was terror and torture, and he was the only sane person alive in this mansion-turned-killing floor.

He missed Edith. He needed her. She was his salvation, his backbone. He wouldn't be alive now if it weren't for her bravery. He'd be strapped to the machine until day five, and his soul would've been removed from his brain via electricity and recorded as nerve impulses—action potentials, whatever hoopla they drummed up to turn their madness into scientific fact—and he'd ultimately be catalogued into the computer and his body wrapped up in a plastic body bag like he'd seen on that VHS tape.

Listen for the machine.

He couldn't take the waiting. Craig checked the cupboard where Dr. Krone's father removed the bottle of scotch. That's when he noticed he wasn't alone anymore. The cupboard had been opened. Someone else had beaten him to the punch.

The machine had kicked on.

Whuuuuuuuuuuum.

A wave of unnatural heat traveled about the room in a hot breeze, even filtering up from the floorboards. Clods of dust rained from the ceiling. Tapes from the shelves were shaken loose. The foundation rattled, jostled from every angle. Craig believed the house would tip over, the force was so powerful. Static electricity was discharged over the room, zapping everything, arching and bending in the shape of branching arteries. He yipped at each low-voltage branch that shocked him. After cursing and curling up into a ball and trying to dodge the blue daggers, the machine finally idled to a soft hum.

The house settled.

Getting up, he stared at the man standing at the cupboard. It couldn't be him. Craig denied the vision, but it was real, and now he had to believe it, like it or not. The man was fishing through the shelf, searching and then claiming a high ball glass and a bottle of vintage whiskey.

"Dad, is that you?"

Brandon visibly trembled. He was on edge, seeking relief by downing a healthy dose of whiskey.

He scanned the room, his eyes wet from crying, though the tears were shed in the name of terror.

Craig's voice caused him to jump, and Brandon temporarily raised his defenses, then relented, "Oh, it's just you. Have you seen your mother?" His eyes darted to the doors. "Is she around? Is she here? Have you seen her? Answer me, son, for God's sake."

Brandon reached out and shook him hard, then he slammed Craig up against the wall. "Boy, speak up! Is—she—around?" Degrading into a coward, he mustered under his breath, "*I must know.*"

"No, no," Craig spat it out. "I-I've boxed us in. It's safe. Nobody's here except us. It's me and you, Dad."

The man was unconvinced. "I don't think so. Nowhere is safe. Your mom's here somewhere. She's after me. Maybe you too. She's after the both of us, I know it."

Brandon inspected the blockaded doors. He closed his eyes and breathed like he'd been running for a long time. Craig looked at his dad and remembered the man had been dead for over a year. Craig had to fact check his father by asking, "What month is it, Dad?"

Brandon thought on it briefly, confused by the question. "It's March. Mom and I were thinking about congratulating you on your new job. A garbage man doesn't pay bad wages. It's guaranteed work. People will always have shit to throw away." He added in confidence, "Tina thinks you need somebody to talk to. You haven't dated. She thinks you haven't been able to move on after, you know, Katie died."

"I haven't," he easily admitted. "It's all my fault. I shouldn't have used my shitty car to drive us to the hospital. And if I would've run for help sooner, she wouldn't have bled to death."

Brandon placed his hand on his shoulder, every word laden with whiskey. "Your guilt is full of 'what-ifs.' The storm wasn't your fault. And you've used your car to drive to work every day. Cars break down randomly, whether old or new. Stop blaming yourself. You're in your prime. You need to get out there and meet people. Find happiness again."

Craig hugged his father close after hearing those words, and his father was taken aback by the gesture, but he soon returned the affection. The moment was short, but necessary.

"Thanks, Dad."

"I should've said something to you before about Katie." Brandon looked him in the eyes. "It doesn't always come out when you want it to."

No shit. After death is pretty late. "Yeah, I know what you mean."

Craig realized he'd forgotten why Brandon was here until the farthest door to the left was rattled, the knob tested. "*Let me in!*" Tina screeched, slamming her fist against the door. The chairs were knocked apart in moments after the repeated round of shoulder ramming.

They were both paralyzed. Brandon gripped the bottle upside down like a club.

"She's lost it," Brandon said. "She wants to cut me up. Tina wants me dead. I've cheated on her for so long, she'll never forgive me. And I know about Parker, and I don't care. Tit-for-tat, you know. I'm a shitty husband, but I don't deserve to have my throat slit." He turned to Craig with a needy gleam in his eyes. "You have to talk her down. Maybe she'll listen to you. Please try. Save me, Craig. I'll be dead if you don't."

Craig could be a world-renowned negotiator, and it wouldn't help. His mother was convinced Brandon must die, and so he would.

The door was kicked open in one wild ramming motion, tatters and slivers of wood bursting and flying across the room. Tina worked through the pieces of the barricade, swiping each of the axes in her hands to complete her mission, the blades audibly swooshing through the air. She wore a white T-shirt stained in sweat and blood and a pair of black jeans.

She aimed one axe at Brandon, as if mentally carving him up. "There you are."

"Mom, stop!" Craig pleaded, stepping between them. "You must listen. Dad's sorry. He admits he fucked up. But you have to calm down. Put down the axes. Please."

Tina's mouth had completely opened, near the point of breaking the jaw. "*No more apologies. No more bullshit.*"

She hurled the axe at Brandon, forgoing words. Craig ducked, avoiding the incoming weapon that spun handle, blade, handle, blade, handle, blade with a wild fanning of air.

Metal splitting into bone, Brandon was struck mid-sternum.

"*Graaaaaw!*" Brandon landed on all fours, paralyzed, clutching the handle that wouldn't budge. He kept watching Tina, more scared of her than the weapon plunged into his body. "Run, Craig—she'll come for you next! She's lost it. She wants to murder every trace of me. I don't know what's gotten into her. She's not rational. She's psychotic!"

Tina hopped on top of the conference table with a twin clop of leather boots. Brandon wheezed, losing blood and the ability to breathe. Blood funneled between his hands and stained the floor. He reached out to Tina for mercy. His eyes were wild, his mouth cringing in deadly anticipation. "*Forgive me, forgive me!*"

"Parker says you're beyond forgiveness." She twisted the axe handle in her hands. "God's the only one who can save you from your sins. Repent. The time of atonement is now."

She raised her head up in a challenge. "Ask for forgiveness."

Craig clutched onto a chair and threatened to throw it at her. "Put the axe down, Mom!"

He realized how crazy that statement was.

An exaggerated grin played out on her lips, one of malevolence. "Dr. Krone has shown me the truth. You can't lie to me."

"*Dr. Krone*," Craig muttered the name, a curse. "This is all his lies. He's manipulated you, Mom. Divorce the bastard. Yes, he's a jerk, but that's not a reason to plunge an axe into his chest."

A bead of sweat trickled across her lips, her words spraying, "Oh, but it is." She hopped off the table, lunging down, and landed in front of Brandon. He was helpless as she raised the lone axe with both hands and plunged it mercilessly into her husband. *Thack! Thack! Thack!*

Craig reeled as a spectator to the brutal murder, each of her laughs the shrill cackle of a true demented killer. Each hack landed mid-skull cap, splitting it down the middle, the flesh audibly parting, the skull creaking open. Then the last two swings connected on each side of the neck as if she were chopping down a tree from the base. After the blows, Brandon's body and head landed independently, the head rolling across the floor and then banging into the wall.

Tina turned to him, the blood drenching her body sullying her motherly image. "You look a lot like your father, Craig. A part of him is inside of you." Spinning the axe handle, his mother aimed the weapon at him. "I must remove him from you. Then I can love what's left of you."

Tina stepped closer. Craig shut his eyes, desperate to deny what was about to occur. He imagined a knife, the Browning, a flame thrower, but none of it happened no matter how hard he focused.

It's because you don't want to hurt her, you fool.

"Please reconsider this," he begged her, cupping his hands together. "I still love you."

"And I love you enough to remove your father from your body." She licked the blood from the edge of the axe, though she wrinkled her nose after tasting it.

"His blood is vile with the taste of sin. So many women he's bedded, he's never been mine completely. But I'm not living that life anymore. Parker has emboldened me with the Holy Spirit. I'm not a battered and abused wife."

"Put down the axe. This isn't you, Mom. You'd never do this in real life. Can't you see it's not right?"

Brandon's headless corpse twitched. He heard blood squirt from the stump three times and then stop. She relished the sounds. Absorbed it. Tina made a bee-line for Brandon's corpse. She touched her finger to his neck and tasted it and raised her voice in demonstration. "His blood is sweet now. I have freed him of his sins!" She eyed the body and her son, the body and her son. "You see—don't you see now, Craig? He's free!"

The corpse seized Tina's body around the back and forced her close.

Craig sprinted out of the room.

the kItchen

RAIg cRAwLed thRough the wreckage of the blockade and slammed the conference room door shut behind him. There was no way to block it, so he ran, trying the other doors in the hallway, though each of them was locked. He attempted to batter them down with his shoulder without success. The doors themselves felt like concrete. Impenetrable.

The top floor had nothing left for him in regards of salvation. Craig raced for the stairs, taking them down two at a time. The mansion would be a labyrinth of memories. He couldn't hide from them no matter where he ran or hid. His mother had already finished off his father, his only friend in this place. He was beheaded, and he would suffer the same fate soon enough, Craig believed, or worse.

He gripped the handrail so he wouldn't tumble forward. Static electricity crossed his body, channeling up from the wood, and it jolted him five times in a row. *Crackle, crackle, crackle, crackle, snap-pop!*

He met the end of the steps, clutching his chest, pained by the electrical surges traveling through his body. Patches of his arms were burned black and smoking.

The bars over the windows and the door in the living room proved this mansion to be a prison. The kitchen was the only logical place to go. He wasn't sure what happened to his rolling pin from earlier, but he was determined to find a better weapon.

The blink.

Oh shit.

There was no cognitive response to the instant change. The kitchen in the mansion expanded. He was in a restaurant-sized kitchen now. Pots boiled with angel hair pasta, rotini, ravioli, and spaghetti noodles on stovetops. On the counter, pork sausage was cut up into discs about to be fried up in a pan. Craig walked past a dish washing machine that was running, steam and burning hot water pounding within the box. So far, nobody was in the kitchen. Carts were heaped with dirty pots and pans, baking sheets, and kitchen utensils waiting to be cleaned. He feared to speak or to make a sound. And that's when he overheard a muffled plea that resounded from the back of the kitchen. "*Nooooooo!*"

He limited his stride. The noise funneled into the room and echoed from a chamber below. The steel shelves blocked that section of the room. Containers of marinara sauce, pesto, boxed noodles, fresh tomatoes, a medley of spices, and walk-in refrigerators kept his eyes busy. Anybody could be hiding nearby.

He swiped a six-inch chopping blade from the magnetic strip hanging above the ovens. He clutched the weapon and pictured driving it into his enemy and then winced, imagining his mother hacking his father's head off.

Craig sucked in a nervous breath. He checked

behind the shelf of boxed items and caught an open door. A stairway. Firelight flickered with varying intensities upon the wall. There were no other lights on below, only fire.

"*Noooooo! Mmmmmmmmph!*"

He teetered on the first step, nervous after hearing the grating screams. In that moment, he whipped around, checking for his safety, and he discovered the kitchen had vanished. A wall was suddenly pressing up against his back, shifting, inching and pushing him down the steps and eventually urging him through the entry below. Crossing that threshold, the wall left him with no escape. There was no other route but forward.

The sweet scent of firewood—cherry and oak— filled his nostrils. That succulent hint of slow-roasting meat attached itself to the air, though he shivered in the cold. It was near freezing. The walls were frosted despite the fire, crystalline. Smoke billowed up to him, but it didn't cloud the room. There was ventilation circulating from somewhere.

Reaching the end of the stairs, he looked on into a room. Meat hooks hung from the ceiling, rusted and without anything to reflect except orange firelight. Naked bodies were suspended in the air. Four dozen at a quick guess, each pitted through the shoulder blades. The blood had long since been drained from their pale and flaccid bodies. Their heads had been shaved along with their extremities and genitals. The cold lent a blue pigment to the skin.

Another square door glowed past the bodies, the source of the firelight. All he could do was cross the room and face the scene.

"*No—stop—don't kill me!*"

The pleas raged from a new victim. They had to be

victims, he thought. Anybody in this chamber was on the chopping block, including him.

You're going to have to walk through them to the other side. Dr. Krone won't have it any other way. Unless you can walk through walls, forward is the only option.

He cradled the knife he'd stolen by the handle, the blade aimed at the floor. "I know how to use this," he threatened. "Don't make me, because I will."

The bodies took up most of the space. He turned to the side and fitted through a row. He brushed up against the bodies, each cold and stiff. The hooks grinded and squealed at the intrusion. He was halfway into the room, into the bodies. Craig stepped over a drain, and nearly slipped, it being iced over. He gripped a man's torso by both its arms to prevent himself from falling. He looked up and unleashed a startled breath. The head was turned down at him. The eyes were forever open, crusted by ice. The mouth was a slit, the purple tongue within arched as if on the verge of speaking.

Craig shoved, and pushed, and collided into the bodies, frantic to evade the room. The screeching hooks reached a crescendo, everybody coming alive at once. Bodies swung back and forth like laundry on the clothesline. He held his breath to contain his screams. Running forward, then battering through them, he ran through the exit.

"Thank God."

He spoke too soon. His hair was wrenched back. Both feet left the ground, and he was yanked back into the crowd. They were alive, crowing, berating, screaming, threatening, lamenting, and cheering. Muscle fibers audibly broke and stretched to seize and grapple him. Blue faces shifted with delight and excruciating agony. Others coughed up black blood. Thin patches of his scalp were uprooted. Warm blood quickly turned cold, streaming down his face and neck. His feet still hadn't returned to the ground. They gripped him underneath his arms, his torso, his shoulders, and his hands to propel him.

He was punched in the jaw before he could scream for help. He bit his tongue mid-blow, the taste of copper and iron filling his mouth. He swallowed twice, and the blood kept flowing.

The corpses couldn't speak words. The ululations and moans carried with the loudness and bass of a boom box. "*Uuuuuuuunnnnnn*." "*Muuuuuaaaahhh*." "*Guuuuuuuuuuuh*."

His knife clanged to the floor. He was defenseless. A hand was shoved into his mouth. It threatened to snuff his airway and strangle him. Craig had no other option. He clamped down, the force of his bite severing halfway through the ice-cold wrist. The hand removed itself, startled by the bite. "*Muaaaaaah!*"

He slithered from their grips, plopping down onto the concrete. Craig crawled on all fours. Claw marks and bites flared up and down his arms, fresh and flaring up. Continuing forward, banging his arms, and legs, and elbows against the concrete, he crossed the threshold of the room. The firelight glowed feet in front of him, urging him on. He couldn't turn back. The victims were pent-up and enraged. They'd surely tear him to pieces if he drew close enough to them again.

He turned his head up at the man's voice.

"And he arrives," the man spoke with an Italian accent. The words were thick and drawn out and conspiring. "It's the man who skipped out on his bill."

Craig's heart seized. The palpitations nearly drowned out the man talking. *Not him. Jesus Christ, not him.*

Rick Margolia's face was bright orange in the dark room. Behind him was an over-sized pizza oven, but now the racks contained smoldering human bodies. Each was blackened and in the fetal position. Human smoke poured from the front and was sucked up by the fans that chopped above them in the ceiling. He caught Hank Pinzer hog-tied inside another oven with a glass front. He was secured spit-style. A steel rod had been forced through his mouth and out the anus.

Craig blathered, "What the fuck is wrong with you? It's a bill. It's not a human life."

This isn't the real Rick Margolia. He made you wash dishes. He's not a murderer, and he certainly didn't do this to anybody. If Hank Pinzer's here, how many more of Janna Cunningham's friends are here too?

Rick stood between the two ovens and a large wooden table. The corpses of Jack Neilson, Alex Cartman, and the rest of Janna's buddies were chained in place on the table. Glazed dead eyes glinted in the flame's illumination. Stomach cavities were hollowed of organs and crammed with stuffed bell peppers and mushrooms. Flesh was glazed with a brown sugar honey layer. Janna Cunningham was also chained to the far wall. Her prom dress was sodden in sweat and the blood that streamed from her temple where she'd been beaten.

"Why didn't you pay the bill?" she pleaded, breaking down into tears. "He's killed them all. He's killed them all because of you."

Rick unstuck the cleaver from the wood table and aimed it at her. "I thought you were dead." He swung the cleaver through the air as a test. "That can be remedied. *Chop! Chop!*"

Janna's head was hacked from the neck in one hard swing. The body jerked and suffered spasms, the stump firing out jets of rich arterial spray. Rick retrieved Janna's head, the "O" of the anticipation of death engrained on her features. The cook opened the oven with Hank Pinzer's slowly cooking body. Rick opened Hank's arms to coddle Janna's head and closed the door.

"The bitch deserved it." He glowered over Hank's body and Janna's head. "I have to be creative. The tastes of hell are quite unique and hard to satisfy."

The crowd of hanging bodies mewled collectively.

Rick pounded the cleaver's handle into the wall, making a *clong* sound. "Silence, all of you. Your deaths will come soon enough."

Craig observed the floor where the blood of Janna's spurting neck had landed. Her corpse was up against the wall, and he noticed the thin gaps like gutter openings on the ground. They emanated the colors of a smoldering charcoal briquette. A black gargoyle hand reached out and seized ahold of Janna's leg. The body was instantly ripped from the chain shackles at her wrists and legs. A shadowy face marked with bear-trap teeth and owl-yellow eyes sucked on the head's stump and then vanished, yanking the corpse into the pit.

"They're hungry for a feast," Rick cheered, amused at the taking of Janna. "Consider that an appetizer."

Rick grabbed a paint brush and dabbed it against

Bryce Johnson's flesh. "Good old-fashioned butter does a dish good." He added pesto sauce and a lemon glaze over the skin, whistling. "He smells ready for the oven."

Craig had to understand what motives Dr. Krone put into this man in order to save himself. "Why are you doing this?"

"What, cooking your friends?" He pondered the question a moment. "My kitchen works hard. I can't have punk kids ripping me off. This is my dream, and you won't ruin it. I'm setting an example. Dr. Krone gave me a place to be rid of the bodies of those who cheat me, and down they go!" He pointed at the floor. "The opening to hell is below us, and the demons wish to feed. I'm their favorite cook. Dr. Krone helped me discover monsters who could truly appreciate my flavor of food. They're culinary experts in the rites of human flesh."

Rick reached to the wall for an instrument that looked like an ice cream scoop. "Come here. You're the last one I need to take care of. I'll scoop your eyes out first. I'll marinate your brain in a basil cream sauce. Then I'll boil you until your skin peels off, and then I'll steam the muscle tissue for ravioli skin."

Craig was backed into the corner where Janna's body used to be. The creature from the floor reached out, but it missed by an inch, and he shouted, "Damn you, stop walking toward me. Stay the fuck away from me."

You're not hooked up to the machine. You have to have some form of control. Dr. Krone can't manipulate everything, especially you.

With the harsh rip of flesh and click of bone, the room of hanging bodies jerked free from their suspension. Feet clopped in unison. The hunched forms were seconds from entering the room. Their moans escalated at the sight of Craig.

"*Muuuaaaaaah!*"

"*Unnnnnnnnnnn!*"

"*Nuuuuuuuuuuh!*"

"They want to be cooked," Rick announced. "They wish to serve Satan, and they know you wish to stall me from my task."

Craig leapt for the opposite corner of the room. Rick was at the head of the group, the frosted-over bodies behind him. He clicked the scoop and smiled at Craig, "Let me have those eyes, huh? I can prepare you dead or alive, it's up to you."

He closed his eyes. Screaming wouldn't help. Pleading for his life would be a waste of breath.

They were seconds away from towering above him.

The hairs on his arms and head stood on end. Static electricity. The energy of souls translated by the machine and translated by Dr. Krone's commands.

Hands kneaded into his shoulders, arms, and legs, the corpses already upon him. They aimed to drag him into the gutter opening and throw him to the monster. The bear-trap teeth clamped shut with a jarring steel clang, enticed by the prospect of eating Craig. *Cah-rrrrink!* Yellow almond-shaped eyes glowed brighter and more corrosive than the fires in the oven. The leather-black talon hand reached out to claim him.

"I guess I won't need to cook you after all!"

Think about somewhere else. It's like you're still connected to the machine. Think. Save yourself!

The blackened hand dug into his flesh, the talons curling bone-deep. "*Graaaaaaaaah!*"

273

Craig was dragged into the pit. He glanced down at the swirling fires below, thousands of burner jets threatening to sear into him. In seconds, he'd be swallowed up by the inferno.

the kRones

"The cLams And linguini sauce are wonderful, darling."

"Thanks, h—"

The conversation abruptly halted. Craig was sprawled on a fringe rug. His clothing was smoking. The thick stench of burnt flesh and cinders exuded from him. He muttered, "I could've thought of a better place than this. *Shit*."

He was within easy eyeshot of the kitchen. Dr. Krone's father and his wife ate at the corner table. A bottle of wine was half-buried in a bucket of ice. They weren't expecting him to drop in, judging by the vexed expression on their faces.

Dr. Krone Sr. was pleased after the initial shock. "It's Mr. Horsy. I knew he had a fire in him. He's going to be more fun than we anticipated."

He noticed the TV screen installed into the refrigerator. It replayed him scrambling from Rick and the frozen bodies.

Craig asked, "How are you doing all of this?"

"The machine has enough of your soul recorded," he replied, "that it can record your experiences even as they happen. But the premises are juiced up with so much brain energy and souls. Can't you feel the electricity in this place? Anything my son wants to happen *will* happen."

Hillary's eyes were concerned. "This man's dangerous. Why not just kill him?"

Dr. Krone Sr. shot down her idea. "Everything's fine. Let's just enjoy ourselves."

"You and your boy are too cocky." She was incensed. Her long straight hair had obviously been dyed ink-black and it shined with a bluish tint. The woman was in her sixties, as old as Dr. Krone Sr. She too had exhausted features. She'd been burning the midnight oil for far too long before her death. "You're not untouchable anymore. He's not hooked up to the machine. He's real. He can fight back."

Dr. Krone Sr. laughed at her concerns, dismissing them completely. He refocused on Craig. "Oh, I'm rude. Mr. Horsy, this is my wife, Hillary. She is ravishing, even eight years' dead."

"I can't say I'm as happy to see you," Craig said bitterly. "And did your son bury you in somebody else's grave too, lady?"

Dr. Krone, the son, ambled down the steps and greeted his family. The three of them stood in the kitchen studying Craig. He was their child. Their creation. And they could do with him as they wished. He was their plaything.

"Don't come near me," Craig shouted.

"I won't have to," Dr. Krone spoke excitedly. "We have twelve hours left before the machine dies down . . . well, eleven and a half now."

Craig leered at the three. "The machine has robbed you of your minds. These souls have turned you into murdering lunatics. You haven't cured anybody of mental illness. You've created a new malady."

They were living their mistake, he realized. They had no real concept of the fact they'd been playing with the souls of the infirm. They were essentially inside the mind and control of insanity.

Hillary swigged wine from her glass. "It was so easy stealing the bodies from the sanitariums. It's like stealing a motherless sleeping baby. We found something greater than curing mental illness. We'll live your memories, and we'll relive them forever. And we have life after death. What can top that?"

"Um, I don't know," Craig shot back, "saving people's lives might be a start."

"But this is so much fun," Dr. Krone laughed. "We'll live through the machine until the end of time. We'll live through people like you, Mr. Horsy."

Dr. Krone Sr. piped up. "We're wasting precious time. I want to see how our subject reacts to new stimulus."

"I still say he's a high risk," Hillary insisted. "He escaped the chef. He's thinking and fighting back."

"That was nothing," Dr. Krone contradicted his mother. "We'll wear him down, but not before one helluva show."

Hillary peered behind Craig. "What do you say to that, Katie?"

Craig's neck was tied with something wet, slippery, and cold. He couldn't breathe, his throat constricted. He yanked back on the coils, which slithered bloody and amphibious through his fingers. The room tilted right-side-up and upside down, and then he was facing the stairway behind him. He'd been flipped. He couldn't focus on any one object, being strangled. His grip over the choking coils was weak and so slimy. Katie's body was tainted, her corpse dripping with each step, skin and muscle tissue turning into liquid.

Katie gritted her teeth. Craig overheard several teeth fall from the gums and land on the wood floor in *plick* noises. She groaned, her throat gargling with liquids, "You owe somebody an apology!"

The Krones lined up at the edge of the kitchen to enjoy the event. Dr. Krone taunted Craig, "He abandoned Alice, Katie. And he allowed you to bleed to death. You and your child died because of his mistakes."

"*Naaawgh!*" Craig choked, his thoughts spiraling. *This isn't real. Katie's dead. For God's sake, she's wrapping the baby's umbilical cord around my neck.*

Picture it.

You have to defend yourself before you die.

But can I die?

He imagined the sliver glint. The sharp edges. The hoops to stick your fingers through. The sound the device made when you sliced through an object.

And there it was in his hands, a pair of sewing scissors. He cut through the purple-black-white umbilical cord. When the sinewy material broke, the flood was released.

"*Hah-hah-hah-hah!*" Dr. Krone's grating laughter carried throughout the house. "This is genius. We should've let one of our patients off the machine a long time ago. It's been years since I've had this much fun!"

Hillary complained, "You're covering everything in blood."

Dr. Krone Sr. guffawed, "Enjoy the moment. Who gives a shit if everything's covered in blood?"

"You'll clean it up, you rascals! I won't have anything to do with the cleanup, you got that?"

Blood had exploded from the umbilical opening in a torrent the second the scissors completed the job. A high-powered monsoon was unleashed, literally tearing Katie in twain, her core turned inside out from the pressure. The wave slammed Craig up against the television and then he bounced, landing on top of the couch. Another wave swept him up like a red liquid hand. He flipped forward. Collided into the kitchen table. He was dunked beneath the water, swallowing a rancid gulp. Hoisted by the next tidal wave, thrown onto his back, thrust upwards, he finally landed in the kitchen and clutched the sink handle to stay anchored in place. The roar of waves crashed against him, the entire house was flooded in five feet of red, creating a crimson wave pool. The Krone family was missing. Katie's flaccid body was floating on the surface, wedged between the floating coffee table and the staircase. Her belly and legs were connected to her torso by thin strips of muscular fabric.

He had pictured the scissors, and they arrived. He imagined them down to the detail, and it worked. *I will make it out of here alive. My ability to conjure objects is growing keener. Maybe it's because the machine's been on for so long.*

"I'm fighting back, you sons of bitches!"

He waded in the blood. It grew thicker by the second into a gel-consistency. He couldn't leave through the doors or windows, so he paddled toward the stairs. That's where Katie's body waited. She was motionless.

Dr. Krone arranged it so she'd explode blood. He can orchestrate anything. Dr. Krone Sr. said the machine has a radius. All you have to do is locate a way out.

"You owe her an apology!"

The words were choked by blood and phlegm. Katie's neck cracked to peek at him. She didn't move except to point at him and blather, "She's coming for you. I can't force you to be sorry. A woman's pain is her own. But not this time. Alice wants to introduce you to her sorrow."

When she smiled, her face broke into five pieces.

Horrified, he asked, "What has Dr. Krone done to you?"

Craig was pleading his case to the wrong jury. She wasn't Katie. Hillary and Dr. Krone Sr. were souls brought back to life, and Katie was merely a replication of a memory. She was Dr. Krone's manipulation made flesh.

The surface of the red water was disturbed. Pockets of air burst. The top of a head. The beginning of ears. The slits for eyes opened. Lips issued a hiss upon the sight of him. The black hair was twisted over her face in a wicked veil. Alice raged, batting the surface to reach him. And she was quick. Craig couldn't react because it was already too late. Hands seized his neck. Then Alice's cold, raspy warning, "You can't run. Not this time. Not ever again!"

He was forced down into the blood, throttled by the neck. The smack against the surface was so intense he nearly lost consciousness. Alice's fingers dug into his flesh so deeply it paralyzed him, drew blood, and threatened to break bone. He was underneath the surface, gasping for air, kicking, scratching at the stairs, battering for breath. He couldn't focus on a single thought.

He was dragged up one stair at a time, closer to reaching the surface and air. Alice's bare feet stomping the stairs was gong loud. She was carrying him up the steps, he realized, not drowning him.

One more step, and he coughed, "*Blaargh!*" He spat out blood, vomited it up, and cleared it from his eyes.

"Almost there." She lifted him up another step. "And you will see it this time."

He caught a door opening down the upstairs hall. Three bodies leaned out to watch.

The Krones.

Alice lifted him up from the floor by underneath the arms. The hallway tilted, and he was suddenly inside Alice's bathroom in her apartment. Random flecks of blood glowed from the white tiles and beige bath rug. The toilet was closed, he noticed, as his face was leveled onto the floor beside the toilet seat. He looked up at Alice, and she was ghostly pale. Blue around the eyes and lips. She wore the face of a long-disturbed individual. Alice grimaced at the sight of him. "It's you who left me to cope with this monstrosity."

"Monstrosity?"

Alice cupped his mouth, enraged that he'd talk to her. "You haven't seen my child. Dr. Krone tried to help me. He said it was too late. If I would've gone to the hospital sooner, my child wouldn't be a monster. You could've helped me make a better decision and snuff this baby when I had the chance." She shook her head, her mouth twitching. "It's much too late now."

Craig fought tears. Dr. Krone was playing on his innermost pain, the kind of pain you forget for the necessity of moving on, but this time, he couldn't avoid it.

He pleaded, "You shouldn't listen to Dr. Krone."

"I shouldn't listen to you!"

She pried open the toilet lid, lifting him up by the neck with her free hand. Craig slammed it shut, throwing his arm up and dodging the sight. "No—you can't!"

Static electricity shocked his flesh. *Zzzt! Zzzt! Zzzt! Zzzt! Zzzt!* The jolts dug into the bone. His marrow tightened, his flesh kicking up smoke. Alice pried his hands from the lid, digging her nails into his back and pounding him in the face with her fists. She bloodied his nose, split his lip, and scratched his right eyelid.

"You—will—see—my—unborn—child!"

Craig reached up with one hand and seized her face by the jaw and nostrils. He shoved her backwards. Alice rolled away, slamming into the floor. Then the door opened. Katie crawled over Alice's fallen body. Her words were blood and slush. "You will see her child!"

Katie's legs were dragging behind her, useless and broken. Bloated and saturated organs were trailing out her torso. Closing in, he was pinned by his arms and back. Alice closed in on him, and she pried open the toilet lid. Alice and Katie's hands gripped his head together.

"Look!"

"Open those eyes."

Bone fingers wrenched back his eyelids.

"No, I'm begging you. Stop this! *Stop!*"

It was too late for words. He witnessed what he battled to avoid. The sight was taken in right before it transformed. The wad of flesh was caked in blood. It had no special features, too ill-formed and underdeveloped to look human.

"I'm so sorry," he wept. "So sorry . . . "

"Yes," Alice said, not in anger but awe. "It's happening just as Dr. Krone promised."

The toilet shattered. Toilet water spilled onto the tiles, gushing in a torrent. The fetus was growing at alarming rates. The wall was covered in tendrils of flesh, and bone, and cartilage. Eyes, mouths, jaws, snapping teeth, arms, legs, breasts, male and female genitals, hearts, lungs, intestines, digestive cavities, and bones were splayed on the living quilt of flesh. Cries of agony and a baby wailing for its mother resounded to eardrum-shattering levels. Every appendage and organ throbbed with life. Veins audibly circulated blood, the flesh squeezing the arteries to spread the life-giving juices. Fingers extended to grab hold of Craig. Fists threatened to beat him to a pulp. The tiles from the wall were plucked free with accompanying crashes. Plaster crumbled and rained overhead. The floorboards were split by the weight of the monster. The living sheet of flesh and warring limbs lurched toward Craig.

The door opposite the room was ajar. The Krones surrounded one of the machines inside, watching the show. Dr. Krone Sr. and his son took turns typing on the keyboard. They showed no fear of the incoming abnormality. Hillary stepped from the room and dared to confront the creature. She shook hands with one of the arms jutting from the wall. Other fingers stroked Hillary's hair and caressed her chin. Dr. Krone joined his mother. He touched lungs that throbbed. "Simply amazing," he whispered. "Astounding."

Dr. Krone Sr. stood beside his son now. "There's so much more we could do with this machine outside this mansion."

"It's a question of souls," Dr. Krone concurred. "The more we receive, the more we can create. It's a matter of extending the electrical current beyond these premises. We need more souls. *A lot more souls.*"

They were obsessed with their creation. And it continued to grow. The wall of flesh covered the entire wall of the hallway and was still expanding. They would continue to harvest souls and create horrors like this, and they would never be satisfied. What if the machine carried on outside the mansion? Everybody's nightmares would come true. And what else could they drum up besides living flesh walls?

Craig eyed the room and the machine. It would be so easy to leap inside and shut it down. But there were two other machines on the premises, maybe more. He was outnumbered and outsmarted. Craig followed his first instinct to attack the three and charged the room. Five hands seized him by the arms and hair before he traveled more than three steps.

Jaws bit into his flesh. Fists battered him. The flesh dripped over his face and smothered his airway, the liquid spreading like a mask. The Krones were delighted at the turn of events.

"He can't do anything." "Watch his pants. I bet he pisses himself." "No, he'll shit." "Not yet." "Give him five minutes." "He'll be dead in five minutes." "I betcha he'll die sooner than that."

Alice and Katie joined the group, Alice speaking dreamily, "My child is so beautiful."

Katie wept, "I wish I got to be a mother."

"You can," Dr. Krone offered to Katie. "We can make children as we wish."

"Like Alice's?"

Dr. Krone stepped toward Katie, Craig catching the outlines of the two through the thin veil of flesh, and the doctor was hugging his wife. "Anything you want."

Hillary joined in. "I want children too. This is so extraordinary. The mind is fun to play in, but this, this is so much better. We have to continue with this progress."

"We will," Dr. Krone Sr. encouraged her. "I promise."

Craig was desperate for air, the flesh mask constricting both mouth and nose passages. How much longer could his body take the strangulation? He fought the arms and flesh, but they were stronger. The mask of flesh was unyielding.

You have to think. Imagine a happier place.

He couldn't imagine much with so much pressure placed on his lungs. His body grew cold against the warm, breathing wall of living parts. No air to breathe, white dots burned his vision. Circulation was cut, the blood pooling in his veins and arteries razor sharp. The blocked flow would be the end of him, and now, all he could focus on was the coldness of his body.

Lake Jacomo

Winter's chill bore deep into him. Craig was lying against the ice. He still couldn't breathe with the flesh over his mouth and nose. His face was impeded by the flesh creation, but it was frozen solid. He cracked and pounded his face against the pond until the skin shattered and cracked. Ice pieces crumbled loose, and finally, he could breathe again. He used his hands and feet to slide on the ice, creating more distance between himself and the monster. The flesh covered half the pond, the monster hidden beneath the snow. Hands and faces could be made out beneath the wintry veil, each smiling, twisted, raging, convulsing, and ultimately, glued motionless.

He breathed in and out, slowly standing up. Frigid air was better than no air, he reasoned. He stood in place, anticipating the next attack. The next living memory.

Ahead of him, the dreaded sight presented itself—all three of them. Dr. Krone was the closest, his parents in the background, checking out the scenery. They were researchers and sightseers as well as killers.

"You can't escape us," Dr. Krone threatened him.

He was angry. *Good*, Craig thought. *They know they're not in total control anymore.* "But this resistance has been a wild ride. I'm sure it will continue to be until you make a mistake, and you're dead. And I assure you, you will die before that machine rests again."

The Krones grouped together and closed their eyes. Lake Jacomo, the slowly falling snow, the frozen-over flesh monster, the slate-gray skies, they collectively vanished. The walls turned into broken plaster and see-through boards. The space was blank of enemies. Craig stood in the first-floor hallway beside the opened door leading to one of the machines. Dr. Krone typed on the keyboard. Static crackled across Craig's flesh, burning him in bright blue zigzag branches.

Craig shouted, "Will you fucking stop that?"

The Krones ignored his statement. Craig caught their eyes light up electric blue for a split second. The static current played over their arms, and legs, and bodies. The voltage was sucked into the skin, parts of the flesh puckering open and feeding on the electricity.

They typed in a new memory.

And it would arrive at any moment.

flesh And blood

The blink,
Darkness.

It wasn't real darkness, but instead, the light was blocked by sweaty palms in front of his eyes. The hands and bodies stank of bread and perspiration. The crowd was hushed. He sensed many, perhaps fifty or more, in the room with him, watching him. He was sitting on a chair, his hands tied behind his back and his legs bound by the ankles with rope.

"Come willingly to God," the throng of people sang. "Come willingly to Him."

He believed Parker Stevens was the one touching Craig's forehead. He escaped them on the street, but here, tied up, he didn't stand a chance. Attempting a strategy of escape, sharp currents of static electricity zapped him, the wounds puckering and sizzling at each connection. "Shit!"

"You cursed in the Lord's temple," Parker bellowed, removing his hands from Craig's eyes as if horrified at the outburst. "You must be cleansed in this church. We all must be cleansed. Craig Horsy's sins reflect our own. This is our baptism as much as it is Mr. Horsy's."

"Mr. Horsy's"? He's talking like Dr. Krone.

He is Dr. Krone.

The congregation stood among rows of pews. This wasn't a small church. Rows expanded in both directions, occupied by hundreds of people. Torches lit the service hall and shed amber-orange firelight, fueled by gasoline and kerosene, judging by the smells. The room had the feel of a ramshackle church, the wooden beams unpainted and without windows. The roof's overhead rafters were exposed. Craig was atop a raised floor, three feet above those in the pews. The congregation's faces disturbed him the most. They were looking for an answer, begging, crying, and ogling over Craig like a messiah or a martyr. Well-clad business types stood amid the poor in rags or wrapped in stained blankets. Grit-smeared faces and the clean shaven were equally matched in the arena. The ravenous and hungry looks about each of them promised bloodshed.

"Every communion, we eat and drink of the flesh and the blood of the Christ," Parker began. "God, the Holy Ghost, our redeemer, has requested his followers to step up and show their true selves. Worship and honor Him, or walk out of this church and forever be banished from this brotherhood."

Parker announced the next sentence with inhuman enthusiasm. "God has finally asked for our flesh in return for his flesh! God wants our blood to be spilled upon this church hall floor in reverence of Him. Call it a reverse communion."

Cheers ripped through the silence, responses forming throughout pockets of the crowd that yes, yes they would tear their flesh asunder for their Christ in heaven. Parker turned down to him, eyeing him with vehemence. "Your flesh, your blood, Craig, will set you apart from the evil that rips the fabric of all our lives."

He couldn't speak through the wadded-up dish cloth stuffed in his mouth and the duct tape securing it in place, though he begged, pleaded, and prayed the man could understand that he wanted no part of this.

"Our flesh, our blood, for Christ!"

"Our flesh, our blood, for Christ in heaven!"

"Our flesh, our blood, shall it rain down and vanquish the fires of hell!"

The chanting was shouted at so many decibels, his eardrums were on the verge of breaking. Suffering the horrible noises, he randomly caught Hillary and Dr. Krone Sr. in ragged clothing, passing about weapons. They ranged from razor blades, double-sided axes, hatchets, beveling tools, scythes, chisels, chainsaws, pinch clamps, maces, baseball bats with nails driven through their core, staffs, sledge hammers, jackhammers, logging saws, and many other implements that were handmade and equally as deadly. He then watched the congregation systematically follow-up on their promises and hack the flesh from their own bodies. The flesh itself slapped the tiles in horrific layers as more joined in the horrible display. Blood pooled and splashed the floor in a rising current.

Parker Stevens removed a boning knife from his white ceremonial robe. He worked three incisions at his hairline, peeling and edging back the flesh to the bare skull. He threw down the scalp after long moments of vocalized agony and raw determination that ended in him delivering a series of raucous laughs. "Your mother was an easy fuck, Craig. She took it any way I'd give it to her!"

The congregation stood with bare, gleaming muscle tissue. Fleshless. Some had worked down to their skeletons, grimacing and crying in revelation and speaking in tongues, eyes rolling in socket pools of blood, hands and faces dripping with gore. Bodies were splayed on the floor, worked over by jackhammers and chainsaws by their fellow brethren. The massacre sparked Parker's lust to shed Craig's flesh and blood, the man's face split and sectioned by bullets of thick running blood.

"It's your turn. The blood is the wine, the flesh is the bread, and Christ is very hungry!"

Parker raised the boning knife to carve up Craig's face.

Craig closed his eyes. He was done being afraid.

You have to be as morbid and creative as the machine.

Craig combed his mind, digging deep, growling from the pit of his throat, and he dredged through the confines of his mind for the help he deserved.

And that help suddenly surged out from the crowd! Brandon was headless from Tina's previous attack, but he could navigate his way up to the podium. He clutched a concrete saw, the blade as wide as a tire, the teeth spokes inches deep. The device whirred and churned promises of mutilation. A shot of white gasoline vapor coughed out from the motor. That's when the blade landed on Parker's face and split it in half. The preacher faltered from the podium, howling in mortal terror, and landed on the cushion of flesh and blood below the pulpit. He drowned in it, lavishing every drop, as he added to the pool of red.

Brandon untied his arms and legs, Craig rising to

his feet. He could think freely, and the thoughts would come to life, he believed, because so much energy was in the air for the taking. Random arcs of static electricity would branch out along the walls and into the members of the congregation.

Craig stared at his headless father. The man patted his back and gave him a thumb's up.

"Um . . . thanks, Dad."

The congratulatory moment concluded as fast as it had begun. Half-fleshed faces, bodies turned inside out, and deviously armed villains watched them, enraged. Phlegm and blood-choked throats roared threats. Exposed eyes sized them up. Parker Stevens was back on his feet. He was soaked in red. He was incensed, his face split in half, the nerves dancing and exposed.

The preacher pointed up at them. "They have chosen to disobey God's word. We must expel them from the house of the Lord immediately!"

Give me the Browning shotgun. No—two of them!

The blink, he clutched the weapons in each hand. Brandon revved up the concrete saw. Two against hundreds, Craig thought, wouldn't suffice. He scrambled to think. Who else was on his side? Who could protect him? His mother, wife, and Alice were out of the question, but he had one other ally.

"It's about time you thought of me . . . "

Edith materialized between him and his father. Her chest was sodden in blood. The bullet wound was a black circle center masse. She was pale as death, but a spark of life glinted in her eyes. She craved payback. It was amazing, Craig thought, that a soul could be called back up from death and become flesh and blood again.

"So what are you arming me with?"

"Well," Craig paused, "what do you want?"

She raised her fists and flipped the congregation off. "*Hmmm*, how about a blow torch?"

Craig imagined it. The device was simple, a large steel tank for the fuel and a long metallic nozzle. Edith strapped on the tank, eager to do some damage. "This is for my children, you bastards!"

Whoosh!

Blankets of liquid flame shot out into the crowd a caustic fiery orange.

Craig opened fire, enjoying twin shotguns. *Ba-boom! Ba-boom! Ba-boom! Ba-boom!*

Brandon swung the concrete saw at anyone who dared to draw close to the stage, swiping arms, torsos—claiming guts—and heads.

Pick-axes, hatchets, spinning daggers, and saw blades were heaved in their direction. Brandon's chest was hit with the saw blade, half of it buried in his chest. The blow didn't faze him. Edith accepted an axe to the shoulder. She didn't bother to rip it out. Craig dodged three knives and a handful of nails.

"Where the fuck are they getting this shit?"

That's it! Think like they do.

He imagined a grenade in his fist. In a blink, there it was. Craig ripped the pin free and lobbed it into the crowd.

Ka-boom!

Shrapnel tore apart the core of the congregation upon detonation. Chunks of the pews exploded and shot across the room in flames. But the group kept coming. The numbers failed to diminish.

Craig dodged a flaming head. "Dr. Krone keeps them coming!"

"Perhaps this isn't the place to fight them," Edith argued, raising her voice. "It's an unending army."

Brandon's neck nodded in agreement, coughing up two spurts of blood.

"You're right."

Craig was out of breath. He narrowly missed a cleaver slicing off his nose. They were backed into the corner.

Edith suffered a nail in the eye.

"It's up to you to think us out of this." Edith's eye coughed out yellow pus and blood. "We're seconds away from being sacrificed to God. Make up your mind, Craig!"

The flame thrower released another caustic plume. Faces melted in waxy layers. Phalange hands and skeletal bodies swarmed behind the row of flames, scrambling, scratching, crawling, shoving, kicking, punching, slicing, climbing, and clamoring for their demise.

"What am I supposed to think up now?"

Edith shouted, "Somewhere safe!"

"But nowhere is safe. Dr. Krone keeps showing up and ruining everything. How can I get to one of the machines? It's the only way to stop this shit."

Brandon was struck by four axes at once. He tipped to the side, but he didn't fall. Craig ducked to avoid the next saw blade.

"What about under the stairs?"

"Under the stairs? What stairs?"

"That damn basement," Edith cried. "We couldn't get through those doors. There has to be something down there. The wires connected to the machines. They channeled into the wall. Perhaps they lead down there, whatever's behind those two locked steel doors."

Craig agreed, "You're right."

A rope with a railroad spike attached to it struck his leg above the knee. He yanked it out with a mean jolt of pain. "Shit—shit!"

"Save us, Craig." Edith clasped his arm. "Take us with you. You can do it. You have no choice."

Static electricity cut into him. The Krones anticipated his next move—or was it the machine? The congregation reached the podium, advancing at once. Skeletons and de-fleshed attackers and burning shells of bones closed in, ready to dismember them.

"I'm as good as dead—again!" Edith barked, throwing her head back in a war cry. "Craig, hurry the fuck up!"

"You're not dying," he shouted. "You can't die twice."

He ducked and rolled to avoid the chainsaw thrown at him. The flames surrounding them were no longer a deterrent. The heat was billowing and the smoke was black and thick enough to snuff him and everybody else dead. He coughed, choking and gagging on what couldn't be expelled from his lungs. He leaned up against the wall and sheltered his body.

Static electricity shocked him one jolt after the other. He tightened his eyes. Held his breath. Listened to Edith and his father fight the crowd. Their footsteps were feet away from him. Fifteen seconds they had left before they would be overtaken.

He refocused again and again on the same image. The static failed to abate. The electric prickles raised gooseflesh and heated the blood beneath the skin. He was zapped and a section of his arm popped with hot blood and melted skin. And that's when Edith unleashed a blood-curdling scream, and Brandon's body toppled onto him defeated.

the STAIRS

Edith WAS SPRAWLED on the stairs, bleeding from numerous wounds. Brandon was slumped below her. He had picked free the axes and knives plunged into his torso, but the saw blade in his chest was stuck. Craig used the guardrail of the stairs as a crutch, his knee still bleeding from the railroad spike wound. They didn't have much time to act before something else would come after them.

Edith gazed up at him with one good eye. "You did it, Craig."

He pointed down the stairs. "Let's move, if you can."

Brandon's father offered a hesitant thumb's up, though three of his fingers had been severed clean. The rubber mat squeaked under their feet. Brandon only carried one Browning—one of Craig's—due to his damaged hand. Edith abandoned the flame thrower pack. She was too damaged to carry the weight. Craig had kept hold of the remaining shotgun.

They walked the rest of the way to the solid steel double doors. "Well, this is it." Craig sized up the door. Blue-white arcs of electricity shot up and down the entrance.

"Hurry it up," Edith demanded. "Dr. Krone's on his way."

He aimed the gun at the door. *Ba-bam!* The connections issued sparks from the door, but it failed to unlock.

The electricity crackled along the walls and stairs in branching lines. Brandon fired at the door to the same dismal effect. Steps pounded from the head of the stairs, loud and incoming. The foundation rattled beneath them. Wooden beams splintered and cried in protest to an unknown, incredible weight.

The stench of death arrived. Female laughter—laughter he recognized—reverberated down to them. Plaster rained in pockets from the ceiling from the pounding of incoming steps.

He gave up on the easy solution. "The guns aren't going to open the doors."

Edith wildly shook her head. "Then what?"

The threats were echoing down to them—

"*You owe her an apology.*"

"*I see your father in you, Craig.*"

"*You abandoned me when I needed you the most.*"

"*You care to slam that barstool over my head again, asshole?*"

"*Come to Christ willingly . . . come to Him.*"

"*I'll feed you to the monsters in hell—you won't dine and dash in my restaurant, Mr. Horsy!*"

"*I'm just an easy fuck to you, Craig.*"

Dr. Krone had enlisted everybody in the fight, Craig realized. Brandon turned from the stairs to Craig. The Browning was directly aimed at him.

"This was all a trick," Craig gasped. "You were never on my side."

Edith's eyes refocused on him. Her mouth was a pink slit, menacing and grim. "I told you, Mr. Horsy, you wouldn't win. You can't. I'm at the helm. The machine grants me everything. I keep feeding it souls, and it keeps feeding me strength. Soon, I will have control over you, and that'll be another soul for the machine. Eventually, the boundaries will expand well beyond this house."

Ba-boom!

He ducked in time. The shot meant for him pinged against the steel door, and the double doors separated. Shadows spread over the bottommost steps. The villains of his mind hadn't arrived, though they were seconds from showing themselves. He charged through the doors, threw them shut, and had just enough time to blockade the entrance before he witnessed the secret in the room.

the Source

CRAIg wedged the steel carts by the entrance at an angle to prevent the doors from coming open. It would only hold for seconds—maybe minutes. The room had no light source because it wasn't necessary. The room was a great chamber, warehouse big. The walls trailed with climbing branches of electricity, bolts of blue-purple-white incendiaries. Static crackles and pops and the hum of an immense power source filled the shadowy room. Flashes of white, flashes of blue kept flickering as miniature strobe lights. His head immediately burned with a migraine from the optical effect. The dank and sweet scent of death was rich enough it gave the air a wet fecundity. He scanned the room for the corpses he'd seen in Dr. Krone Sr.'s tape, and finding them in heaps and outlines at the far corners of the room, he also discovered the shape of many machines.

Dr. Krone lied. The coward said there were only three machines. There's at least fifteen!

The static flashes and the intensity of the current tripled. Crackles exploded in great plumes of smoke and silvery sparks. The machine was fired up, working on all cylinders. They were designed replicas of the ones upstairs—a simple metal refrigerator shape with a chair soldered into the end. The wires trailed to the ceiling and connected to the rafters, hanging like knotted threads of a monstrous sized spider web.

"It's the house," Craig muttered, astounded at the sight. "The wires are hooked to the house. The whole place is one big machine. That's why the walls can change into different scenes. That's why my memories become real anywhere I am."

The silver streaks of light allowed him to study the bodies closer. The corpses were kept hidden in clear body bags, positioned with their backs against the wall, torsos up to the head propped up as if watching the show. Many of the bags contained magpie skeletal remains. He caught maggots writhing within the skin of many, eating away the layers of soft human flesh to the bone and core. The corpses were colored in the flickers of electricity. There were hundreds of corpses, and there were many more standing in the back of the room or piled on their backs and bellies in cordwood stacks.

The barricade rattled from a giant shove.

"*You owe her an apology.*"

"*I'm not just a fuck!*"

"*My baby rots inside of me. Care to see, Daddy?*"

"*Hell is hungry, Mr. Horsy.*"

"*The next drink will be on me, compliments of your best friend, Willis.*"

"*It's too late, Craig. My soul isn't my own. Listen to me, Craig. You can't win. We tried. Give up.*"

"No, Edith!" Craig shouted back. "I refuse to give up."

The barrier wouldn't hold much longer. He had seconds to think. He was alone in a room of hundreds of corpses—maybe a thousand.

He darted to the closest machine in a last-second decision. The computer monitor glowed blue. The screen was blank.

Bam! Bam! Bam!

Two of the carts were shoved back, knocked onto their sides. Two were still lodged in place.

"What the hell do I do?"

He feared touching anything, but he had no choice. He touched the *Enter* key. The screen displayed a menu. The selections were simple. *Enter Memory. Enter Name. Enter Place. Enter Change.* He selected *Enter Name.* He typed, *A.* A list of names popped up—Andrew, Andy, Allison, Alex, Alan, Andrea, Anderson, and the list carried on down the letters of the alphabet. He scanned downwards with the mouse and selected all the names. The screen counted 1,800 names. *Enter Place.* Craig typed, *Dr. Krone's mansion. Enter Memory.* He guessed on this one. *Alive. Enter Change.* He paused on the command. What did it mean, he thought. It made sense to enter person, place, and the memory, but he couldn't decide what to enter for the change.

"*The door is weakening.*"

"*You will apologize to her, you bastard.*"

"*My child rots in my womb! Why won't you acknowledge our child?*"

"*You could never turn down an open bar, you fucking alcoholic.*"

"*I'll char your flesh for added flavor.*"

"*You can't just throw away this fuck. Not this time.*"

Craig's fingers trembled at hearing hands bang against the door. Sweat trailed down his arms to his wrists. He shivered in anticipation of the door being thrown open.

He entered all the information he could on the final tab. *Protect Craig Horsy. Murder Dr. Krone and his family. Destroy the machines. Find an escape route out of the house.*

The double doors shot open.

He struck the *Enter* key.

the entRAnce

nothing hAppened. The machine didn't react. The electricity continued to pulse from the machines. Silver sparks were shed in all corners, illuminating the incoming enemies. The wall of flesh and human limbs, infant limbs, and bones spread out along the walls. Alice was close at hand, mesmerized by what was once a miscarried baby in a toilet. Susan wore a brown sheath dress. She was heartbroken, her face weighed down by discomfort and regret. She clutched two knives, each glinting in the refractions of unnatural light. When she caught sight of him, her face turned wicked. The bent smile. The bloodlust in her eyes. She had reinforcements behind her. Rick Margolia wielded a clever in his hand as he coasted the room for his next entrée. Willis was burned up from the bar memory. Pockets of fat popped throughout his skin, still boiling. Tina clutched a razor blade, and beside her, Parker Stevens was slathered in blood and clutching onto the concrete saw Craig's father had used on him previously. Brandon, headless, swept the blue nozzle of the Browning across the room, ready to pull back the trigger at any indication his son was near. Katie and Edith stayed near the back of the group. Edith was war-torn, bloodied, and she had reclaimed the flame thrower. This time it would be intended for him. Katie was further along in her decomposition. Both eyes had turned to broken grapes. Loose flesh hung from her jawline, the clacking and gritting of misshapen and missing teeth creating a strange rattle. Black blood leaked from the ends of her dress. Her legs had somehow been repaired, and she could walk at will. Her stomach was extended, but concave in the middle. The flesh sank and rose with the shape of a hand reaching through the flesh to escape, but the infant kept failing to break the barrier.

These were his executioners.

Dr. Krone and his family finally entered behind the initial throng. Dr. Krone Sr. was tickled to be leading the "Murder Craig Horsy" expedition. Hillary was engrossed with the wall of flesh as much so as Alice, both caught up in the maternal turn-on.

Dr. Krone stared right at him, spotting him instantly. "I warned you would die."

The doctor marched to the nearest machine. His hand was arched over the keyboard to type in his fate. "Who will get to murder you? *Hmmmmm.*"

Katie raised her hand, gritting those bleeding teeth. Susan clanged both the knives together in response. Brandon blasted a shot into the air. *Ba-boom*! Alice was too busy running her hands through the flesh wall to care, mesmerized by her prolific baby. Edith unleashed a jet of flames. *Whoosh.*

Rick Margolia and Willis stood side by side, and Rick guffawed, "I'll cook him like this bastard." He pointed at Willis. "Well fucking done."

Dr. Krone smiled, impressed by his creations. "Yes, yes, they all want to be the killing hand. What does that say about your life, Mr. Horsy? You as a person? Everybody's past has a time or two—or like you, many times—they're not so proud of. You can't sweep it under your cognitive rug here. You must face it."

Craig glanced at the machine he'd typed on. It asked a final question—*Proceed with command?*

Dr. Krone realized what he'd done. "No—don't you touch it. Don't do it, you son of a bitch!"

It was Craig's turn to laugh. He looked up at the pieces of his past. They were jilted. Unreal. Dead. These weren't memories swept under his cognitive rug. This was Dr. Krone's machine at work. And now he would put the machine to a new test. "We all have memories we're not so proud of, Dr. Krone. You must face your past. That's what we do here."

He punched the *Enter* key.

the bAttLe

R. kRone LAnded on his knees, flabbergasted, as the life in him seemed to drain out through his feet. "*No . . . you didn't . . . WHAT DID YOU TYPE?*"

Hillary was alarmed. "I told you it was dangerous to let him roam the mansion. He's not hooked up to the machine."

Dr. Krone Sr. refused to be defeated. "No, it's not over. The machine works both ways. I can reverse the command."

Dr. Krone Sr. raced for the closest machine, but Craig tackled him. "It's time to enjoy your treatment, you sick asshole."

"You can't stop us," Hillary cheered. She was already standing at the machine, ready to type in new commands. "My husband's right. We can reverse your commands."

And that's when they trudged out from the darkness. Body bags were ripped to shreds. Corpses limped toward them, coming alive. Rotten muscle audibly tore and bones clinked loose beneath the softening flesh of their bodies. The previous stench was light compared to this new moment. The ripe fog carried so thick, everything was demurred by a see-through gray net thick enough to be sticky. Hillary was the first to be forced to the ground. She was surrounded by two dozen walking corpses, pushed from one to the other, each rendering a mouthful of her face and throat until she was screaming and faceless.

"Save me—anybody!" Hillary's tongue was bitten from the mouth after an intimate kiss from a hungry corpse, and then she vanished beneath the dog pile of feasting corpses, batting her arms for her life and delivering soggy screams.

Dr. Krone Sr. dove into the pile to reclaim his wife. He was forced onto the ground beside his dissected wife. Heads bent down and lifted up from his resisting body, pecking and rendering his flesh. "*Aaack— Guagh—Ahhhhhhh!*" Blood-laden cries were quickly smothered until he was dead once again.

Craig didn't know where Dr. Krone had hidden himself. The enemies were still after him. The room bustled with activity, and he was the only living person who owned a real heartbeat.

He flopped onto the floor when Edith shot an arc of flames at him. The heat grazed his back, the flames inches from burning him. A daring corpse of desiccated flesh and browning bones—over a century dead—removed the fuel line from the tank.

Edith screamed, "Oh shit!"

Craig worked to his feet to sprint in retreat.

Kaboom!

Edith and the corpse were engulfed in caustic explosions. Half the room was lit up, firelight dancing alongside the branches of static electricity. Across the room, Brandon drove the concrete saw ahead of him and split four corpses down the middle. If the man had a head, he would've boasted a grin. The flesh wall of malformed body parts sucked in corpse after corpse, and after burying them in layers of living, breathing, and deadly skin, they were spit out bones, blood, and organs. The wet splashes and muffled groans—tranquilized wild animals—of the snuffed dead continued unending. Katie strangled a corpse with an umbilical cord, lifting it from the ground and driving it face-first into the floor with a bone-crunching impact. Rick Margolia flanked as many corpses as he could with his cleaver. Brandon was finally overpowered in the opposite corner. Four corpses were tugging on each of his arms and legs. Soon, his limbs were forced from the sockets with wild blasts of blood.

The concrete saw was stolen from his father and claimed by one of the undead, and Rick's head was dismembered from his neck in one swipe.

Craig eyed the machine within four steps of him. He could type for the war to vanish completely.

He decided not to waste another second waiting.

"We are your family, you can't destroy us!"

The cold and wet umbilical cord wrapped around his throat. It was so tight, he heard a soft snap. His throat burned and radiated razor-sharp agony. He couldn't breathe. The pain was as stunning as it was paralyzing. He was on his knees, bent forward in struggle. He couldn't shrug his wife from strangling him.

Her belly was pressed against his back, the protrusion wet. "Can't you feel her kick?"

Craig indeed felt the soft touch against his back from a dead foot.

"She could've been someone special," she wheezed

from the effort of choking him. "Someone different than you, someone much better!"

The room spun in a dizzying frenzy. The loss of air was stealing his equilibrium. The room was upside down, right-side-up, and then murky and in focus again.

"*Aack! Pahlease!*"

His concentration spread out across the room. Corpse hands smothered Susan and clenched their nails into her flesh. In one death-delivering effort, the flesh over her sternum and face were removed with the smoothness of butter. She was punched through the torso by six hands and lifted in the air in a grotesque presentation. Willis crumpled on the ground, burning to cinder and ash in the aftermath of the flame-thrower tank fuel explosion. Corpses throughout the chamber reached and battled over the squares of skin and human anatomy they tore from the wall of flesh. Alice stood her ground until she was swallowed up by fifty corpses and eaten alive.

Craig's eyes rolled into the back of his head. His vision failed to refocus. Katie's cold dead breath played against his neck. She kissed behind his ear, leaving a slimy patch of skin and mucus. "I will see you in hell, and then we'll finally be a family."

His brain boiled with the need for oxygen. His lungs spastically tried to inhale and exhale to mimic the act of breathing. Each attempt issued the raw agony of broken ribs. Seconds from death, Craig let himself go limp.

He kept thinking, where had Dr. Krone disappeared to?

the deAL

he blink happened AgAin, The umbilical cord disappeared. He could breathe again. He coughed and gagged to set his breathing back to normal, being on his knees. His eyes watered, and a line of spittle fell from his panting maw. The corpses were in their body bags. The enemies from his mind had also vacated the area. They were simply gone.

He waited and listened.

"Mr. Horsy," Dr. Krone spoke, his throat trembling and giving way to his fear. Craig was proud to realize he'd terrified the man who'd delivered so much heartache and horror to him for the past three to four days—or God knows how long, he thought. "You made a smart play. You're a special case. Mom was right. It wasn't safe for you to roam freely. It's not safe for anybody to be free in this mansion. Don't you see why it'd be impossible to allow the world to enjoy this? It would simply spiral out of control."

"Like it hasn't already?"

"It's ours and ours only to enjoy," Dr. Krone said, staying hidden. "That could include you, Mr. Horsy. Would you like to experience only good memories? I could permit it."

He's trying to bargain with me. Why the fuck would I trust him after all of this? He's crazy.

The hairs on his arms were raised. The electric impulses hadn't ended. Blue arcs traveled up and down the walls and the glow encased each of the machines. He eyed one of the screens and noticed words were being typed out on it.

Craig cracked a smile. *Ah, I see his game for what it really is.*

He poised himself over the machine. "Would you really allow me to relive only the good times? God, I miss Katie every day. Could you make it so our child was really born?"

"Yes," Dr. Krone replied, happy to hear Craig was interested. "A burping, farting, healthy little girl, she can be anything you want and everything you ever wanted her to be."

He searched between the machines. He caught Dr. Krone's shadow. The man was hunched over the computer screen. His eyes never left the console.

"You can fuck Susan into oblivion." Dr. Krone fidgeted and couldn't shrug the nervous ticks and tremors in his head. "You want Alice too? She'll do anything to pleasure you. You can have them both at the same time, and they'd like it. You want to relive your regrets and make a change, then let's do it. You know how to run the machine. Once you've been hooked in so long, you don't have to be hooked in anymore to travel the memories of your past. The machine has memorized them already . . . you simply type in the change."

Craig closed in for the finalizing blow. He leveled a fist into Dr. Krone's jaw, coldcocking him, swinging like a prize fighter. "I want my life back the way it was before you tried to take it away from me!"

Dr. Krone landed as a helpless pile onto the floor. He waved his hands, pleading, begging, desperate to bargain for his life. Tears glazed over his eyes and wet his cheeks. He blubbered and whimpered, "It's my machine, and you're under my control. You do as I say. You can't be doing this. No, you just can't!"

He anchored his foot over Dr. Krone's chest. "We're in real life now. We're no longer in each other's minds. I have free will. You're helpless in your own skin. I bet that's a new feeling for you."

Dr. Krone refused to make eye contact. He was a child in full temper-tantrum mode. His chubby and waxen skin cringed and frowned. He pounded the floor with his fists. "It's my machine, and you do as I say! I'm in charge. You're the patient, and I'm the doctor."

"I've heard that shit before. Sure. It's your machine, but you'll do as I say."

He throttled Dr. Krone by the neck. The man was covered in so much stinking sweat Craig's grip was slippery. He managed to lift him up by seizing his collar. Craig forced him onto the chair of one of the machines. "It's your turn to be introspected to death."

Dr. Krone was at a loss for breath. "It's . . . not your . . . not your machine . . . you . . . you don't know . . . you don't know how to use it . . . "

He leveled another punch across the man's temple. The man was stunned by the blow, and Craig was able to strap Dr. Krone into the machine. The doctor came back to life when Craig walked to the other side of the machine to type in his command.

"I know the machine better than you. There are so

many intricacies, secrets, and better ways to produce the greatest memories. You want that? I can give it to you."

Craig scoffed. "No thanks."

"Tina followed her dreams in your mind and killed your dad. Do you want to know how she did that? And why? It's not as simple as typing in a command. The words have to be special. Specific. You can only learn from experience. My experience. I can teach you. I will, Mr. Horsy. I swear it. Release me. I'll let you be my assistant. The more souls we collect, the realer they become, and we'll experience every soul out there, and they'll be unique and new and extraordinary in their own special way. The possibilities are endless. We'll have millions of souls, Craig. Why stop? Why ever stop?"

Dr. Krone's skin glistened with panic. He was terrified, and the doctor couldn't mask it. And then his fear changed into scorn. Accusations. The words throbbed so deep and vicious, Craig stopped thinking about what commands he'd enter into the computer.

"You're naïve beyond comprehension. The machine can drum up a command, but it reads what's in your mind. It creates what you've thought in your subconscious and the subconscious of others. Deep down, your best buddy Willis wanted to harm you for what you inflicted upon him. The souls can tweak that reaction and exaggerate the impulse, but there's a seed of truth in the people of your past. Are you willing to destroy this marvel for the sake of revenge? So you were scared, it's over now. You're not hooked up to the machine. You'll be on the side that has control. Anything you please, it's yours."

The doctor's registry of sanity and insanity and

murder and life was obscured. The man didn't flinch at suffering. The machine had warped those natural emotions, and Craig wouldn't have anything to do with promoting his cause. Craig stared out at the bodies strewn against the wall in clear body bags. This wasn't science. It wouldn't better society. Some things in the mind weren't meant to be understood, and people's innermost thoughts weren't designed to be spelled out to an audience.

"You haven't saved any lives with this device. You tell Edith and the others like her what they died for? You believe in your machine, so then relax. Enjoy your family's work."

Dr. Krone sputtered and begged to be released, but Craig ignored him. He was exhausted, craving a cigarette, hungry, and most of all, he felt the urge to shower and rid himself of this place.

He poised his hands on the console. Craig couldn't figure out what to type. It would be too easy to type in, *Die, Dr. Krone*. He wanted more than his heart to stop. Dr. Krone hadn't been on the receiving end of terror. He enjoyed the fruits of his memories and others' suffering. Now it was his turn.

Craig typed in the command.

dIe, dR, kRone

he ReAction wAS InStAnt. Blink-instant like everything else had been. He typed in the command: *Dr. Krone will suffer the nightmares of everybody who's ever been hooked up to the machine*. Craig felt the heat emanate from the device. The crown of needle prongs was inserted into the doctor's head with a teeth-grinding *thack*. The circle of low-gauge needles was rammed into his eyes. The thrust shook the doctor in place. He was stunned. The man drooled and moaned, "*Uhhhhhhhnnnnnn . . .*"

Craig attempted to look away, but it was too mesmerizing.

Milky foam spittle launched from the man's lips. His face scrunched with each seizure-spasmodic twitch. "*Whuuck—whuuck—whuuck!*"

Dr. Krone went stiff, his mouth quivering. His skin changed from white to raw-meat red to cut-circulation purple. His eyes gushed blood and so did the needles that penetrated his brain. The stink of singed hair and burning plastic followed.

WHUUUUUUUUUUUUUM!

The machine smoked and static electricity branched out from all directions and cracked in lightning-sharp crackles. Craig fled from the scene, but not before catching Dr. Krone's final moment. The machine was clearly overloaded by Craig's command. The needles in the doctor's brain were wrenched out so quickly, his skull cap was removed and the boiling soup-mush-for-brains billowed down his face in steaming, clotted lines. Dr. Krone's mouth was locked in agony, his tongue rigid and extended.

Craig couldn't dote on the man's death when blue-white branches and webs of high voltage electricity—unnaturally bright and near-blinding with each crackle and surge—randomly spat out across the room. He dodged the machines and anything metal. He was near the double-door exit. The walls were blanketed by flames. The electric jolts ended once he crossed the door and threshold. He pounded down the rubber-matted floors and doubled up the stairs. He stopped and looked about the living room with relief. The bars over the windows and doors were missing.

It was the machine the whole time. Dr. Krone wanted to protect his investment. The machine was his security system.

He lunged out the door in case the electricity decided to shoot out at him without warning. Escaping through the front door, the night was thick and starless. He viewed the treetops of woods. The mansion was unassuming, he thought. The air was still. Absolutely calm. The din of fire eating the walls, the foundation expressing its distaste of its slow disintegration, Craig looked on down the long gravel driveway and snow-covered lawn. He shivered in the freezing cold. There were lights on in the far distance, perhaps a quarter of a mile from his standing point. He could knock on a door for help.

He watched the smoke pour from each window and the fire climb to the upstairs quarters. The electricity branches were gone. The machines had been damaged enough by the fires to be rendered useless, he believed. Craig prayed the secrets Dr. Krone uncovered about the human mind and their connections to the machine remained un-recovered.

Take your time getting help.
Let the house burn some more.

CRAIg chAnged out of his hospital gown into the clothing his mother brought him yesterday—a pair of blue jeans, a button-up, orange-and-white-checkered shirt, and new Sketchers shoes. Three days, he stayed at St. Luke's Mercy Hospital. He wasn't critically injured, he learned, after the doctor ran his tests. The CT scans proved he had no brain damage. Dr. Robyn Chambers, a physical therapist, tested his joints and their reaction to stimulus, and garnered positive results. His main doctor, Dr. Hank Herman, was adamantly concerned about the wounds to the eyes and skull he received. Dr. Herman claimed he'd never come across such strange and accurate insertions. They didn't harm any critical junctures in the brain.

"It's amazing how precisely these insertions were made," Dr. Herman repeated during the checkup. "Most people with this deep of brain trauma would suffer memory loss, nerve damage, or lose basic motor function—or brain function would terminate altogether. Whoever created these knew what they were doing."

He kept his comments to a minimum. The long walk to reach the house of Dr. Krone's neighbor allowed him time to think. Nobody would believe his amazing story. How would he explain the events? "Dr. Krone stuck me in the head and eyes with needles and my memories projected onto a screen. Oh, and then I was hooked up to this machine, and I got to travel back in time and replay my memories. And if that's not interesting enough, Dr. Krone typed in commands on this machine, and my memories became flesh and blood too. They were monsters, some of them. My wife was a rotting corpse. My best friend, Alice, her miscarried baby was a . . . well, never mind. Can you imagine it, though?"

He also feared who could learn the truth. He wasn't sure how much of the mansion burned down. He'd drive down to the property today and check it over. He prayed the VHS tapes and the machines were destroyed. What if he did tell the truth? Somebody would be interested. There were enough psychiatrists and doctors who'd love to enter people's brains and tinker with their processes and live their patients' memories as their own. The souls of the insane had ruined what could've been an honest scientific breakthrough. It could've cured a lot of unsound minds.

Some things are too crazy to be true.

He walked past the emergency waiting room and out of the rotating doors when he was blindsided by a detective. He wasn't dressed as the atypical detective. The wardrobe was simple—brown leather coat, Chicago Bulls ball cap, and black khakis pants. The man was in his early thirties, clean shaven, and his face beaded with a healthy zeal. He smiled at Craig. The detective flashed his identification.

"My name's Robert Williams. I'm investigating

what happened to you, Mr. Horsy." He motioned for Craig to come into the parking lot. "Let me buy you lunch."

Craig was starving. The hospital food left something to be desired, and three-quarters of his stay, he couldn't eat due to the testing. Tina tried to sneak him a Snickers bar, but he had to turn it down. When it came to his health—and near death days ago—he couldn't leave anything to error.

"Sure, lunch sounds good. I'm guessing you want to know everything about Dr. Krone."

Robert offered a wry smile. "That'd be a start."

He was driven to a restaurant called Arthur Bauman's Stack. On the way to the entrance, the detective asked, "I hope you like ribs and meat sandwiches. The doctor said you could use some good food. You've been on IV fluids all week."

"That's what Dr. Herman told me." Craig's stomach rumbled. Despite the temptation, he couldn't forget what he vowed. He couldn't disclose the complete truth. It was simply too dangerous. "You picked a good place to eat. I'm already salivating like a dog."

Inside, they were guided to a table under a giant bison head. The table was rough-cut wood as if right out of the tree, it seemed. Robert ordered a stack of ribs, coleslaw, and fries, and Craig decided on a braised pork sandwich with pork and beans. Now that they'd ordered, Robert's professionalism arrived. His eyes zoomed in on him. "I waited for you to receive your treatment, Mr. Horsy. You've been through a lot of trauma. Dr. Hill said you had needles jammed through your eyes and skull that were over three inches long. Any normal insertion would leave you a drooling vegetable. That's what makes your case, your survival, so interesting. Plus, our investigative crew has sifted through the remains of the mansion. It's all burned up. Nothing really left except for more questions. I hope you can help. We need your account of things, so how about it?"

He wet his lips and cleared his throat. It bought him time to plan his words carefully. "I can put it in a nutshell, though my memory isn't one hundred percent, I'm sorry. I was kidnapped from my apartment, and I woke in a room with a couch. It appeared to be a psychiatrist's office. A nurse said I'd slipped outside on ice and hit my head. I believed her, for whatever reason. I waited for my appointment, and a man named Dr. Daniel Krone talked to me. He mentioned the fights I'd gotten into at school as a kid and my court appearance.

"So after the questioning, I was somehow sedated—that's what I'm guessing. I woke strapped to a chair." This was where Craig started to lie. "Dr. Krone asked me personal questions about my family and my childhood, and then I wake up, and I don't know how long I was out, and the place is burning. I was able to escape. I don't know what happened to Dr. Krone or that nurse. All I know is that he wanted in my brain—my memories, you know?"

He'd said too much, but it was too late.

Robert arched his brow. "So nobody's told you anything else about the crime scene?"

"No." He was genuinely confused. "Is there anything you want to tell me?"

"Dr. Krone owned ten asylums," he then paused, bracing himself for the telling, "and he co-operated twenty others. What that means is he had access to thirty asylums. We've found approximately twelve hundred dead bodies in his mansion. They were sealed up to reduce the smell. Each of the bodies had received their fair share of poking and prodding. The range of decay also indicates these bodies are centuries old. Someone remarked that one of the bodies was wearing a confederate uniform, and another was from the American Revolution." He paused, allowing the statement to sink in for Craig. "Their damage was similar to yours, Mr. Horsy. "Their eyes were ragged with needle marks. Their brains were either diced up or removed completely. Dr. Krone owned enough surgical devices for ten medical teams. Some are even of medieval origin."

He opened up a little to come off convincing. "Dr. Krone mentioned dissecting the brain for its potential. He really wanted to somehow capture a person's memories. He believed it would solve mental illness. The details of that work, though, I have no idea about. It all sounds morbid. And how many bodies? Twelve hundred? Jesus Christ."

"You're a very lucky man to survive. Our investigation is still in the running. We're tracing the bodies and trying to identify every last one. So far, they've each been traced back to Dr. Krone's asylums. The man sold the establishments about ten years ago. Dr. Krone's father, David Krone, has been missing for years. He up and disappeared for no real reason. There's so much going on in the investigation, we ask you stay quiet about this. That means not talking to the news or friends or relatives about this."

The food arrived, and Robert thanked the waitress. The woman heard tidbits of their conversation and was expedient to leave them to their meal. Robert didn't touch his food, and Craig hesitated. "What else should I know, Detective?"

"What do you know about the machines?"

He placed a confused expression on his features. "Machines? What kind of machines?"

"Do you have any clue?"

He shrugged his shoulders. "I'm not sure. I was sitting in a chair when Dr. Krone was interrogating me. Whatever my back was against, it was hot. It sounded like a motor too. But I couldn't turn around."

Robert was excited. He was making a mental note. *Shit.*

He tried to relax. What could they do with the information he was giving them. Craig had to learn what Robert understood about the machine, so he asked, "Did you find machines? What did they look like?"

"They were burned up pretty good. There were twenty-five machines counted on the premises. They were simple. I'm not sure it means anything, but they were located in the basement level of the mansion, the same level as all those bodies. I'm not sure what the hell was going on. We did find a room of melted VHS tapes, but they're useless. The fire got to them. It's a shame a trusted doctor stole patients from his asylums to do private research. The state's going to take some hits for this. Those asylums will be turned inside out. The news will have a parade with this shit. I suggest you lay low, Mr. Horsy. We'll do our best to protect your anonymity. That's why you shouldn't talk about it to anyone."

"I'll keep my mouth shut."

Robert began to eat his food. "This is only the

beginning of the investigation. I assume you'll be available to answer questions again anytime?"

"Of course. I'll tell you anything I know."

tINA hoRSy

The **wouNdS oveR** his eyelids and scalp had healed to light pink scars in two month's time. Tina said he looked like he was wearing purple eye shadow. She was concerned about the damage as any mother would be, but he kept the explanation of his injuries to a minimum. He served up the condensed version that he'd given Detective Williams, keeping everything damning a secret. He visited Tina every Thursday after he recouped. They frequented Half-Time now that Craig and Willis had made up, and that was where they were now sitting during happy hour. Fifty cent beer draws. Tina was on her sixth. Craig had just downed his eighth. Willis was busy with the happy hour crowd. Joey, his brother, was pouring three shots across the bar for a pair of men in business suits.

Craig watched Willis and Joey. Their faces would randomly smolder and blacken to the skeleton beneath. Sometimes in his everyday life, he couldn't shrug Dr. Krone's drummed-up scenarios. *Nobody can forget something like this, so try and deal with it the best you can.*

Trying to distract himself from the horrible visions, he talked to his mom again. "You look a lot younger than you used to. You dyed the gray out of your hair. You got a facial. One of those mud treatments at Club La Feminist too."

"Club La Femme, you idiot." She rolled her eyes, speaking to him as a friend as much as a mother. "I don't want men checking out my ass when I'm working out. You're asking for unwanted attention."

Willis stepped up to them. "You two want another draw?"

Tina clapped her hands. "Yeah, yeah. Two more, barkeep."

Craig studied the man's scar above his temple. It was shaped like a sideways "U." Willis sensed an apology coming. "And I forgive you. Again. You're receiving help. Let's move on and drink and be jolly, okay? Forget about the past."

Willis delivered the draws moments later and toured the rest of the bar and its patrons. Alone with their drinks, this was Craig's chance to bring up Brandon. He wanted to talk about his dad for a time, among other things Dr. Krone had opened up. He had to know what was true and what was a manipulation.

He blurted out, "Dad was an asshole."

"Craig Ryan Horsy, you watch your mouth."

She was stern. The fun expression on her face had been erased.

"I'm sorry, but it's the truth."

She hiccupped. "I know!" Tina busted out laughing. "He really was, and it took forever to realize it."

"He was an abusive creep. He cheated on you so many times. What a bastard. He couldn't be happy with a wonderful woman such as yourself."

"He had a little man complex. A lot changed

between now and say thirty years ago. Women were subpar to men in every category, and now we make more money than them and we don't really need them. We're independent, and some men couldn't handle that change, such as your father. It's old-fashioned bullshit. He kept me down by cheating on me, and other things."

"And that stupid basement," Craig added, "and his nudie posters. That was his room, don't interfere with the business he's conducting, and dear God, don't interrupt his special time in his special room."

"Macho machismo asshole." She sipped on her draw. "A part of me misses him, you know, the part of him that loved me without his complexes and hang-ups. Deep down, he wanted to be a good man."

"You shouldn't have stayed with him. Not for me, not for him, but for yourself. You should've jumped the shark. You should've jumped Jaws."

"Live and learn. But I've lived a good life. I have you. I lost you for a while after Katie. I never got to really console her death with you." She touched his arm. "I'm so sorry, Craig."

He smiled. "Console me with fun now."

Craig raised his glass, and they toasted each other.

He couldn't resist bringing up another piece of information that could be true or not. "Did you ever cheat on Dad?"

Tina kept a straight face, but the side of her lip twitched. She contained the lying smile.

"No."

"Are you certain?"

She pushed him. "Craig, what kind of a son are you by asking me these questions?"

"I'm a son after the truth. Hey, I went to those

court-appointed psychiatrist visits. Dr. Herman has introspected me to death. 'How do you feel?' 'What does that mean to you?' 'Did that hurt you?' 'How are you, emotionally?' Psycho-babble hokey-pokey bullshit. I've always suspected you had a man on the side." He stared her down. "Am I wrong? You can tell me. I won't judge you. And I already know who it is."

Tina played with her coaster, spinning it back and forth. After fighting herself for thirty long seconds, it burst out of her like a confession, "Parker Stevens, okay? *Man*, that felt good! I've held that in for so long. Not even my sisters know about him."

"Do you still talk to him?"

"I broke it off so long ago," she confessed. "It felt wrong. Maybe it was revenge for me, and maybe I cared about Parker, but I couldn't distinguish between the two feelings. It wasn't fair to him and it wasn't fair to me."

"So you slept with him?"

A hard elbow to the ribs. "Craig Ryan Horsy, you're full of questions today—and juicy ones too. That's between a man and a woman and God."

"That's sounds like something Parker would say. I imagine out of everybody in the history of the world, God has heard every private story and juicy secret. I'd kill to have a drunk conversation with God. I'd hear *some* stories." He let the issue dwindle. "What's Parker up to these days?"

"You didn't hear?" She was excited to disclose the nugget of truth. She always enjoyed fresh gossip. It was a prerequisite for any receptionist and part-time manicurist such as herself. "He had a falling out of faith. He renounced the church, and now he works as a zookeeper in Florida. I think his father forced the church on him from such an early age, he couldn't decide between personal faith and his family's faith. I haven't heard from him in a long time. But I miss him. He helped me through some hard times."

"He even tried to bless me without Dad knowing. That was scary."

Tina checked her watch, ready to move on from the talk of her philandering. "Are you up for a movie?"

"We're stinking drunk."

"So? The theater's just down the street."

"You're right, why not?" He finished his drink. "Let's saddle up and hit the road."

Tina looked him in the eyes. "I have to ask you something. I really kept that a secret, you know, my affair with Parker." She came in close. "How did you find out about Parker and me? Seriously?"

ALIce denny

ALIce denny WAS Craig's final obstacle, post-Dr. Krone's machine. He waited in her apartment complex's parking lot in limbo. Visit her or leave. He couldn't remove her from his mind. Months had gone by since his escape, and he couldn't summon the courage to visit her. She still lived in the same apartment. What had she done since her miscarriage? And what a way to remember somebody, he scolded himself. The hardest part would be breaking the ice. What would he say to an old friend?

"Sorry" would be a start.

He opened the car door. The door was halfway open when he paused. *You can do this. You want to do this. If she doesn't want to see you, she'll make that clear.*

He brought flowers. Carnations. In high school on Valentine's Day, students could buy them for one dollar and have them delivered to their sweethearts during class. He sent them to her. She wasn't the type of girl to catch any boy's admirations, but he always had a special feeling toward her. He couldn't describe it. Friendly love or just friends, he couldn't decide, and at the time, it didn't matter as long as they stayed friends.

Craig silently wished himself luck and approached her apartment. "Here goes nothing."

Once inside and up the stairs to her floor, he knocked on her door once. There was a shuffle from within, and the door was unbolted and thrown open. There she was, Alice Denny. Her face was blank. Unreadable. She wasn't mad, or excited, or angry. They stared at each other. She noticed the carnations. Her eyes teared up, and she finally smiled. Alice hugged him so hard he had to take three steps to absorb the impact.

He hugged her back. "I'm sorry, so sorry for what happened . . . "

She wept and clutched onto him, refusing to let go of him. "You can't leave. I'm not letting you leave again."

"No, I won't. I promise."

"I scared you off, didn't I? I'm sure that night overwhelmed you. How couldn't it?"

"You needed me." He kissed her forehead. "I care about you so much. You were overwhelmed. You needed me."

"I love you."

And that's when she kissed him on the mouth. It happened so fast, he was taken aback, but he wanted it. It was a sweet kiss. Craig kissed her back. "This . . . this is good."

After a moment, she let him in. "What brought you back?"

He couldn't give her an honest answer. Not the truth. He sighed, unable to commit to one explanation. "I have a lot of regrets I'm trying to address."

"You mean ever since your ordeal? I heard about

that in the news. Are you okay?" Alice traced her hands along his eyelids and the indentions of his skull. "A paper said a doctor was experimenting on his patients at the mental asylums. What did he do to you?"

"Wow, people are finding so much out about this. I thought it was kept quiet. Boy, I was wrong. The police swore there was a media blackout on this thing. Information seeps through the cracks, I guess. I can't say exactly what he did to me," he lied. "I was hooked to a machine. Poked and prodded. Why and for what purpose, it beats me. Investigators are still piecing it all together from the burned remains of his home. Hundreds of bodies were found there. I'm lucky to be alive."

"Your eyelids, they're scarred from . . . "

"Needles. I was going to visit Dr. Herbert, a psychologist, and undergo sessions for some issues I'm addressing. But I was kidnapped by this Dr. Krone asshole. He had access to my file information, and this doctor misled me into thinking I was undergoing a session, and then the rest is, well, a blur."

She petted his hair and kissed his eyes and the scars. Then they sat together on her couch. "I'm so glad you're back. I thought I'd never see you again. I believed I'd catch you in public, or something, but that never happened. And here you are. Is your visit *just* because of your near-death experience?"

"Yes and no," he admitted. "Yes, because I'm trying to change my life; no, because I've always regretted the way things turned out between us. It's about time I made a change. Losing Katie and my child marked a decline for me—and more so than the normal person, because I was already dealing with deep-down psychological shit and avoiding it. Katie's death unraveled my coping mechanisms and I had nothing left but anger. My near-death experience was actually beneficial in some ways, though Dr. Krone wasn't the right person to help me through my ordeal. Definitely not him."

He smiled, digging deeper into the memories to share with her. "I should've followed you to your house that Halloween night and gotten drunk with you and become your blood brother."

Alice's face slackened. "Huh? Your blood brother?"

"Yeah, you remember that Halloween back in high school. You invited me back to your house, but I turned you down."

"How did you know I wanted you to be my blood brother?"

Craig clammed up, then said, "I—uh—um, well . . . you told me about it once."

"Gosh, that was forever ago," she whistled. "I got really drunk that night. And high. Yeah, you missed out, buddy."

She let it go, too happy to see him to be caught up in the details of high school. Instead, she clasped his hands into hers. "I've loved you for the longest time. You didn't know it, though."

"I didn't," he admitted. "I was a fool. But whatever we do, let's take it slow."

Alice kissed his cheek. She was still trying to catch up for lost time. "I'm so sorry about your father. I wanted to go to the funeral, but I wasn't sure if seeing me would hurt you, or confuse you, or scare you, or what. Believe me, I wanted to be there for you. I know you and your dad weren't the closest, but still, it's hard for anybody to lose a father."

"You have nothing to apologize for," he reassured her. "It's an awkward thing. I was going through some bad shit. It's probably for the best I was left alone. I was drinking hardcore, hating my job, hating everything."

"Your ordeal really turned you around. It's amazing how much you've changed. Have you been in contact with your mom?"

"We're drinking buddies now. Did you know she cheated on my dad?"

"I don't blame her for one second. Everybody in the neighborhood knew your dad was philandering. A new girl every other month is what I heard. No offense."

"It's true, and none taken. She's a strong woman. And she deserved better, though my dad had his winning qualities despite his less desirable traits. Did you know who her fling was?"

"I have no clue."

He paused for dramatic effect and then said, "Parker Stevens."

She playfully slapped his arm. "Oh, you've got to be kidding me! Parker Stevens, the priest? Seriously? Wow, that's amazing. I remember when she tried to get you baptized when Brandon was at work. People gossiped like crazy about that. Your poor mother. What he put her through, I'm sure she's living it up now being single."

"God rest his soul, that man was an asshole. I had a strange childhood. I keep remembering more and more about it. My memories are pretty strange."

"Then let's give you some new memories."

She kissed him full on the lips, their tongues meeting for the first time. He wrapped his arms around her, and they folded onto the couch, Alice on top. Their bodies grew naturally closer, and he couldn't help but enjoy the warmth of a woman. "You're such a good kisser."

"It'd say practice makes perfect, but it's been a while."

"Me too. But that's okay. Two tenderfoots make a chief."

"What does that mean?" Craig laughed. "No seriously, explain it to me."

Alice nibbled his ear. "I don't have a clue. It makes no sense."

"This does," he said, kissing her nose. "I'm such an idiot. How come I didn't come to my senses sooner? I'm so stubborn."

"It's in the past now. You're here. It's me and you and that's all that matters. We have so much to catch up on."

"We have all the time in the world," Craig said, holding her in his arms. "Like you said, two tenderfoots make a chief."

About the Author

Alan Spencer lives in Kansas City with his amazing wife and two dogs. Ever since being a background extra in the shot-on-video film Zombie Bloodbath 3, he has been obsessed with everything horror. His favorites are cheesy and gory films. He is the author of over forty novels, including *T-Rex, Meet Your Favorite Serial Killer,* and *Washing Machine Holocaust*. You can find the author on Facebook and Twitter, or drop him an e-mail at alanspencer26@hotmail.com. He would love the attention.

All Art is Junk by R. A. Harris

Lana Rivers, a girl with paintbrush hair, is missing and it's up to Lancelot, her cyborg knight, and his bionic conjoined twin, Cilia, to find her before her evil father, a disrespected artist turned mad-scientist, performs a terrible experiment on her.

Cherub by David C. Hayes

Cherub wasn't like the other boys—too slow, too rough—but he didn't deserve what that hospital did to him, and now he will make them pay.

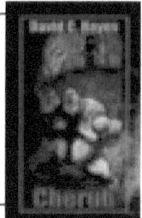

Skinners by Adam Millard

Los Angeles, the City of Angels. At least, that's what the brochure says. What it fails to mention is the earthquakes. Oh, and the flesh-eating creatures lying dormant beneath the concrete, waiting for the chance to surface once again. Their wait is over . . .

The After-Life Story of Pork Knuckles Malone by MP Johnson

What's a farm boy to do when his pet pig becomes an evil, decaying hunk of ham with slime-spewing psychic powers?

A Lightbulb's Lament by Grant Wamack

A gentleman with a lightbulb for head wakes up in a world full of darkness, hooks up with a beautiful ex-prostitute, and an old man who can heal people; he travels down south to find the mysterious Creator.

PseudoPsalms by Peter Adam Saloman

Bram Stoker nominated author Peter Adam Salomon has laid bare the intricate horrors of the human condition in this poetic compilation; PseudoPsalms: Saints v. Sinners.

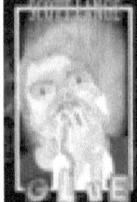

Bizarro Bizarro: An Anthology

The finest bizarro short stories from 2013.

Notes from the Guts of a Hippo by Grant Wamack

A rugged journalist travels to Brazil in search of a missing hippo researcher and the notes left behind lead to something earth shatteringly revelatory.

Day of the Milkman by S. T. Cartledge

In a world dominated by the milk industry, only one milkman survives after a terrible storm sinks all the ships and throws the Great White Sea out of balance.

Moosejaw Frontier by Chris Kelso

An unapologetic disaster of metafiction

Notes from the Guts of a Hippo by Grant Wamack

A rugged journalist travels to Brazil in search of a missing hippo researcher and the notes left behind lead to something earth shatteringly revelatory.

Industrial Carpet Drag by Bruce Taylor

Chemicals make you do great things!

Necrosaurus Rex by Nicolas Day

Necrosaurus Rex tells the tale of Martin, a simple janitor, who takes an unfortunate trip through time, becomes a violent mutant, and the father of us all. There's 14 billion years crushed inside these pages, and most of them are pretty nasty.

The Boy Who Loved Death by Hal Duncan

From blackest humour to bleakest horror, with twisted relish, Hal Duncan's eighteen tales dig into death—and the life that goes with it.

X's for Eyes by Laird Barron

Between the machinations of the disciples of black gods and good old corporate skullduggery, it's winding up to be of a hell of a summer vacation for the Tooms Brothers.

Omega Grey by Seb Doubinsky

When professor Todd Bailer embarked on a psychedelics quest to discover if the land of the Dead really existed, he had no idea he would threaten the cosmic balance of the universe by triggering a real-estate conquest of the new Frontier.

Berzerkoids by MP Johnson

The first short story collection from Wonderland Book Award-winning author MP Johnson

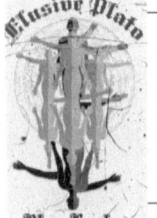

Elusive Plato by Rhys Hughes

The last in a long decadent line of piratical Spanish eccentrics, Bartleby Cadiz grows up in isolation to be as mad, bad and metaphysical as his ancestors. But he feels there is something different about him. What can it be?

Boiled Americans
by Michael Allen Rose

Boiled Americans is a puzzle box in book form, inspired by the violence of living in urban America and exploding the tendency to forget or ignore.

Great American Slasher
by David C. Hayes

Baseball, apple pie . . . and murder.

The Bohemian Guide to Monogamy
by Andrew Armacost

Here, a strange labyrinth of interlinked short fiction assembles itself into a darkly moving novella that deftly explores the bottomless pain and pleasure of love and commitment.

Surreal Worlds edited by Sean Leonard

An anthology of surrealistic compositions created by some of the finest names in genre fiction. A showcase of international talent undaunted by the conventions of language and common narrative structures. Here is timelessness. Here is Surreal Worlds

How to Succesfully Kidnap Strangers
by Max Booth III

Do not respond to bad reviews. If you must respond to bad reviews, please do not kidnap the reviewer.

ADHD Vampire by Matthew Vaughn

He came, he conquered, he was distracted a lot

Static/Orgone by Jamie Grefe

A double-novella of literary grindhouse nightmares and theoretical post-apocalyptic vengeance.

Retch by David Bernstein

What would you do if you were cursed to puke right before you reached orgasm? You'd do anything, right? (You know you would.) Find out what one wealthy, good-looking, playboy will do to try to end his abhorrent curse.

Battering the Stem by Bob Freville

A darkly comic urban crime novella. What would it take to make you beg?

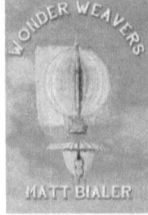

Wonder Weavers by Matthew Bialer

An epic poem about a mysterious sighting in 1896.

Cartoons in the Suicide Forest
by Leza Cantoral

When we're dead
You know she'll adore us